The

Weight

of

Feathers

The Weight of Feathers

Anna-Marie McLemore

THOMAS DUNNE BOOKS
St. Martin's Griffin ✿ New York

THOMAS DUNNE BOOKS.
An imprint of St. Martin's Press.

THE WEIGHT OF FEATHERS. Copyright © 2015 by Anna-Marie McLemore.
All rights reserved. Printed in the United States of America. For information, address
St. Martin's Press, 175 Fifth Avenue, New York, N.Y. 10010.

www.thomasdunnebooks.com
www.stmartins.com

Designed by Kathryn Parise

The Library of Congress Cataloging-in-Publication Data is available upon request.

ISBN 978-1-250-05865-2 (hardcover)
ISBN 978-1-4668-7323-0 (e-book)

Our books may be purchased in bulk for promotional, educational, or business use.
Please contact your local bookseller or the Macmillan Corporate and Premium
Sales Department at (800) 221-7945, extension 5442, or by e-mail at
MacmillanSpecialMarkets@macmillan.com.

First Edition: September 2015

10 9 8 7 6 5 4 3 2

For JEM,

for holding your hand out to me,

and keeping it there until I took it

Acknowledgments

Of the people I have to thank for bringing this story to life, there are many who have, unwaveringly, believed in me. There are others who have worked hard on this book without ever having met me. And others still have given generously of their time and expertise even though they barely knew me. To all of them, I am deeply and humbly grateful. A few, I'll mention here:

Taylor Martindale, for your faith, your fearlessness, and your friendship; I am truly lucky to have you as my agent and my advocate.

Kat Brzozowski, for being a dream to work with, a pleasure to get to know, and a brilliant editor who helped this book find its heart and its grounding. Lisa Pompilio, for designing such a beautiful cover that captures so much of this story. The wonderful team at Thomas Dunne Books/St. Martin's Press: Tom Dunne, Michelle Cashman, Stephanie Davis, Marie Estrada, Karen Masnica, Jeanne-Marie Hudson, Lauren Hougen, NaNá V. Stoelzle, and everyone else who touched this book;

whether or not I got to work with you directly, I am so thankful for everything you've done.

My fellow authors who helped this book along the way: Caroline Richmond, for your invaluable notes on the earliest incarnation. Kelly Loy Gilbert, for your insight on some of the most important moments in this story. Mackenzi Lee, for being one of this book's earliest and most enthusiastic fans. And the Fifteeners; I am lucky and proud to share a debut year with you.

The experts who helped make this story more accurate and authentic: Romani scholar Ethel Brooks, for answering questions about everything from pluralization in the Romani language to the history of *Sara-la-Kali*. Jen Cowitz, for giving me a look into your life as a professional mermaid and character actor. Catherine G. Anderson, for kindly and cheerfully enduring my e-mails about French phrases and proverbs. Stefanie von Borstel, for checking my Spanish, and for some perfect *dichos*.

My father, for every book you gave me, every question you welcomed, and for making me believe in the risks that are worth it. My mother, for showing me the strength that comes with being a woman, and for teaching me never to believe that I am less than anyone else. My family, without whom I would not know the kind of fierce loyalty at the root of this book.

My husband, for reading every page of every story. For being the boy I fell for so hard and so fast that I will never forget what it feels like to be seventeen.

And readers, for believing that stories count. For making them count.

The Weight of Feathers

Una golondrina no hace verano.

One swallow does not make a summer.

The feathers were Lace's first warning. They showed up between suitcases, in the trunk of her father's station wagon, on the handles of came-with-the-car first-aid kits so old the gauze had yellowed. They snagged on antennas, turning the local stations to static.

Lace's mother found a feather in with the family's costumes the day they crossed into Almendro, a town named for almond fields that once filled the air with the scent of sugary blossoms and bitter wood. But over the last few decades an adhesive plant had bought out the farms that could not survive the droughts, and the acres of almonds dwindled to a couple of orchards on the edge of town.

The wisp of that black feather caught on a cluster of sequins. Lace knew from the set to her mother's eyes that she'd throw the whole mermaid tail in a bucket and burn it, elastane and all.

Lace grabbed the tail and held on. If her mother burned it, it would take Lace and her great-aunt at least a week to remake it. *Tía* Lora's hands were growing stiff, and Lace's were new and slow.

Her mother tried to pull the tail from her grip, but Lace balled the fabric in her hands.

"Let go," her mother warned.

"It's one feather." Lace dug in her fingers. "It's not them." Lace knew the danger of touching a Corbeau. Her *abuela* said she'd be better off petting a rattlesnake. But these feathers were not the Corbeaus' skin. They didn't hold the same poison as a Corbeau's body.

"It's cursed," her mother said. One hard tug, and she won. She threw the costume tail into a bucket and lit it. The metal pail grew hot as a stove. The fumes off the melting sequins stung Lace's throat.

"Did you have to burn the whole thing?" she asked.

"Better safe, *mija*," her mother said, wetting down the undergrowth with day-old *aguas frescas* so the brush wouldn't catch.

They could have cleaned the tail, blessed it, stripped away the feather's touch. Burning it only gave the Corbeaus more power. Those feathers already had such weight. The fire in the pail was an admission that, against them, Lace's family had no guard.

Before Lace was born, the Palomas and the Corbeaus had just been competing acts, two of the only shows left that bothered with the Central Valley's smallest towns. Back then it was just business, not hate. Even now Lace's family sometimes ended up in the same town with a band of traveling singers or acrobats, and there were no fights, no blood. Only the wordless agreement that each of them were there to survive, and no grudges after. Every fall when the show season ended, Lace's aunts swapped hot-plate recipes with a trio of trapeze artists. Her father traded homeschooling lesson plans with a troupe of Georgian folk dancers.

The Corbeaus never traded anything with anyone. They shared nothing, took nothing. They kept to themselves, only straying from the cheapest motel in town to give one of Lace's cousins a black eye, or leave a dead fish at the riverbank. Lace and Martha found the last one, its eye shining like a wet marble.

Before Lace was born, these were bloodless threats, ways the Corbeaus tried to rattle her family before their shows. Now every Paloma knew there was nothing the Corbeaus wouldn't do.

Lace's mother watched the elastane threads curl inside a shell of flame. "They're coming," she said.

"Did you think they wouldn't?" Lace asked.

Her mother smiled. "I can hope, can't I?"

She could hope all she wanted. The Corbeaus wouldn't give up the crowds that came with Almendro's annual festival. So many tourists, all so eager to fill their scrapbooks. That meant two weeks in Almendro. Two weeks when the younger Paloma men hardened their fists, and their mothers prayed they didn't come home with broken ribs.

Lace's grandmother set the schedule each year, and no one spoke up against *Abuela*. If they ever did, she'd pack their bags for them. Lace had watched *Abuela* cram her cousin Licha's things into a suitcase, clearing her perfumes and lipsticks off the motel dresser with one sweep of her arm. When Lace visited her in Visalia and they went swimming, Licha's two-piece showed that her *escamas*, the birthmarks that branded her a Paloma, had disappeared.

Lace's mother taught her that those birthmarks kept them safe from the Corbeaus' feathers. That family was *el Diablo* on earth, with dark wings strapped to their bodies, French on their tongues, a sprinkling of gypsy blood. When Lace slept, they went with her, living in nightmares made of a thousand wings.

Another black feather swirled on a downdraft. Lace watched it spin and fall. It settled in her hair, its slight weight like a moth's feet.

Her mother snatched it off Lace's head. "*¡Madre mía!*" she cried, and threw it into the flames.

Lace's cousins said the Corbeaus grew black feathers right out of their heads, like hair. She never believed it. It was another rumor that strengthened the Corbeaus' place in their nightmares. But the truth, that wind pulled feathers off the wings they wore as costumes, wasn't a strong enough warning to keep Paloma children from the woods.

"*La magia negra,*" her mother said. She always called those feathers black magic.

The fire dimmed to embers. Lace's mother gave the pail a hard kick. It tumbled down the bank and into the river, the hot metal hissing and sinking.

"Let them drown," her mother said, and the last of the rim vanished.

Her mother spit out the words like a bad taste, but Lace couldn't blame her. The Corbeaus would've let a Paloma drown any day. Eight years ago, Lace's older cousin Magdalena got caught in a fishing net the Corbeaus had set in the lake. She would've drowned if her *novio* had not seen her stuck in the nylon threads and pulled her out of the water, half the net still tangled around her costume tail.

The Corbeaus had been setting nets to trip them up for years, and the *sirenas* learned to spot them and get out of them, the same as colanders. But the one that got Magdalena was nylon, not rope. The dark water made those thin threads and tight knots invisible.

Lace's father had filed a police report about what happened to Magdalena. The report went nowhere, but it had scared the Corbeaus off nylon nets ever since.

Lace went to break the news about the tail to her great-aunt, but *Tía* Lora had already seen. Lace found her watching from the motel window.

"Which one?" *Tía* Lora asked.

"The blue one," Lace said. "One of the new ones." She waited for sadness to wash over her great-aunt's face.

Tía Lora showed little more than a wince. It crept into the muscles around her mouth, but barely reached her eyes. "It's okay. We'll make another."

She accepted it with such quiet. This was her work, every stitch born from the pain in her fingers. Lace could help, but she didn't have *Tía* Lora's years and instinct. Even with her eyes going, Lora Paloma's sewing by touch came out better than Lace's by sight.

They were lucky *Tía* Lora had stayed with them. No one had been so good with the costumes since Lace's great-grandmother died. Four years before Lace was born, *Tía* Lora had every reason to leave. The Corbeaus had killed her husband, the man who had given her his name and made her a Paloma.

But *Tía* Lora stayed, and Lace's grandmother made sure the whole family knew they would not leave her alone and widowed by Corbeau hands. That *Tía* Lora had no Paloma blood meant nothing. The Paloma name she had fastened to herself on her wedding day was still hers.

"*Lo siento,*" Lace told her great-aunt.

"I'm used to it." *Tía* Lora turned her face from the window and smiled. Light gilded her brown cheek. "Every year your *abuela* brings us back here and pretends we can keep the feathers away."

Lace gave her great-aunt a smile back. A few weeks earlier, Lace's grandmother had drawn the family's route on an age-softened map of California, announcing they would set up in Almendro even earlier this year.

Now *Abuela* sat in the motel parking lot with her coffee, smug smile ready to greet the Corbeaus' Shasta trailers when they realized the Palomas were already here.

What she was hoping for, waiting out there with her Styrofoam cup of Folgers and powdered creamer, Lace didn't know. A good brawl, maybe, between the Corbeau men and Lace's cousins. A shouting match, *Abuela* screaming in Spanish, Nicole Corbeau shrieking in French.

Either way, her grandmother was disappointed. Lace's cousin Matías brought her the news that instead of taking a block of rooms at the River Fork, the Corbeaus had rented a run-down house, like they knew the Palomas had gotten ahead of them.

"Where?" *Abuela* demanded.

Matías told her it was somewhere near the campground, if he could even call it that. Five years ago the state had cut the funding to keep it up. Now it was just a cluster of fire pits, the root growth of porcelain vine and wild roses turning over the earth.

"At least they'll be out of the way," Lace said.

Matías folded his arms. "I don't know what they're doing. That house is only half as big as they need for all of them."

"I bet they make their children sleep outside," *Abuela* said. "*Los gitanos* and their trailers."

Abuela drained the last of her coffee and crushed the cup in her hand. She tossed it over her shoulder, knowing Lace would throw it out.

This was her grandmother's pride. If she wanted Lace's father and uncles to make the *aguas frescas,* she would pelt them with lemons until the mesh bag was empty. Instead of asking for *la Biblia* from her trunk, her brown, ring-covered hand pointed until the nearest grandchild obeyed.

Lace bent toward the asphalt. If *Abuela* left her coffee cup on the ground, any Paloma daughter knew enough to pick it up.

Volez de ses propres ailes.

Fly with your own wings.

❧

A knock shook the trailer door.

"Ten minutes," Cluck said, scrambling to replace a broken wire. During the season, fixing wings was a full-time job. His mother's *qu'il pleuve ou qu'il vente* policy meant they performed through every summer storm, rain damaging the feathers and wind warping the frames.

"Five," his mother said. Her shoes crunched the ground outside.

He tied his hair back. *Pépère* hated when he did that. He thought ponytails were odd on both boys and girls, something strange and American. He'd fluff the back of Cluck's hair with his hand and say, "What is this?"

But *Pépère* was already down at the show site, checking Cluck's work. Without the wings, there was no show.

Chemical smells blew in through the window. Boiling water. Rusted metal. Hot adhesive in the nearby plant's mixing tanks. Reminders that his grandfather used to check the temperature and pressure gauges, the pipe-washing logs, the vent gas scrubbers.

That was twenty years ago. Now the plant ran so hot the smell of plastic and ash blew clear to the highway. One day the whole system would overheat and shut down like a fried car engine, his grandfather said. The owners hadn't replaced the old overflow tank, just to save a hundred thousand dollars. And the plant's trainings didn't even cover how workers shouldn't wear cotton near the tanks. Last year, a pipe burst, and a spray of cyanoacrylate burned through the shin of a man's jeans.

Cluck's mother kept the show coming here because of the Almendro Blackberry Festival. Each year the town celebrated a variety of blackberry first cultivated by a local fifty years earlier. It was a point of pride around here, the berries growing so easily in backyards and ceramic planters that the brambles trailed on brick walkways and crabgrass lawns.

The festival brought in enough tourists for a quarter of the season's ticket receipts. But if it were Cluck's call, they'd go west to the coastal forests, or north and east, where wildflower fields fringed the groves of trees. They'd never stop in the town that had turned on *Pépère*.

A pebble bounced off the trailer's window. "Cluck," one of his cousins yelled through the pane.

Cluck cut a few feathers. He wished all his fingers worked. He'd gotten used to three being nothing but dead weight, but when he had to rush, he missed them.

"Did you go back to France to get the feathers or something?" Cluck's cousin laughed at his own joke. A few of his younger cousins gave him an echo.

"We didn't wear wings in France, *crétin fini*," Cluck said under his breath. In Provence, the Corbeaus had been *les fildeféristes*, tightrope walkers. They'd moved from town to town, fastening their ropes to church steeples. Onlookers swore *les Tsiganes* had sold their souls to the devil so he would take from them their fear of heights.

Now the Corbeaus were a tentless circus, performing anywhere they found enough trees. Their *fildefériste* blood had thinned out enough that they now walked branches, not tightropes.

Cluck came out of the costume trailer, arms full of feathers and wire, and put the repaired wings on the last few performers.

He had to dodge to keep from bumping into anyone. The ring of travel trailers was busy as a yellow jacket's nest. Performers cycled through the pink Airflyte to get iodine for their feet. Cluck's mother and Yvette kept the books, receipts, and maps in a half-white, half-red 1962. Lights and cables came out of the aluminum 1954 Cardinal. Anyone with a twisted ankle or a cut palm waited for Georgette in the 1956 Willerby Vogue with the melamine-green underbelly. And a 1963 Airstream was the junk drawer of the trailers, half schoolroom for the younger Corbeaus, half workshop when *Pépère* and Cluck needed the extra space.

Cluck watched Clémentine and Violette skip off into the trees, carrying burlap bags of petals. Each night they refilled them with cornflowers and seven-sisters roses that grew wild in the woods, the same kinds they wove into flower crowns.

They looked like wood fairies, their wings made of forest and sky colors.

His mother snatched the spare feathers from his hands. "What were you doing, trying to grow wings yourself?" She followed after the performers, her shoes clicking on the rocky ground. Only his mother would wear high heels in the woods.

Cluck got to the show space in time to see the performers taking their places in the boughs. The wings drew the audience in, but they made the performers' jobs harder. It took years for a Corbeau to learn to wear them without knocking the wide span into branches or snagging them on leaves.

Cluck knew. His grandfather made him climb trees wearing a set of wings when he was fourteen. Cluck had been scrambling barefoot up maples and oaks since he was old enough to walk, hiding in the higher branches Dax couldn't get to. But his first time up with those wings took him twice as long. The weight pulled him back or pushed him forward. Hitting the outer wires on the boughs made him fight to keep his balance. "If you've been up there wearing them, you will be better at making them," *Pépère* had called up from the ground.

Now Cluck only went up into the show's trees twice each run, once to hang the glass chimes and once to take them down. In each town where his family stopped, he had his own trees, always far from the show space.

Pépère found him and put a hand on his shoulder. "Good work."

"Yeah, tell that to my mom," Cluck said.

It was *Pépère* and Cluck's job to make getting up there easier. For the climb, the wire frames folded against the performers' backs like lacewings or stoneflies. Once they reached a high branch, a few tugs on two ribbons or cords opened the feathered span.

Thanks to the width his mother and aunts insisted on, the wings, once open, acted as sails. They caught all wind. If a performer didn't have the strength and balance to fight the pull, they fell. A generation before Cluck was born, a sudden gust knocked a great-aunt from a silver maple, and she fractured two lower vertebrae. She walked again, but never climbed.

"Don't worry about my daughter," *Pépère* said just when Cluck thought he hadn't heard him. "She doesn't like to see you do anything better than her precious *vedette de spectacle.*" He moved a few trees away to light up a cigarette, far enough that the wind wouldn't bring the smoke to the audience.

Cluck smiled. Only his grandfather could call Dax the star of the show and make it sound like an insult.

He watched the trees. The performers let themselves be seen, looked as though they meant not to. They leapt onto lower branches. The strongest ones, like his brother, pulled up the lightest ones quick enough to make them look like they were flying. The women danced as if the thin boughs were wide as the sky. The men stood as their partners, lifting them, offering their hands, and hoisting themselves higher up so easily it looked like their wings had done it. The more graceful of his cousins ventured far onto the boughs of valley oaks, their weight bowing the wood.

He would've loved to see any Paloma try it.

Cluck's mother stopped a few steps from him. Every Corbeau, from five-year-old Jacqueline to Cluck's grandfather, knew her stare was an order, a flight call keeping a flock together.

"You're slower this year," she said, a warning, and then left to count ticket receipts.

Cluck put his hands in his pockets and let a long breath out. "No, I'm not," he said when she'd gotten far enough not to hear him. "I just hate this town."

Más vale pájaro en mano que
ciento volando.

A bird in the hand is worth a hundred flying.

Lace didn't have to ask why her family had set out for Almendro so early. *Abuela* wanted to make sure the Corbeaus
couldn't steal the lakeside.

The Corbeaus had held their own shows there twenty years ago,
forcing the Palomas to set up along the river. But after the night the
water rose up onto the shore and swallowed the Corbeaus' favorite
trees, the Palomas claimed the lake. Those trees, now on the lake floor,
were the only ones near the water strong enough to hold the Corbeaus' bodies and wings. But *Abuela* still worried that their *magia negra*
could make birches and young magnolias grow big as sycamores.

"Those *cuervos* should never have taken the lake for themselves
when we're the ones who need the water," *Abuela* said. "And now we'll
keep it. I don't care if it means we come here in February."

"We're gonna freeze our asses," Alexia whispered as the mermaids wriggled into their tails at the river's edge.

But none of them could blame *Abuela*. This was the town where the Palomas and the Corbeaus always crossed paths. Sometimes, in other counties, they overlapped for a couple of days, the end of one family's run coming up against the start of the other's. But Almendro was their battleground, even before that night at the lake twenty years ago. And if one family didn't show, the other won by default.

Lace and her cousins slid down the bank, the heat fading with the light. The water felt cold as the first minute of their motel showers. Their skin puckered into gooseflesh. They held their grumbling under their tongues, but their grandmother still sensed it.

"The spring in Weeki Wachee was colder than this," *Abuela* said. "Seventy-two degrees."

A shiver of excitement crossed Lace's *escamas* whenever *Abuela* talked about Weeki Wachee. In that little spring-fed town, *Abuela* had performed with a dozen other women in ruched elastane. Playing to the aquarium glass built into the side of the spring, they combed their hair with carved conch shells, chased each other's spangled tails, kissed sea turtles. They smiled underwater without making bubbles, something Lace practiced in every motel pool from Magalia to Lake Isabella.

In a little more than a year, she'd be there, sharing the spring with wild manatees, swimming in the town that made her grandmother a famous beauty.

The Paloma *sirenas* weren't Weeki Wachee mermaids. They didn't perform in front of plate glass. They were less like circus girls and more like the world's tallest thermometer (134 feet, for the record high in Baker, California), mechanical dinosaurs made out of scrapped car parts and farm equipment (Lace and Martha snuck off to see them in Cabazon), or the world's largest concrete lemon (ten feet long, six feet wide, five miles outside El Cajon).

But the real tourist trap was the Corbeaus' show. Lace had never seen it herself, but from what Justin told her, all the Corbeaus did was climb trees with wings on their backs. At least the Paloma mermaids were quick, darting through the water, dancing in the drowned forest. Vanishing and reappearing.

"They want to work to see you," *Abuela* reminded them. "Don't start *la danza* too early. You let them find you first. They find you, they feel smart."

"Half of them are here for a festival about a berry," Lace said as she fixed Martha's smudged lipstick. "How smart can they be?"

Abuela stood over Lace, her shadow great as a jacaranda tree. "You make them feel smart. You make them feel special, or you're not doing your work. *¿Entiendes?*" She looked around at Lace's cousins. "All of you. You understand?"

"*Sí, Abuela,*" they murmured.

Abuela turned back to Lace. "*¿Entiendes?*"

Lace did not round her shoulders the way Martha or Reyna did when *Abuela* looked at them. She kept her back straight.

"*Sí, Abuela,*" Lace said, barely parting her teeth. Always *Abuela,* never *Abuelita.*

Emilia—*Abuela* called her *la sirena aguamarina*—leaned toward Lace. "Don't worry," she whispered. "That's a good sign. The day she starts calling you fat and saying your poses are sloppy is the day she's decided you're one of us."

Emilia would know. Her hair glittered with strands of paillettes and river pearls that marked her as a lead mermaid. She swam in last, perched in the center of those sunken trees, posed for tourists. But when she first joined, it was months before *Abuela* even let her choose her own tail, a blue-green like Colorado turquoise.

They all wore tails bright as tissue paper flowers. Butter yellow. Aqua and teal. The orange of cherry brandy roses. The flick of their fins looked like hard candy skipping across the lake.

Lace's own, pink as a grapefruit, branded her as the youngest, in her first season. Same with her hair, loose, no decorations. At the end of this season she'd earn a gold-painted shell or a strand of beads.

Then another every season after. When the light hit Martha's wet hair, sequins shimmered like constellations. Reyna and Leti wore clusters of shells at their hairlines. Her older cousins had so many strands clipped in that their hair looked made of paillettes.

They used those same plastic coins, sheer as beach glass, to cover their birthmarks. Their *escamas* were not some spectacle to be displayed in the show. *Apanchanej*, the river goddess who had blessed them with their love for water, had given them these marks, and they were not to flaunt them. Lace had barely gotten the high school equivalency all Paloma girls had to earn to join the show when *Abuela* filled her hands with paillettes and told her, "I don't care if you have three GEDs. You cover your *escamas*, or you don't swim." So every *sirena* did, even though the waterproof glue made their skin itch.

Lace touched up her cousins' cream eye color, fixed the pins in their hair, and then slipped into her own tail.

"Don't let the water keep you, *la sirena rosa*," *Tía* Lora whispered.

The sun turned the trees to fire and gold, and *Abuela* called them to their places. Lace's uncles sold their *aguas frescas* to the audience at the lakeside. Mothers charged their camera flashes. Fathers held video recorders, speaking the year and month and panning across the lake. Children held up plastic binoculars, seesawing the focus bars. Couples soaked up the light off the water and the fever of looking for mermaids.

The stretch of river Lace's grandmother had her swimming from ran through deep woods, the edge of where the Corbeaus would set up their show.

"But you are a good girl," her grandmother said. "So you will not go into the woods." A statement and a warning. *¿Sí, mija? ¿Verdad?*

Lace clutched an algae-slick rock and listened for the hollow whistle of her uncles' *zampoñas*. To start the show, three of them blew into the long pipes. The *arundo* reed gave back clean, full sounds.

Those thin walls meant louder notes, but only a few of her uncles knew how to hold them without snapping the pipes.

"*Los turistas* are gullible, huh?" they said as they warmed up the *zampoñas*. "They think we can call mermaids with these things."

But it added to the show's mystery, one man, silent and sun-weathered enough to look wise, standing on a near bank, two others in the trees across the lake, where the audience could spot them. All three played those wooden pipes, fastened with strips of cane and braided bands, the notes long and steady as their breaths.

Lace kept listening for the deep call of the *arundo* wood. Tangled river roots gave the air the scent of cool earth. It mixed with the tart fruit of the *aguas frescas*.

She took the deep breaths she'd need to stay under. The tail was heavy, and if she didn't have the air to kick against it, it pulled her down.

A few low trees shivered. A handful of night birds scattered. Lace crossed herself, like her mother told her, to keep away feathers.

The silhouettes of branches trembled in the fading light.

"Hello?" Lace called out, but the wind choked the sound.

She ducked behind a rock, ready to dive into the current. She'd never been quick on her feet, but she could swim away so fast anyone would think she was a trick of the light, the flicker of a candle in a glass jar. Half her job was disappearing.

The branches parted, and a pair of enormous wings emerged from the woods. Their shape stood black against the sky. They loomed over the bank. A few more steps, and their shadow would find Lace. If the wearer brought them down, they could crush her. The Corbeaus' *magia negra* would harden them into flint.

The feathers vibrated with all the evil that family carried. These crows had left Lora Paloma nothing. There were reasons a flock of crows was called a murder.

Lace waited for the figure to click his back teeth like the rattle of a comb call. If she let him, he'd get those teeth into her, his bite sharp as a beak.

The water grew colder against Lace's back. She peered around the rock, looking for the frame of a Corbeau man big enough to make the trees shrink away from him.

Her breasts stung from the chill. The current pulled at her hair. She'd only ever seen pictures of the Corbeaus' wings, all those feathers fastened to arched wire. They were wide as a hawk's span, so tall she wondered how the wind didn't tip them.

They twitched on the back of their wearer.

Lace squinted into the dark, making out the body attached to these wings.

It wasn't a man, but a woman, smaller than the shortest of Lace's cousins. How did she stand up against wings that size?

She stumbled, lost or drunk. Her feet grazed where Lace had hidden her dress in the undergrowth.

The woman tripped on the underbrush, and her hand bumped her lips. A smudge of red-orange came off on her thumb and forefinger.

She pinched her fingers, making the imprint of her mouth move. She laughed at her own hand.

Then she noticed Lace.

She turned her head and took in the pink of Lace's tail, the matching cream eye shadow, the plum-red lipstick.

The woman's stained fingers froze in the air, a tethered balloon.

"Ah, *ouais?*" she asked, as though Lace had said something.

Her hair was cut to her chin, with thick bangs, like the girls in Martha's old postcards. By the light of the candles Lace's father left burning in glass jars, it looked orange like flowering quince. Her crown of flowers and leaves reminded Lace of fruit topping a *tarta*.

She was iced as a cake, her eye shadow the mauve of new lilacs. Painted wings spread from the bridge of her nose across her eyelids and temples. Rhinestones glinted at the corners of her eyes. The blue and bronze peacock feathers on her back rippled like wheat. Not the black ones Lace and her mother kept finding. Those, her cousins swore, grew from their heads like hair, another mark of *el Diablo*.

Lace's fingers dug into the rock. She and this woman could tear each other's hair out. Lace could scratch at those feathers. The woman could wade into the river and shred the soft fabric trailing from Lace's fin.

Lace could take off her costume top and swing it at the woman. The scallop shells and fake pearls would leave her lip bloody.

She didn't.

If the woman pulled a wire loose from her wings, she could put Lace's eye out.

She didn't.

Lace slid down into the water.

The woman backed toward the woods until the tree shadows swallowed her whole.

On ne marie pas les poules
avec les renards.

One does not wed hens with foxes.

They didn't want money. If they did, they would've gone for his wallet as soon as they'd gotten him on the ground and then just left him outside the liquor store.

In the dark, he could only tell them apart by size. The biggest one. Another a little shorter, quick enough to get him in the stomach before he could tense. The third a couple of years and a few inches behind them both.

"You don't talk, *chucho?*" the biggest one asked. He hadn't hit him for a couple minutes. He let the other two get the practice.

The smallest of the three got Cluck in the jaw. He hit the hardest. More to prove.

The salt taste thickened inside Cluck's cheek.

"You speak English, *chucho?*" The quick one kicked him in the shoulder.

Pain spread down Cluck's arm. Letting them get him on the ground was his first mistake. He knew that now. But it always worked with Dax. Once Dax got him down, Cluck wasn't fun anymore. Better not to fight back.

This was about territory. These guys didn't like him in their part of town after dark. He'd figured if he went slack, they'd know he'd gotten the message.

Next time, he'd just walk the extra half-mile to the grocery store.

"¿Hablas español?" the quick one asked.

It wasn't the first time Cluck had gotten mistaken for something he wasn't. Women often asked him for directions in Spanish. His mother said it was his Manouche blood. His whole family had it, but in him it came through like a stain spreading. It made him darker than anyone in his family except his grandfather. It streaked red the feathers that grew in with his hair, made him *le petit démon* to his mother.

"You don't speak none of them, *chucho?*" the smallest one asked.

Cluck tongued the blood on his lip.

The oldest one grabbed his shirt. "Talk, *chucho.*"

The cornflower came unpinned from Cluck's vest, and the blue-violet bloom tumbled to the dirt. He still didn't look up.

The oldest one shook him. "Talk."

Cluck's shirt collar came off in his hand, and he fell back to the ground.

The oldest one's lip curled up. He'd probably never heard of a detachable collar. Cluck wouldn't have either if his grandfather hadn't worn them when he was his age. The buttonholes had grown soft over the last half a century. The collars came off more easily than they once did.

"Used to be very fashionable," Cluck said. "The mark of a gentle-man."

The oldest one hit him in the temple. The force spun through his head. He felt his brain whipping up like one of his aunts' meringues. Beat to stiff peaks. Just add sugar.

Something about Cluck always rubbed somebody the wrong

way. If it wasn't his clothes, it was his left hand. These three hadn't noticed it yet. Too dark. The light from the liquor store barely reached them. The ring of red-orange stopped just short of the ground where Cluck braced his hands.

A shadow broke the neon. The shape of a girl, hands on her hips. She set her shoe down a few inches from the fallen cornflower.

Cluck looked up. The red-orange caught one side of her face and body. It lit up the hem of her skirt and one sleeve of her jean jacket. It brightened her lipstick to the color of pincushion plants, and streaked her hair. Black or brown, he couldn't tell. She had on a thin scarf tied like a headband, the tails of the bow trailing on her shoulder.

She cleared her throat.

All three of them looked up. The bigger one dropped Cluck's collar.

The girl tilted her head toward the road. The three of them backed away, like Cluck was something they'd been caught breaking.

"You gonna say anything?" the youngest one asked as he passed her.

"Still thinking about it," she said.

She held out her hand to Cluck. He hesitated. She wasn't as little as Eugenie or Georgette, but he was still more likely to pull her down than she was to get him on his feet.

The muscles in his left hand twitched. He kept it still. He never could talk his body into believing it was right-handed.

She grabbed him just above his elbow and pulled him to standing. The force of her surprised him, her small hands stronger than he expected. He stumbled, stopping himself from falling forward.

"You got an arm on you," he said. "Well, two of them."

"I do a lot of swimming."

"Around here?" He brushed off his hands on the front of his pants. "I don't recommend it. Not with the colanders."

She stared at him, her lips a little parted.

He picked up his collar, dusted it off. "The roots of the trees growing in the river tangle together, form these big strainers."

"I know what a colander is," she said.

"Of course you do." Anyone who lived around here did. He buttoned his collar back on his shirt. "Do you always have that effect on men?"

"I know their mother."

He blew the dirt off the cornflower and pinned it back onto his vest. "Same sewing circle?"

"Something like that," she said. "You could've fought back, you know."

"Oh yeah?"

"You take out the biggest one first. Do you have any brothers?"

"Just one." He folded his collar down. "He's the biggest alright."

He straightened up, collar and cornflower and the rest of him all put back in place. He had about six or seven inches on this girl, her body small but not willowy. There was enough on her that she seemed soft instead of fragile like the thinnest and shortest of his cousins.

He wished he hadn't noticed. Noticing came with the thought of touching her, and a sureness that she would not break under his hands.

"What's your name?" Cluck asked.

"None of your business," she said.

"How's that look frosted on a birthday cake?"

She laughed, but didn't want to. The corners of her eyes fought it.

"What are you doing out here?" he asked.

"You first."

"My family needed milk."

"You couldn't have gotten it in the morning?"

"They get up early."

"First shift at the plant?" she asked.

The plant. Two words, and Cluck's tongue tasted dry and bitter as the charcoal off burnt toast. *The plant*, where his grandfather once worked as a safety engineer, making sure everything ran clean. He oversaw the safety measures, implemented new ones. That was before the plant let him go, all because of what the Palomas did.

Now his grandfather traveled with the rest of the family, the life he'd never wanted. He'd gone to school to get away from it. All he'd wanted was to work, use what he'd learned, live in a house that was his. He'd had these things—the position at the plant, the house with a lemon tree that blossomed every May—until the Palomas took them.

But none of that was anybody else's business, so Cluck just told the girl, "No, they don't work at the plant."

The girl pointed at Cluck's left hand. "You should get that looked at."

That was a new one. Strangers usually assumed it was a deformity, that he came this way, his fingers balled into a fist at birth and never fully opening. His hand had been that way for years, the ring finger and pinkie stuck curled under like talons, the third finger always bent. He could only straighten his thumb and forefinger, only had full range of motion in those two. Even if he could spread out his whole hand, his fingers wouldn't match. The third, ring, and pinkie would never get as big as the ones on his right hand, the growth plates cracked and knocked out of place years ago.

"Too late," he told the girl.

Then came the few awkward seconds that made her hunch her shoulders as though she were tall. Her ear almost brushed her jean jacket. She looked caught, like strangers when he noticed them staring.

"Let's get you some ice," she said.

Her guilt made him wince.

"You don't have to do that," he said.

But she waved him into the liquor store, slid quarters into the ice machine, and filled a plastic sack. The light from the refrigerator case shined through the soda bottles, casting bands of color on the linoleum. Stewart's Lime, Cheerwine, Blue Vanilla Frostie, all bright with dyes his grandfather said were no better than the chemicals the plant mixed up a hundred thousand gallons at a time.

The girl pulled the scarf off her hair. Her messy bun came undone, her hair falling down her back. She plunged her hand into the ice and wrapped a fistful in the sheer fabric. The water darkened the flower pattern, turning the white space between the roses gray.

She held it to his temple. "That's gonna be blue by tomorrow morning."

Cold water dripped down his cheek. "Don't worry. They look good on me."

She switched hands and shook out her fingers. "This happens a lot?"

"Must be my sparkling personality."

She put his hand on the scarf. "Could be the way you're dressed."

"Eye-catching, isn't it?" Cluck had the same thing on he wore most days. Collared shirt, sleeves rolled up from working on the wings. Vest and trousers. "Fetching, you might say?"

The girl filled her arms on the way to the counter. Soda bottles, caramel corn, praline cashews from a farm one county over.

The man at the counter jerked his newspaper to straighten it. "More popcorn, eh?"

The girl flicked him off. The man chuckled, an almost-friend laugh. Almendro was so small nobody bothered to renumber the town sign after the census a few years ago. The man probably knew the girl's mother and all her sisters if she had any. She'd probably been coming in to buy sour worms and neon sodas since she was in grade school.

They probably did this every week, the man's teasing, her middle finger, his laugh.

"You want anything?" the girl asked Cluck.

Cluck wondered how someone her size ate all that. "You don't mess around, do you?"

Her hand paused halfway to a bag of peach rings. "Excuse me?"

He braced to talk himself out. He forgot girls didn't need to be heavy to feel heavy. Last summer, half his cousins lived on honey and chili powder, a diet they read about in a magazine. Eugenie planned on doing it again this year before they got to Stanislaus County, where she had a park ranger who thought he was her boyfriend.

"I didn't mean it that way," he said. "Here." He tried to take the bags and bottles. "Let me buy. Least I can do."

She dropped everything on the counter, bag of ice and all, and walked out. The bell on the door jingled and knocked the glass.

Cluck followed her out. "I can do this all night."

She stopped and turned around, arms crossed tight. The wind fluffed up her skirt, like the bottom half of her was underwater. "Do what?"

"You say something and feel bad about it," Cluck said. "I say something and feel bad about it. Just warning you though, I say a lot of stupid things, and I'm good at feeling bad. You'll get tired before I do."

She walked off, the thin film of her dress lapping at the backs of her knees.

He still had to get the milk. The man at the counter grunted to his newspaper, huffed at the mess of packages Cluck had made the girl leave on the counter.

"Sorry." Cluck paid for a quart of milk, and put everything else back. Soda bottles in the refrigerator case, dried mango and a whole jicama with the other fruit.

The man looked over at him like he might shoplift. He should've combed his hair. His grandfather said wearing it as long as he did, down over the collar, wasn't doing him any favors. But his grandfather knew why he never cut it shorter. He knew what it was hiding, why Cluck never pulled it back in public. It would've been as bad as turning his head over, showing strangers the red.

Cold water dripped off the sides of Cluck's palm. He still had the girl's scarf, full of ice.

He ran outside after her, but she was already gone.

A mal nudo, mal cuño.

Meet roughness with roughness.

❧

Oscar and Rey saw Lace holding the bucket of motel ice and knew they were in for a show. But she hitched her thumb toward the door to order them out. They grumbled and took their soda bottles and *chicharrones* down the hall to Matías' room.

Justin lay sprawled on the other bed, the motel's patterned spread crumpled under him. He snored the low drone of june bugs, one hand shielding his eyes from the TV.

He and Matías could get away with anything. They were *Abuela's* perfect little *soldados*. Matías was ready for a fight whenever a Corbeau looked at one of them. Justin always had some plan to sabotage the Corbeaus' generator or spread vegetable oil on the tree branches.

They were *Abuela's* good boys, *sus niños buenos*, and *las sirenas* were clumsy fish. *Abuela* always pointed out when one mermaid was looking a little soft, another too bony. One of them had put on too much cream blush, another hadn't speckled enough paillettes over her body, so the ones covering her *escamas* were too obvious.

Abuela saw only their screwups, while Matías riled up the Corbeaus, and Justin beat up locals when no Corbeau showed.

But even Matías wouldn't have pulled what Justin did tonight. The only locals Matías ever beat up were a couple of guys throwing corn nuts and M&Ms at Emilia and Martha, trying to feed the mermaids like animals. Matías might have been one made-for-TV movie away from slapping a Corbeau in the face with a glove and challenging him to a duel, but he took pride in a fair fight, even with the Corbeaus. When Justin stole the Corbeaus' extension cords, he did it behind Matías' back. Matías never would've let him do something that pulled in the Corbeau women. His *caballerosidad* was as firm as his fists.

Lace upended the ice bucket. The flat cubes spilled onto Justin's chest and scattered out, hitting his chin and arms.

He startled awake and jumped up. "What the . . ." He shook off his body.

"What is wrong with you?" Lace asked. "Do you want your mother getting the call to bail your ass out of the county lockup?"

"You think I'm stupid?" He ripped the spread off the bed and shook it out. "We were never gonna get caught."

"You don't know that." She tore the bedspread out of his hands. "What was that?"

He snatched it back, forehead creasing. He and his brothers looked so much like his father, with that hard brow bone and lips as full as any woman's. The girls liked him as much as the women liked his father. But now his father was gone, taking his mother's Chevy and leaving nothing but three sons who had his last name instead of Paloma.

"Why'd you do it?" Lace asked.

"What are you, my mother?"

"Worse. Your mother's too nice to do this." She smacked the side of his head.

He flopped down on the plain sheet and bunched both pillows under his neck. "Get out of the way, will you?" he said to Lace's body cutting through the TV's light.

She put her hands on her hips, blocking it worse. He was gonna listen. He was gonna know that if he broke his mother's heart, she'd break him.

Justin stared at Lace's rib cage, trying to see through her.

"That guy was what?" she asked. "Fun?"

"I didn't like how he looked at me."

"Bullshit." She slammed her hand into the side of the TV. It went dark. She'd stayed in this room last season, and knew the right spot to turn it off.

Justin still stared at her stomach. "Oscar and Rey, if nobody teaches 'em how to fight, they won't know."

"That wasn't a fight," Lace said. "That was the three of you beating on a local. You know what happens when you beat on the locals? They don't come. If they don't come, we don't get paid. Word spreads that we're the kind of people who beat up anyone we feel like. Then guess what? We're not welcome in this town anymore. Then we're not welcome in the next town, or the next county. My father goes back to a job the school district cut. Your grandfather goes back to selling *champurrado* where, Echo Park? You want that?"

He sat up. "I had it handled." His yelling turned her face hot.

"Oh, like you had it handled with the horse?" Lace asked.

Justin's cheek grew sunken, back teeth biting the inside. "Low, Lace," he said. "Low."

The guilt hit her, small, but sharp. He was right. Her bringing it up was low. Justin was only eleven when he, Alexia, and Alexia's older brother "borrowed" a Camargue colt from a family that ran a traveling horse show. They'd planned to bring it back before dawn, but it had spooked and gotten away from them, and in the moonless night they couldn't spot its pale coat.

The three of them thought they could get away with it if they kept their mouths shut. But then Alexia, a new mermaid, could not get near water. She shied away from it like a foal that had never seen a river. Her brother and Justin startled as easily as fillies, jumping at the sound of every closed door or chittering squirrel. They realized the horse family knew about the Camargue, and had cursed them.

Justin, Alexia, and Alexia's brother stayed up three days and nights, searching for that horse. The Palomas, including Lace, all stayed up too, praying, fearing that the lost colt would make the horse family hate the Palomas as much as the Palomas hated the Corbeaus. But they could not help them look, because to lift the curse the three would have to get the horse back themselves.

They finally found it grazing in a salt marsh. They returned it, their eyes never leaving the grass as they apologized. The next day, Alexia loved water again, and her brother and Justin were bold as hawks. The family who owned the Camargue figured they had learned their lesson, and lifted the curse that made them like skittish horses.

Lace sat on the edge of the bed, back to Justin. All the arguing seeped out of her. It wasn't fair of her to bring it up. Justin had been the youngest of the three of them, and he and his cousins had made it right.

If only the feud with the Corbeaus came down to a single lost colt.

"Somebody's gotta look out for us," Justin said.

"We look out for each other," she said.

"*Abuela* puts us in the same town with them."

Them. The word twisted his lips. He couldn't even speak the name Corbeau.

He was saying what nobody else would. *Abuela* chose wrong. Every year, she chose wrong. And every year, the Corbeaus got one of them. Last year Matías spent half the show season with a cast on his right arm, though he swore it was worth it and he'd do it again. The year before that a *sirena* came home with her dress strap ripped by a Corbeau. Her mother had thanked God she could run faster than any of her cousins.

Every year, they wondered what the Corbeaus might do next. Send crows to bring sickness on the Palomas. Use *gitano* magic to curse a Paloma child, stopping her from growing the birthmarks that showed up on all other Paloma girls. Leti was sure they'd murdered *Tío* Armando years ago, slaughtered him in the woods. The story about the coyote was just that, she said, a story.

Lace put nothing past the Corbeaus. Twenty years ago, they'd caused the flood at the lake, killing *Tía* Lora's husband. Eight years ago, they'd almost drowned Magdalena with that net. There was nothing they would not do.

Justin punched his pillows, fluffing them up.

"I'm not gonna go looking for a fight," he said. "All I'm saying is, they come here, they're gonna get one. And I'm gonna make sure my brothers are ready."

"And whose show do you think that guy's gonna go see now?" Lace asked. "Ours or theirs?"

Justin grabbed the remote and clicked the TV on.

"If you want to look out for us, good," she said. "Look out for us. Keep Oscar and Rey out of fights."

He flipped the channel. "If you don't want me beating on the locals, don't go out so late."

He knew why she went out late. She starved all day so when she slid into her tail, her stomach wouldn't look soft with baby fat, *Abuela* poking it with the corner of her Bible and saying, "You're still not a woman, *mija*." But after the cleanup and the costume mending, hunger drove Lace to the snack aisle at the liquor store. So she stayed as she was, not soft enough for her grandmother to pull her from the show, not thin enough to be one of the finned beauties who draped their tails on wide rocks, posing for pictures.

Justin threw the remote in the air and caught it. It smacked against his palm. "Guys around here gotta know they can't look at my cousins."

"He wasn't looking at me."

"He could've been."

Thank God Justin didn't have sisters. "But he wasn't."

She almost felt bad for the guy. He'd either been too scared to fight her cousins or thought it was no use. He wasn't built like Justin, but he was just as tall, and he had enough muscle on him that he could've tried if he'd wanted to.

Maybe Justin didn't like his hair, how it was almost long enough to touch his shoulders. According to Lace's uncles, no man worth anything wore his hair past his ears. She didn't know if it was that wavy and messy on its own or if that was from her cousins kicking him around. And she couldn't quite tell what he was, his features strong but not sharp.

Lace's cousins didn't like not knowing what someone was, not knowing what to do with them. Poor guy didn't stand a chance.

"Sorry, Lace," Justin said, as quickly as if he'd stepped on the fin of her tail.

"Don't tell me. Tell the local guy. Tell your mother."

"I thought you didn't want my mother to know."

"Then don't do it again." She pulled the door shut behind her.

Her feet brushed the hallway carpet, picking up static. Her fingers sparked on the knob of her room. Today had been the first day dry enough for it. The rain was coming again, her father said. They were waiting on a wet summer, one that would dull tourists' taste for outdoor shows. The Palomas would fight the Corbeaus for an even smaller audience.

Martha had fallen asleep before Lace went out. So bony her upper arms were as thin as her forearms, Martha couldn't keep weight on, even with her mother always pushing stone pine nuts at her, swearing they would help her grow hips.

Poor, good-hearted Martha. She'd once made the mistake of saying they shouldn't call the Corbeaus gypsies. She'd read somewhere that the right word was Romani. The glare *Abuela* and Lace's mother gave her could have singed the green off an ancho chile.

Their tails hung over the shower bar, the pink and orange fins dripping into the bathtub. Martha's arm stuck out of the comforter, long fingers grasping the TV remote. Lace clicked off the set.

Makeup covered the pressboard dresser. Base and mascara. Cream eye shadows in a dozen shades. Red lipsticks. All waterproof. Sea-colored rhinestones to stick at the outer corner of each eye and on their false eyelashes. It was Lace's job to put color on each of her cousins, the same as it had been before she joined the show.

If her cousins showed for call late from flirting with local men, Lace barely had time to do her own makeup. Not that it mattered. *Abuela* kept her in the background, a mermaid who flicked her tail and then disappeared into the shadows of sunken trees.

Lace took off her dress and twisted to look at her *escamas*, jeweling her lower back like coins of water. Each one was round, the size of a dime, raised a little like a mole. They shone like the cup of an abalone shell. A sprinkling of scales off a pale fish, a gift from the river goddess *Apanchanej*.

Las sirenas all had them. Alexia's spotted the back of her neck. Sisters Reyna and Leti wore theirs on opposite shoulder blades.

Martha was lucky. Hers encircled her lower calf like an anklet, hidden by the costume tail. Any paillettes she wore were for decoration.

Lace sank down on her side of the bed. Her skirt fluffed, and a wisp of black wafted out. She pinched the air and caught it between her fingers. A feather, dark as obsidian, streaked with the red of wine and pomegranate seeds. She'd never seen one like it, with all that red.

The color turned her throat sour. It made her lower back prickle. If it brushed her birthmarks, it might make each one peel away like a scab.

She took the feather out to the parking lot, struck a match from one of the motel books, and lit it. The fire ate through the plume. She let it fall to the ground and then stamped it out until it crumbled to ash.

Entre l'arbre et l'écorce il ne faut pas mettre le doigt.

Don't put your finger between the tree and the bark.

Cluck watched his grandfather lean an elbow out of the Morris Cowley's driver's side window. The wind from the highway made the end of his cigarette glow.

"Those things'll kill you, you know," Cluck said.

"So will the things they eat in this country," *Pépère* said. The soda in the liquor store horrified Alain Corbeau, those colors bright as neon tubes. He thought Kraft Singles contained, within a few square inches, all American evils. His career at the adhesive plant had only strengthened his belief that chemicals belonged on the flaps of envelopes and between layers of pressboard, not in the stomach.

Cluck laid two new peacock feathers out on the dashboard, both pale as swans' wings, thanks to a recessive allele. Leucism. It left nothing but white, and the faintest flashes of sunrise colors if the light hit the barbs the right way.

Locals swore the white peacock of Elida Park was a myth, no more real than a green flash at dusk. But today the bird had dragged his train across the grass and left behind these two perfect tail feathers.

Cluck's grandfather lifted one off the dashboard. It let off a little blue. "What will you do with them?" he asked.

Cluck held the passenger door handle. Whenever the truck up-shifted, its weight pulled on his fingers. The latch was so old that if *Pépère* sped, it might come unhooked, and the door might fly open. "Same thing I do with the blue ones, I guess."

His grandfather set the feather down. "Your hard work will never be worn, then. You'll never catch anyone in this family in white wings."

Pépère parked the Morris Cowley behind the Craftsman house, their home for the weeks they'd be in Almendro. The plumbing squealed, the floorboards groaned back and forth, and on windy nights, the attic murmured to the second floor.

Cluck didn't have to hear it though. He slept in the costume trailer, a blue and white 1961 Shasta Compact. It saved his cousins from argu-ing about who had to sleep in the same room with him, calling *not-it* like they were still in grade school lessons. To them, his left-handedness and the red in his feathers made him dangerous as a *matagot*. Worse luck than a black cat brought across a stream. When the family went to church on *la veille de Noël* or *le Vendredi saint*, they did not bring him. So *Pépère* stayed home with him, reading from Luke. "Let them have their Latin and their *hosties*," he told Cluck.

Pépère pointed out the window. "*Regarde.*" He lifted his hand toward a flitter of movement. A red-winged blackbird, all dark feath-ers except for a brushstroke of deep coral on each shoulder, crossed the sky.

This was his way of telling Cluck not to mind the red in his own feathers.

Pépère set the parking break. "I left Eugenie's wings for you. She tore the right one."

"Again?" Cluck slammed the door.

"*Malheureusement.*"

"I'll get to it."

First Cluck got the tire pressure gauge from inside the costume trailer. If the Shasta would sit for the show's run here, he had to make sure the tires weren't sinking into the ground.

He'd just put the gauge to the front right tire when Dax grabbed him by the back of the neck.

"You just had to go start something, didn't you?" Dax slammed him against the side of the trailer. He caught a handful of Cluck's hair, pulling at the back of his scalp.

"What?" Cluck asked.

"Don't ask me what." Dax flicked Cluck's temple. "This."

Pépère had made Cluck forget the bruising, the soreness. He always made him forget, no matter who gave him the bruise. Locals. Dax. His mother, when he was small, catching him in the eye with her elbow and then telling him "*Le petit imbécile,* stay out of my way."

"You went to start a fight," Dax said.

The smell of Dax's aftershave dried out Cluck's mouth, his tongue a parched sponge.

"I didn't start anything," Cluck said.

"Then where'd you get this?" Dax pressed him into the aluminum siding so hard the ridges cut across his body.

"Some guys in town," Cluck said.

"What guys?"

"I don't know."

"Don't lie to me." Dax pulled him off the side of the trailer enough to slam him into it again.

Cluck held himself up, but didn't fight. "I don't know." A metal seam pressed into his cheek.

"If you went to settle the score, you better tell me now."

"What?" was all Cluck could get out.

"Don't go near them." Dax held him harder, wringing out the muscle at the back of his neck. "Got it?"

"Who?" Cluck turned his head.

The rage in Dax's face shifted, the edges ground down.

He loosened his grip, dropped his hand. "You don't know."

The back of Cluck's neck cooled.

"They're in town," Dax said. "That family."

That family.

The Palomas were already here. They came back every year, never any guilt. Because of them, Clémentine's oldest brother had lost his first wife twenty years ago. Cluck had heard stories about her, the woman with so much grace on the highest branches none of them could believe she had no *fildefériste* blood.

La magie noire the Palomas carried in their birthmarks had taken her.

The Palomas meant for every performer to die, drowned with those branches when the water flooded up onto its shores. All to steal the lake they thought belonged to them. It was only by the grace of God that the rest of the Corbeaus managed to swim against the pull of their own wings, scramble onto rocks, claw at the shore.

The Palomas lost one of their own too, a man who must have been at the lake to draw the water onto the land, *la magie noire* ready in his hands. But the Palomas still set up their show where the trees had been, on that man's grave and the grave of a Corbeau.

Cluck's family moved to the other side of the woods, as far as that stretch of forest would let them get from a family that danced where one of their own had died.

Cluck's neck prickled to hot again. This was where the Palomas had ruined their grandfather. And every year they came back to rub it in.

"Does *Pépère* know?" Cluck asked.

"Since when is it my job to tell him?" Dax shoved him, this time to let him go. "You swear the fish didn't do that to you?"

The fish. Dax didn't like saying the name Paloma any more than Cluck did.

Cluck pulled on the hem of his shirt to smooth it. "It was some guys from around here."

"You're sure?"

"Another local told them off." The girl in the red lipstick knew the man at the liquor store enough to give him the finger and get a laugh. And Cluck would have known a pack of Palomas. He would have seen *la tromperie* in their eyes. His mother called the Paloma girls *les sorcières*. They must have been, she said, to draw an audience when all they did was swim.

"What are they doing here this early?" Cluck asked.

"They know our schedule," Dax said.

"We should've canceled the stop."

The words drew their mother's shadow toward the trailer. The idea must have summoned her, called her like a spirit.

She stood with arms crossed, thin elbows resting in her palms. "This family hasn't canceled a stop since we came to this country." She'd starched her linen shift dress so well the breeze didn't move it. Her eyelashes looked sharp as chestnut spines. "Not for rain. Not for the earthquakes. Not even for snow, not that either of you would remember that year."

It was what set them apart from the Palomas, who had to cancel their shows every time it rained. The drops disturbed the water too much to let the audience see them.

"Not another word about canceling shows, understood?" his mother asked.

Dax's "*Compris*" and Cluck's one nod satisfied her. She went back inside, slamming the kitchen door.

"Don't go near them," Dax told Cluck.

"I never have," Cluck said under the screen door's rattle.

"But you're thinking about it."

Every Corbeau thought about it. Cluck never did anything though. Dax and his cousins were the ones who used to place nets where the Palomas swam. They'd only stopped when Dax and Cluck's mother ordered them to. "Only cowards set traps for little girls in costumes," she told them; true men did not go after women. Cluck had tried telling them before that someone would drown, and all he'd done was earn a few more bruises from his brother. Dax only listened to their mother.

But Dax throwing out the nets hadn't kept the Palomas from slicking the tree branches with petroleum jelly last year. The Palomas had even been smart enough to pick branches shadowed by leaves, so the performers wouldn't see the light shining off them. They were lucky Aunt Camille had broken her leg and not her neck.

Pain throbbed through the roots of Cluck's hair. "I won't do anything," he said, though God knew he wanted to sometimes. Fighting was the only safe way to touch a Paloma. Half this family believed if they ever let a Paloma brush their arm or bump their shoulder, they'd wither and die like wildflowers in July sun. But fighting was safe. The rage made it true and good. The anger and honor of defending this family shielded them like a saint's prayer. Hitting and kicking were safe. Anything else could bring sickness.

"You better not." Dax followed their mother, his slam of the door as fast and loud as hers.

Cluck set a hand on the trailer door frame and pulled himself up the step.

Eugenie sat on the trailer's built-in, her skirt rippling over the threadbare mattress.

There were only two reasons Eugenie showed up in the costume trailer. Cluck only had to check her hands to know which. Sometimes it was a torn dress, usually one of *Mémère's* chiffons or silks, skirts she had danced in at Eugenie's age. Eugenie would hold the fabric out to him, and he stitched up the tear.

This time his cousin's palms cupped not one of their grandmother's dresses, but a plastic bag of freezer-tray ice cubes. She said nothing, just held it out to him the same way she offered a ripped dress.

He took it, his nod as much of a thank you as he had in him.

She got up from the built-in and hopped down from the trailer door, the hem of her dress dragging after her bare feet.

The bag wet his palms. He didn't know where she meant him to use it. His temple, the back of his neck, where his ribs hit the trailer siding.

Cluck made out the sharp, far-off call of red-winged blackbirds. *Pépère* always meant for the sight of them to make Cluck feel better about his own feathers. Cluck could never bring himself to remind his grandfather how easily crows killed them.

*Una oveja que arrea a los lobos
vale más que la lana.*

A sheep that herds wolves is
worth more than her wool.

Lace's uncles stood at the picnic tables in silence, half-juiced fruit filling their hands.

They were never this quiet when they made the *aguas frescas*. Every afternoon, their laughing carried all the way to the motel with the scent of limes and oranges.

Had they just killed a crow? Last summer, Lace had seen a black-feathered bird peck the heart from a halved passion fruit. Her uncle loaded the Winchester 1912 her father used for scaring off bears and coyotes, and shot it. Lace could still remember its eyes, shining like mercury drops.

Lace searched for the crow or the shotgun. Instead she found *Abuela*, standing between wooden picnic tables, her presence hushing the men.

"Rosa," *Abuela* said. The wrinkles in her face thinned to cracks.

Rosa. Pink, the color of Lace's tail. Her name to her grandmother.

Tía Lora caught up, her eyes tight. Worry pulled at her mouth.

"After the show, you stay," *Abuela* told Lace.

This was it. Tonight *Abuela* would tell Lace off for throwing ice on Justin. He and Matías, *los soldados. Abuela* blessed the work of their hands. It didn't matter that Justin knew Lace was right. To *Abuela*, it would never be Lace's business to correct him.

Lace nodded.

"After the show you make yourself pretty and show your tail," her grandmother said. "Let them take pictures of you."

"What?" Lace asked. Only *Abuela*'s favorite mermaids draped themselves on rocks after the show. "Why?"

Abuela put her hands on Lace's shoulders and pressed down, like she did to bless her when she was sick. *"Una oveja que arrea a los lobos vale más que la lana,"* she said.

The sound didn't break the squish of fruit under the men's hands.

A sheep that herds wolves is worth more than her wool.

This was a reward. This was for Justin and the bucket of hotel ice, for telling him to keep Rey and Oscar out of fights.

Abuela understood. She knew even better than Lace did that if Justin and Rey and Oscar hit whoever they wanted, soon the Palomas would get run out of town. *Abuela* treated as sacred the fights with the Corbeaus, all those bruises and the broken arms. But *Abuela* would not bless sending a local home with a black eye.

Lace would never have Martha's shape, thin and jeweled as a violet eel, or Emilia's wide, pageant-queen smile. But she had thick hair that fell to her waist, mermaid's hair, and she was *una niña buena.* A good girl.

Her grandmother had decided this was enough.

"Gracias, Abuela," Lace said, accepting the blessing.

Her grandmother crossed the afternoon shadows, the crepe myrtles and salt cedars casting the shapes of their leaves.

Lace's great-aunt squeezed her shoulders, laughing like she'd remembered a joke. Each of her uncles picked her up and spun her once, for luck, *"Para que nada cambie tu rumbo."* *So nothing will turn you around.* It was always their blessing to *las sirenas,* because the river's depth was so dark a mermaid could forget which way to the surface.

An hour before the show, Lace layered on pink eye shadow, added a last coat of red lipstick, rubbed in more cream blush. At the sound of their uncles' *zampoñas,* the mermaids swam in from their different spots along the lake and river, like creatures called from far-away grottos.

They held their breath and took their places in the underwater forest, made of trees the Corbeaus had sunk twenty years ago. This was *Abuela's* greatest triumph, that every time they came to Almendro they used the stage the Corbeaus had built them, the grove the Corbeaus once called their own. Now audiences who sat on the ridge just above the shore could see down to the lake shelf, where the trees locked together into tangles of branches.

The mermaids treated those branches like a coral reef, settling into the hollows, perching on the edges of submerged boughs. They swam in pairs, then clusters, then each out in a different direction. They circled, then broke away. Their bodies formed the shapes of hearts or stars. They lined up so their tails made a rainbow.

No canned music. Just the reed pipes and the soft rush of the river emptying into the one side of the lake and flowing out the other. The applause came in bursts, like the mermaids were fireworks blooming into sparks.

They draped their bodies to look as though they were sunning themselves, even though they were underwater and the light had fallen enough to turn the edges of the lake copper. A few of them dove in and out of the lake like flying fish.

It was being under that Lace loved most. The lightness of her own body, the water trying to lift her toward the surface. The silhouettes of the underwater trees, like a forest on a fall night. How everything looked blurred like she was seeing it through stained glass. How water that had felt cold when she slid into the river now felt as warm as her own body. Even the sharp sting in her lungs as she swam out of view to take a breath.

Just as the audience began to believe they were spying on unknowing mermaids, *las sirenas* looked at them. They swam up to the rocks, hiding and flirting like water nymphs. The tourists caught those flashes of color on camera.

At the end of *la danza de las sirenas*, Lace and Martha posed on the steep bank, fanning their tails out on a rock. The trees filtered the last sun, and the sequins lit up like raw quartz. *Los turistas* left the low cliffs where they'd been watching and took the path down the slope, to the narrow stretch of beach.

A girl in jelly sandals the color of hibiscus flowers took a few steps toward Lace. Her eyes wavered between the shimmer of Lace's fin and her painted face.

"Do you want to touch my tail?" Lace asked, like she was told to, in the voice she'd heard her older cousins use, soft as the whispers of river sprites.

The girl opened her small hand and stroked the fin, first hesitant as touching a snake, then surer, like petting a cat. To her, the soaked elastane and sequins might feel a little like a mermaid's scales.

Their season's receipts were at the mercy of children and their favorite *cuentos de hadas*. The Corbeaus called her family's show kitschy, as artless and plastic as souvenir snow globes. Matías and his brothers had thrown punches when Corbeau men made fun of the bright colors, the glitter, the wide-eyed looks *Abuela* made the *sirenas* wear, as though dry land was magic they'd never imagined. But Lace's mother told her that tourists probably couldn't even take their children to the Corbeaus' show. "They're French," she said. "I bet they take their clothes off halfway through."

When the crowd thinned, and the families left, the mermaids watched *Abuela*. At her nod, they slid back into the water, smooth as knives. Martha swam toward her far corner of the lake, Lace back to her spot up the river. She kicked down to where the river's current didn't pull.

A shriek like a car alarm echoed through the water.

Lace startled, losing her rhythm, and the current swept her.

She spread her arms to swim, but her tail jerked her back.

Her fin fabric was caught. A colander had gotten the end of her tail.

Lace doubled her body over and felt at the fin. Her hands found not just river roots, but tangles of slick threads.

The nylon of a fishing net.

The Corbeaus. They hadn't put a net in the water since what happened to Magdalena. But tonight they'd left one in the river for Lace and her cousins.

She pulled at her tail. The fin stayed. The net had balled and wrapped around her, holding her to the colander. She twisted and swam, but the roots and the net only gave enough to let her fight.

A string of bubbles slipped from Lace's lips, the last air she had left. The dark water turned to stripes of light. Red like the Cheerwine in the liquor store refrigerator case. Green as lime soda. Electric blue like the Frostie bottles.

She'd been taught to protect her tail like it was as much part of her body as those little girls thought. But now its weight and its trailing fabric were killing her.

She braced for ripping the fabric to hurt, and tore the fin in half. The tail split up the side. She kicked out of the river roots. The empty tail dangled from the colander, leaving her naked except for the fake pearls of her costume top. She floated toward the surface like a bubble.

Her grandmother would wring her neck for leaving her tail, but not as hard as she would if Lace washed up dead. A mermaid drowned in the North Fork. What would that do to their ticket sales? *Abuela* would use every *yerba buena* in her suitcase to bring Lace back to life just so she could kill her again.

The net came with her, caught on her fingers. The threads, aqua as a swimming pool, almost glowed in the dark water, this awful thing like the one that nearly killed Lace's cousin.

She shook the nylon threads off, and they sank back toward the river roots.

Lace surfaced to the noise of far-off screaming, and a long call like a tornado siren. Louder than her gasping. Louder than her coughing. Louder than her sucking the air from the dark.

Her half-drowned brain fizzed at the edges, making her hear things. She got her breath back and shook her head to clear it all.

But the screaming stayed. So did the siren's yell. She rubbed her eyes and temples, circling her bare legs to tread. She pressed behind her ears to clear the water. But the noises kept on, joined by a thrumming through the ground. A whole town running at once.

She lifted her head to the sky, a shade of blue from dark.

A cloud swirled over Almendro, so thick it seemed made of liquid. It looked deeper as it moved, solid as water. Tilting her head up made her dizzy with wondering if it too held a current and tangles of roots, a mirrored river banding the sky.

Qui vivra verra.

He who lives will see.

❦

*I*t took Cluck ten seconds to get up the cottonwood. He didn't even have to paint iodine solution on the soles of his feet the way his cousins did. Climbing had turned his rough as bark.

The moon looked wedged between the hills, yellow as tansy buttons. It got free and rose, paling. He could almost make out the ringing of distant glass chimes, the show's only music.

Then sound broke the sky open. The moon shuddered. The siren's first scream filled the dark, turning the stars to needles. It grew, spreading out from the plant like air thinning a balloon's skin.

Cluck put his hand to the tree's trunk and steadied himself. His heartbeat clicked in his ears. Another drill. By now, Almendro had gotten used to them. When Cluck's grandfather worked as a safety engineer, the plant ran drills more than regulations mandated. Now they just blared the sirens to make the plant sound compliant, while telling employees to ignore the noise and keep working.

The ground wavered like a pond's surface. The porcelain vines flickered with life, lit up with the chatter of small creatures. Sparrows flitted to their nests. He made out the dark shapes of wild rabbits and prairie voles darting into burrows. Squirrels scratched up trees. Two stray cats slipped into a hollow trunk, a gray fox into its den. They scrambled like wasps into a nest, sensing rain coming.

Cluck lifted his eyes to the moon. Wisps of white-gray cut across its gold, like curls of smoke off his grandfather's cigarettes.

He looked over his shoulder. A ball of cirrus clouds rose from the chemical plant, a nest of white thread. He swore he felt the cloud reach out through the night, the threads tangling in his hair, cutting through his throat toward his lungs. The closest he'd ever come to *le vertige*. Not from height, but from the distance across Almendro's sky.

The moon pulled back. The cloud spread out from the plant, a blanket unfurling. The siren throbbed between his temples.

Cluck half-climbed, half-jumped down.

He ran through the woods, calling his grandfather. *"Pépère,"* then "Alain," then *"Pépère"* again.

Cluck ran down the hill. He found his mother sitting on a costume trunk, counting ticket receipts.

He caught his breath. "We have to stop the show."

She looked up from her ledger, pencil paused.

"We have to stop the show now," he said.

She shook her head and went back to her numbers.

He slammed the book.

She backhanded him. He knew that kind of slap, meant to knock sense into him as much as to reprimand. Suggesting they stop a show was little distance from cursing the family name. They'd gone on through sprained wrists, jammed shoulders, nosebleeds. If one fairy twisted her ankle, the rest kept on. The first night Margaux took off with a local, they put Violette in her place, like changing out a light-bulb.

Cluck turned his face to his mother again, his cheek hot.

"What's the matter with you?" she asked.

He lifted his hand, toward the siren's swell. The glass chime sounds died under its rise. But even the audience ignored it. The sirens annoyed the residents of Almendro, but they were used to them. The tourists took their cues from the locals and figured no tornado or air raid was coming.

"It's not a drill," Cluck said. He pointed to the sky. The ball had thinned to a veil. It spread out over the town, opening like a trumpet flower.

To his mother it must have looked like cloud cover. Nothing more. She had begun to tip her chin back down to her work when Cluck heard his grandfather's voice.

"He's right," *Pépère* said. Cluck could see the readiness in those hands, his fingers half-bent. But what would he do with those hands? The plant had locked him out years ago, so he wasn't there to check gauges or turn off valves.

Cluck's mother watched the sky. The veil thickened and grew uneven, like *la religieuse,* the hard layer coating the bottom of a fondue *caquelon.*

The pen fell from her hands. *"Et maintenant que faisons-nous?"* she asked Cluck's grandfather. *What do we do now?*

It was the first time Cluck had heard her sound like *Pépère*'s daughter, her voice open and fearful, instead of annoyed, put-upon, as though the old man were an aging dog. Her words so often brimmed with *"Et alors?" What now?* Now they were full of *"Papa,* take this, fix it."

The three of them didn't whisper. The audience couldn't hear them. A hundred yards, the trees, and that siren took the sound.

But the audience saw the cloud. Children watching for fairies spotted it first, thinking it was the magic of winged beings. They squealed and waved at the fairy cloud.

Their parents followed those small hands. That cloud drew a shared gasp from mothers, a *what-the-hell* from fathers. The siren swelled from background noise to a shriek, and they registered the sound.

Pépère closed the space between him and them. "Ladies and gentlemen, my apologies," he said, his voice level but loud. It carried, pulled their eyes from the sky, covered the faint breath of glass chimes. "We're going to have to cut tonight's show a bit short."

Cluck watched him, his own muscles sparking and restless. How did Alain Corbeau keep such stillness in his voice?

"I'm going to ask you all to proceed to the road," his grandfather said. "There's a service station very close. Everyone go there. Stay inside or under an awning." He spoke in his safety engineer's voice, a pilot directing passengers. *Stay calm. Breathe. Brace.* "Do not try to go to your cars. Do not try to go home."

Cluck's cousins climbed down from the boughs, light as cicadas. Never rush when they can see you, Nicole Corbeau had taught them. The women moved no faster than the blooms that pulled loose from their flower crowns and drifted down.

The audience scattered.

"If you need assistance to the road, ask any of us," *Pépère* said. "If you're wearing anything cotton, and you can remove it easily, then do so, but the important thing is to get to the service station."

"Cotton?" a man with a camera strap around his neck asked the question Cluck could see on every face. "Why cotton?"

"The fallout may contain adhesive intermediates," his grandfather said. "Cotton will stick to the skin worse than other fabric."

There was no screaming, no flurry of clothes tossed aside. Alain Corbeau's voice calmed them like a song. Men took off cotton pullovers. Mothers urged children out of cotton jackets. But shirts, pants, and dresses stayed on, and the audience streamed toward the gas station at the road's edge, quick, but not running. Alain Corbeau's stillness assured them that, cotton or no, they would be fine as long as they took cover.

Cluck pulled his grandfather aside. "Cotton. They're all wearing cotton."

"They won't be hurt," his grandfather said. "Between the station and the pump awnings there's enough cover." He eyed the sky, gauging how long they had. "Half of them are already there."

The cloud balled like chewing gum. Soon it would break into rain. Once that cloud fell, full of the plant's adhesives, polyester would stick to their skin just as bad.

"Why did you say cotton?" Cluck asked.

"Think, boy," *Pépère* said.

He heard these words from his grandfather more than his own name. *Pépère* always asked him questions to make sure he stayed *vif*, sharp. What was the difference between primary and secondary remiges? What were the components of structural coloration? If Cluck didn't give the answer as easily as the day of the week, he heard "Think, boy."

But his grandfather was choosing now to quiz him?

Pépère walked a few paces behind the last audience members, a wary shepherd. "What do they make at the plant?"

Cluck went with him, his muscles tense with wanting to run. "I don't remember."

"You remember," *Pépère* said.

There had to be somewhere Cluck needed to get. The mayor's house? Not that he knew the address. The police station? Anyone who could do something about the strands of cloud tangling overhead. This town was deaf to those sirens.

"What do they make, boy?" his grandfather asked.

"Cyanoacrylate, okay?" Cluck shouted.

The feeling of the word stayed on his tongue. *Cyanoacrylate.* Those six syllables rooted his feet in the underbrush. The memory of *Pépère* crumpling newsprint crawled up Cluck's back. A one-paragraph story in the paper. The worker who had never been given enough safety training to know not to wear cotton. The spray of chemical eating through the man's jeans.

Cotton and cyanoacrylate. An exothermic reaction. It ran hot and quick.

The need to run, to do something about the truth in those sirens, came back to Cluck's legs.

"Why didn't you tell them?" he asked.

"You don't set off a gun in a field and then try to herd sheep," *Pépère* said. "It would have panicked them. It would have taken twice as long to get them to the filling station."

Cluck looked where his grandfather looked. The cloud swam and twirled, the surface of a bubble a second before bursting. It would rain the same cyanoacrylate that had burned through a plant worker's jeans.

"Get to the house," *Pépère* said. "Now."

"What about you?" Cluck asked.

His grandfather nodded, a lift and lowering of his chin meant to say, *Yes, I'll be there.*

He wouldn't. He would stay until everyone who'd come to see the show found shelter. This had been his work once.

Cluck's cousins drained from the woods.

He hadn't seen Eugenie. It gave him the feeling of stopping short just before a hillside. He noticed the lack of her, a missing pair of wings.

"Where's Eugenie?" Cluck asked.

She never flaked on a show altogether like Margaux or Giselle, but a little too much Melon Ball wine and she couldn't find the ground, forget the grove of cottonwoods and maples.

Pépère searched the wings. "She wasn't with you?"

Cluck didn't bother going back for his shoes. The wanting-to-run feeling broke, and he took off toward the stretch of woods Eugenie wandered when she got lost.

"Boy," *Pépère* called after him. "Your shirt."

Cluck heard those three syllables. They reached him. But they didn't register.

He got halfway across the woods. Then the cloud condensed into beads and fell. The sky rained hot, sticky drops. He kept his head down, shielding his eyes. The rain seared his neck and arms. His back felt scraped, stung with vinegar. The pain augured into his chest.

His shirt gave off a low hiss. He looked down. The fabric let off steam.

The hiss went deeper, eating through his shirt.

Cotton. His pants, the ones his grandfather once wore, were flax linen, but *Pépère's* dress shirt and Cluck's own undershirt were cotton. They were burning him like an iron.

It was getting into his body. His skin would give up and vanish. The heat would singe his lungs and his rib cage.

He ripped open the buttons on his shirt, tore it off. The rain on his hands found the cotton. The pain made him bite his cheek. Blood salted his tongue.

He pulled off his undershirt. It covered him with the feeling of wrenching away thread stuck to a scab. It left him raw to the hot chemical. It fell, and all he could do was grit his teeth against it.

Nunca llueve a gusto de todos.

It never rains to please everyone.

S he got out of the water, legs free of her tail, sirens pinching her forehead.

The cloud fanned out and crept across the sky. First it looked like white cotton candy. Then it thickened, like milk curdling in tea.

She followed the lights her father left for her, candles in glass jars to help the mermaids find their way. She felt for her dress in the underbrush, pulled it on over her costume bra. Buttoned it quickly. Ran for the motel.

Then it started to rain. The canning jars hissed and flared. Whatever had blown up at the plant turned the flames different colors, like light through prisms.

First the rain felt warm, like bathwater. But then it seeped through Lace's clothes, and she felt the sting of a shower turned all the way up. Even under her dress. Especially under her dress. Her arms and calves, her hands and feet went numb to it. But her breasts and shoulders, her back and thighs felt scalded. The searing feeling ate through her, singeing her lungs, and she couldn't get enough air to run anymore.

Pain sucked away the tail end of a breath, and she dropped to her hands and knees. She opened her mouth for more air, but it only sharpened the feeling that each bead of rain was a little knife cutting down through the sky, piercing her hard and fast.

The woods spread out in front of her. All those trees and all that distant darkness pressed the truth into her like a hand on her chest, that she did not have the air to get up and run again. She could not get up until those little knives stopped falling. Even if she crawled to the nearest stretch of road, it would offer less cover than these branches.

But she couldn't even move enough to crawl. All she could do was pull herself under the nearest tree, gritting her teeth against the feeling that her dress was soaked and heavy with poison. She squeezed her eyes shut, hoping to keep out what was falling from the sky. If she blinked enough of it in, it might leave her blind.

The rain burned into her. She curled up tighter, cheek against her sleeve. She shut her eyes tight enough to see comet trails of light. She tried to keep out the feeling that the rain was a million lit matches. And the strange smell in the air that was a little like apple cider if apple cider was the venom of some night creature, the rain and stars its teeth.

Cherchez la femme.

Look for the woman.

∗

The moon showed Cluck a stripe of water. He knelt at the river's edge and plunged in his hands, still burning from touching his shirt. The cold water hushed his palms.

"Cluck?" said Eugenie's voice.

"Eugenie," he called out, looking around. "Eugenie."

Cluck stood up, fingers dripping river water. A dozen little flickers of motion pulled his eyes. The rain weighted down the tree's branches, making them bow. Older greenery that couldn't stand up to the chemical withered and slipped down.

The night was coming apart, because this town hadn't let *Pépère* save it.

"Eugenie," he yelled out.

"Cluck."

He would have missed her if it weren't for the wings looming over her. She had her back to a tree, leaves sheltering her. Her wings shone with the chemical. It slicked her flower crown and made it look heavy as glass.

Whatever she'd been drinking had flushed her cheeks, but her eyes stayed wide. The moon filled her pupils like milk in a bowl.

Cluck grabbed a handful of her dress. "Is this cotton?" He stretched the fabric, trying to tell.

She sucked air in through her teeth and pointed to his chest. "What happened?"

"Is this cotton?" His shouting cut her off.

"Silk," she said, the word startled out of her. "*Mémère's*."

"Come on." He pulled her with him, and they ran, the ground sticky under their feet. "Watch your eyes," he said. Drops had fallen onto his cheeks and forehead. The fumes made him tear up.

The animals had all taken cover. No rustling in the underbrush. Only the steady rhythm of siren calls.

Eugenie stopped cold and slapped Cluck's arm. "Look."

About thirty yards off, a girl was curled under a tree, sparser than the one Eugenie had picked. Drops of the chemical rain trickled down.

The girl shielded her head with her arms.

Cluck knew the shape of her. He knew her hands. He'd seen her set them on her hips. He knew her hair, now frosted with chemicals.

And he knew with one look that her dress was made of cotton.

The rain would eat through her dress to her skin, and she would not know why. She was following the rules every teacher since kindergarten would have taught her. *Cover your face. Protect your eyes.* It held true for earthquakes, debris, hail, but not tonight. Because she was smart, and followed those rules, the rain would dissolve her.

Cluck held Eugenie's elbows. "Get back to the house. Stay inside." The rain on his palms cooled. He dropped his hands before they stuck to Eugenie.

"Cluck," she said. Her pupils spread, the twin moons growing.

"Dammit, Eugenie." He was shouting again. "Do it!"

She froze. She must have thought he didn't know how to yell. But he wasn't Alain Corbeau. When the sky started falling, he yelled.

She wasn't hearing him. She only heard the panic in him. He saw it in her face. She picked up on his fear, tuned in to it like the static between radio frequencies, because she knew what fear looked like on him. She'd just never seen anyone but Dax put it there.

It threw her. He needed it not to throw her. Not now.

He grasped for something that would get to her.

"You need to make sure Noe and Mason get inside," he said.

Georgette would have herded all the younger cousins into the house by now. But the names of Eugenie's little brothers was all it took, and she ran.

Jugar con fuego es peligroso juego.

To play with a flame is a dangerous game.

T he feeling of hands throbbed through Lace's body.

"Don't fight," said a voice she couldn't place. Those hands tore at the back collar of her dress. She cried out at the sound of ripping fabric. The back of her dress being torn from her felt like getting her body slit open.

She wrenched her head up, away from her shoulder. Heat stabbed through to her mouth. Her cheek evaporated like water on a dust road. There was nothing but pain spreading through her face.

Her hair tethered her, tangled in the weeds. She pulled, but it held her.

The boy from outside the liquor store held scraps of her dress in his hands. Her bra had gone with the fabric. Only a thin layer of nylon stuck to her breasts. The fake pearls had melted, the plastic stuck to the buttons on her dress.

She looked down at her body. The small movement seared her cheek. Shreds of her dress had stayed, burned to her breasts and stomach. Her body let off wisps of smoke, like steam off a lake on cold nights.

But there was no cold; she was all heat. Everything was. Her back and the riverbank. Her breasts and the underbrush. Her hips and the sycamores, all melting like the clocks in her father's favorite paintings. Each losing drops until they were gone.

The boy from outside the liquor store didn't have a shirt on. No undershirt either, just the silt brown of his chest.

What happened to your shirt? she tried to ask. The sound didn't come. Her lips mouthed the words, but her throat didn't help.

Had her cousins laid into him again?

The boy was talking at her, asking her things, beating her dress like it was alive.

She didn't hear him. She watched a black feather drift from the back of his neck like a fallen piece of hair. The wind swirled it down to her arm, and it stuck. She jerked her elbow to shake it off, but it stayed. A single plume, the tip stiff with barbs, the lower half fluffy with down. Black, streaked red.

Pain spread through her cheek and neck. It burst open like a peony. The lights her father left for her flickered in their glass jars and went out.

El pez grande se come al chico.

The big fish eats the small one.

🪶

"Can you say your name?" the nurse asked. Lace knew the woman was a nurse without opening her eyes. She had all the nurse smells. Powdered latex gloves. Ballpoint pen ink. Unscented fabric softener.

The back of Lace's scalp throbbed. She bit her tongue to keep from crying out.

"Do you remember why you're here?" the nurse asked.

Lace's lips scratched against each other. "The cotton candy," she said. The cloud in the sky had looked so much like spun sugar. Waiting for a paper cone to whirl through. "Because of the cotton candy."

She tried to curl onto her side, shifting her weight. The pain in her head rushed through her body. In the dark of her clenched-shut eyes, she saw it, the night twenty years ago. She may not have been there, but she'd heard the stories, all those trees sinking into the water. The lake swallowing the trunks whole.

No one in her family, not even the few of Lace's uncles who saw it happen, knew how the Corbeaus had done it, except that however they did came from the strange power of their feathers. Their *magia negra*.

"What if they're doing it again?" Lace asked, the sound barely enough to make the words.

"Shh," the nurse said, soft as a faucet running in another room.

Lace and her cousins had never been allowed to talk about that night. What the Corbeaus did was like death; the women in her grandmother's village would not speak of it because they believed the word *muerte* burned the lips.

"They could be out there doing it again," Lace got out, but all she got back was more *shh*.

Lace had not been born twenty years ago to see what the Corbeaus had done. But she had heard the story. First when she was four, the day she picked up a crow feather off the ground, all the barbs perfect and pure black. When she came inside twirling it in her hand, her mother had grabbed it from her small fingers so hard Lace braced for her mother to slap her. Instead, her mother told her about the awful thing Lace had not yet been alive to see.

The Corbeaus had meant the accident twenty years ago to ruin the Palomas' stretch of river, spoiling their stage and killing as many of them as they could. All at once the slow, steady current had grown turbulent, like there was a storm under the surface. Loose branches stabbed through the water. Sudden rapids tumbled in from the lake. The Corbeaus had wanted the *sirenas* trapped in the river's root tangles like figurines in snow globes.

The mermaids had all escaped those waters, rough as a wild sea. And the Corbeaus' own *magia negra* had turned on them. They did not love the water, so they could not control it. The lake rushed up onto its beaches, and the grove of shoreline trees where the Corbeaus held their own shows went into the water, pulled in quick as if the current had grabbed them by the roots.

Tía Lora's husband was swept into the lake with those trees and drowned.

Lace opened her eyes, the lids heavy and swollen. The light made her forehead pulse, like having her hair pulled.

The nurse's lilac eye shadow matched her scrubs. She wrote on her clipboard, the cap of her pen chewed like a licorice stick.

One corner of a ceiling panel lifted away from its frame, just enough to let in a black feather. Lace watched it dip and rise. It spun down and landed on the back of her hand. She brushed it away. It slipped off the sheet and through the guardrail.

But another fell.

"See?" she asked the nurse, but the nurse didn't see.

Lace shook it off, but two more fell, then six more, then a dozen, until there was no more ceiling. Only a sky made of black feathers, brushed with the red of candy apples. Red glaze made of the same sugar as that cotton candy sky.

She screamed. Her screaming made another nurse appear, this one all blue. She came with a needle and a vial and a bag of water. Lace looked for the goldfish in the bag of water, but they'd forgotten the goldfish.

Lace said so. She told them they needed to bring back the bag of water and the candy apples and the cotton candy. Give it all back for a bag of water with a goldfish.

"Did you hear me?" Lace asked. "They forgot the fish. They didn't give you the fish."

But there was still no goldfish, and the feathers kept falling.

Drowsiness settled over her. Her weight fell against the bed. Her eyes shut without her shutting them, like a doll tipped backward.

Her pulse ticked under her skin, like a watch under tissue paper.

She was the fish, raw and sliced. The bag of water was for her.

Qui trop embrasse mal étreint.

Grasp all, lose all.

A nurse stopped in the doorway, hand on the frame. "You been here all night?"

"No," Cluck said. Another nurse had sent him home around one in the morning, promising, "We'll take care of her, don't worry." So he'd gone back to the trailer and changed his clothes. It took him fifteen minutes to get his pants off. Thanks to the adhesive, the linen took half the hair on his legs.

He'd come back with a milk bottle full of Indian paintbrush, bachelor buttons, a burst of wild roses. It had taken the better part of an hour to find flowers the adhesive hadn't ruined, ones low enough to the ground that taller stalks had shielded them. On the walk back to the hospital, Cluck had almost stepped on a tourist's Polaroid, left on the side of the road. The hot adhesive had burned through the film. Except for a corner of sky, the image never developed.

The nurse stepped into the room. "Visiting hours aren't until eight, you know."

"I can hide in the supply closet until then if you want," he said.

She chuckled and joined him at the window. Cluck parted the blinds. It bothered him how much Almendro looked the same as it had yesterday. If he didn't look too close, he couldn't see the adhesive glossing the roof shingles like rubber cement, or the stray cats and dogs, their fur matted with it, or how it frosted cars and mailboxes like drying Elmer's glue.

The difference was how the air felt, hot with the faint sense that the smallest noise would make everyone in this town flinch at once. The things that had changed were harder to see than the wilted plants and the tacky sidewalks. The ruptured mixing tank had left three plant workers dead, and a dozen others injured. Every family who relied on paychecks from the plant held their breath still in their lungs. And everyone else kept quiet, stunned by the noise and the rain, afraid to go outside.

None of it had to happen. None of it would have happened if the Palomas hadn't ruined *Pépère*, cost him his job. Cluck's grandfather was the only man pushing for the plant to run safer, and when they let him go, they dropped his safety procedures one by one in the name of efficiency. When the Palomas wrecked *Pépère*'s good name, they destroyed the credibility of all the work he'd done.

"Did you lose anybody?" Cluck asked the nurse.

She checked an IV line. "Nobody close."

Cluck had heard the nurses talking about some workers' wives, friends, a few others picketing at the fence, wanting answers. He didn't have to ask why the plant workers weren't there too. He could almost hear Almendro pulling at its own seams. Half the town would demand justice, an admission from the plant's owners, and the other half would beg them to shut up. If the plant pulled out, there were no jobs. So the workers swallowed the last-minute shifts, the blowdown stacks that made the air sting their eyes, the non-regulation safety gear.

The nurse put her hair back with a rubber band that matched her scrubs. Her nails, that same light purple, clicked against her pen. He couldn't imagine liking one color that much. Not even the red in his feathers. Especially not the red in his feathers.

"Try not to get me in trouble," the nurse said, checking her watch on the way out.

The girl in the hospital bed ground her teeth in her sleep. The solvents they'd used to get the adhesive off her skin left her rawer.

Where she'd held her cheek against the sleeve of her dress, she now had a deep red burn in a blurred heart shape.

She'd probably never know that all of this was the Paloma family's fault. She'd never know that it started twenty years ago, the night the lake had flooded onto its shores like a creek bed overflowing, and those trees sank straight down like hands had pulled them under. His mother said they disappeared under a surface so calm it must have been *la magie noire*, the same dark magic that gave the Palomas their scales.

The Palomas started some rumor that Cluck's grandfather caused it, that it was some failed experiment, as if his engineering degree had taught him how to make a lake swallow trees. Cluck couldn't prove they'd started it, but he knew. The rumors had tainted the rest of Almendro like fire blight, and *Pépère* had lost his job. Now he had to travel with the family, Cluck's mother and aunts not caring that he might not want to come back to this town.

One day Cluck would go to school the way his grandfather had. He'd keep things like what happened to this girl from happening to anyone else.

Maybe his family would cut their run here short because of the accident. Maybe they'd move on, give this town space to stitch itself back together. They could move up their stop in Tuolumne County. They always got plenty of tourists there, and some of the best climbing trees Cluck had ever seen. Sturdy, well-spaced boughs. Full greenery that let the light through like tissue paper. In those branches, his cousins looked like oleander blossoms in a sea of leaves.

The girl stirred, making noises that could've been pain or waking up. He saw the shape of her moving in the windowpane.

"*Tío* Lisandro?" she asked. "Aren't you dead?"

Any other morning, he might have laughed. Thanks to his grandfather's clothes, he probably looked like an old black-and-white photograph in one of her family's albums. A ghost come to life, complete with suspenders.

"Nope." He turned around, hands in his pockets. He didn't want her seeing his fingers. Pulling off his shirt and her dress had left them blistered and burned. Every time the nurse spotted him, she made him cover them in something greasy that smelled like a citronella candle. "Not dead. Not Lisandro either."

But the girl wasn't looking at him. She patted the bed around her.

He wondered when she'd notice her hair. Last night it fell to her lower back. Today it stopped just below her collarbone. The rest had been so tangled, so full of brush bits and cyanoacrylate, they'd had to cut it off.

He rubbed at the back of his neck. The falling adhesive had turned his skin raw, and now the starched collar of his grandfather's old shirt made it worse.

She pulled at the loose fabric around her waist. "Where are my clothes?"

The strips of fabric that had once been her dress were long gone in a hospital waste bin. Her bra hadn't made it either. It had some kind of plastic beading on it that melted like sugar.

"Hospital gown," he said. "It's cute. Got ducks on it."

Her fingers found her IV. She pulled it from the inside of her elbow. The long needle flopped out, limp and bloody, and she climbed over the guardrail.

"Hey. You're supposed to hit the button, not pull the thing out. Hit the button." He put his hand on the rail.

She saw it before he could pull it back. He couldn't tell if her stare was because of the blisters, or because of his third, fourth, and fifth fingers, always curled under.

He tried giving her the call button, but she was staring down at the hospital sheet. One of his feathers had fallen onto the bed, a brushstroke of red and black. Scratching at the back of his neck must have knocked it loose.

She looked up at him, eyes red from solvents and morphine, and registered that he wasn't an orderly or a dead relative. She smelled like blood and acetone.

"What did you do to me, *gitano?*" she asked.

He dropped the call button. It hit the sheet and bounced.

Gitano. The Spanish was close enough to the French. *Gitan.* Gypsy.

She thought he'd done this to her, that the feather on the sheet meant he'd put a *gitan* curse on her. Her burns, her cut hair. She thought it was all him. He could tell from how she'd said the word.

This was why his family never let people see their feathers. If they hid them, they were just show performers. But if anyone saw them, they'd think what this girl thought, that they were full of dark magic.

She grabbed the water pitcher from the bedside table, holding it up like it wasn't cheap plastic, but ceramic. Something she could break over his head. The spout splashed her hand and her hospital gown.

"Get out," she said.

Cluck held up his hands, not caring what she thought of them, and backed out of the room.

Eugenie leaned against the hallway wall, painted the same dull salmon color as the water pitchers and emesis bins. She stood out, a brighter pink. She'd taken the cyanoacrylate worse than he had.

Cluck was out in it longer, but Eugenie was paler. She'd been wandering each floor of the hospital, still in her ruined silk dress, looking like she'd taken too hot a bath. The frog who didn't feel the water boiling.

She handed him a Styrofoam cup, and sipped from the one in her other hand. "From the cafeteria," she said. "It's awful, but I can't stop drinking it."

He followed her toward the stairwell.

A man in a suit caught his eye. He stood outside a patient's room, looking in.

The suit was too nice for a hospital. For a funeral, maybe, but if whoever he wanted to see had gotten as far as the mortuary, he wouldn't be here.

The suit was navy. No man in a town like Almendro paid their respects in anything but a plain black suit.

"Risk something," Eugenie said, answering the question Cluck had almost spoken. "Risk assessment? Risk management? Something like that."

Cluck turned his head.

"I heard him talking to one of the nurses," she said. "I pretended I was waiting so I could get a look at his card."

Cluck touched Eugenie's shoulder, to tell her he'd be right back.

Eugenie grabbed his arm. Hard. He'd forgotten from when they were kids how her small fingers could dig in. When it was her and him against the bigger cousins, that grip always wore them down. She didn't hit or kick, but she held on like a ferret, not letting go until whichever cousin she was on surrendered.

"Don't," she said. "It's not worth it."

Risk managers were his grandfather's opposite, a photographic negative to that undeveloped Polaroid. They found so many corners to cut, they turned everything to confetti.

"None of this had to happen," Cluck said. The Styrofoam heating his palm made him want to throw coffee on the man's silk tie. "Don't tell me it's not worth it."

Eugenie felt him pulling away, and held his arm harder. "We're not worth anything to anyone here. We don't even have names. We're just *les gitans,* right?"

He cringed. She'd heard everything the girl said. And like him, she'd heard *gitan* when the girl said *gitano.*

Eugenie shook her head and shrugged. "So why bother?"

Si quieres tener enemigos, haz favores.

If you want to make enemies, do favors.

El gitano. She'd touched him, held ice to his bruises. The liquor store's salt and sugar smells came back. They crept down to her stomach. She turned onto her side, fighting off the sick feeling.

Her cousins hadn't known what he was either. If they'd been beating up a Corbeau, Justin would've told her, knowing Lace couldn't have said a word. Fighting was the only way to touch a Corbeau without taking on their curse. His Corbeau blood was the thing about him Justin didn't like, even if he couldn't name it.

It was worse than her helping him up and putting ice to his temple. He'd gotten her out from under that tree, to here. How much touching had that taken?

But she knew now. That feather had told her.

A nurse in green scrubs tried to put her IV back.

"No," Lace cried out, wrenching her arm from the woman's grasp. "No, I don't want it."

She wasn't letting them make her numb to how the Corbeau boy had touched her. How he'd left that net for her, even if he didn't know she was the one he'd left it for. There was no other reason for him to be in that part of the woods. He'd set a trap for *las sirenas* and then saved her only because he didn't know she was one of them.

"He did it," she tried to tell the nurse, but the nurse didn't listen. "It was him."

The nurse got a better grip.

"I don't want it." Lace jerked her elbow away. Her forearm banged the bed rail.

The nurse dropped her arm. "Fine."

So Lace lay there, needleless, seething at the knowledge that she had touched him, he had touched her, that her body had been against his.

The stick site prickled. The longer she had the needle out, the worse her skin stung. It shrieked with the burns and the stain of the *gitano* boy's hands.

When she got so thirsty she couldn't swallow, the nurse told her she needed to take the IV again, that she wasn't ready to drink water.

Lace said no. After the nurse left, she drained the pitcher next to the bed. But then it was empty, and she was still thirsty. So she stumbled to the bathroom sink without turning on the light, and drank from the tap.

As soon as she swallowed, the water came up again, yellowed with stomach acid.

The nurse flicked on the light. The overhead fluorescent bleached her blond hair white. "You want it back in yet?"

Lace shook her head. Pain shot through the muscles above her jaw, and she threw up the last of the water.

"All right, girly," the nurse said. "Have it your way." She flipped the lamp off.

Lace ran water down the sink. The changes in light made her forehead throb.

The mirror showed a face reddened like a half-ripened apricot. The skin was tight in places, gathered like rippling water in others. The right cheek looked bloody as a garnet, but her fingers found it dry, rough as sandstone.

Her hospital gown gaped away from her body. The cotton billowed, showing her shoulders, her breasts, all the way to her thighs.

Her family might never see the blight the boy left on her. These burns veiled it. *Abuela* and her mother might never know if a Corbeau touching her had seared off her *escamas*. Lace wouldn't look, but she knew. The rain had already burned them away.

A nurse, the blue one this time, pulled her away from the mirror. "Come on, honey." She slipped the needle in, taped it down. Lace took it, and the fishless water made her sleepy, quiet, less likely to climb over the guardrail.

A square of fabric sat on the nightstand. Filmy, printed with roses, folded. The scarf she'd forgotten in the boy's hands, when melting ice soaked it.

She balled it up and threw it. It fluttered to a chair and then slipped to the floor.

Her hand knocked a milk bottle she hadn't noticed. It stood at the back of the nightstand, bursting with wildflowers. The dusk blue of bachelor buttons. The white and yellow roses that grew wild on the hillsides. Red blossoms like blooms of flame.

She must've looked even worse than she thought. Nobody in her family brought flowers to hospitals unless someone was dying or having a baby.

Her fingers worried the tape on her IV as she slept.

The purple nurse came back, woke her up, tried to get her to eat. Lace shook her head at the plate, because everything tasted like her dry lips.

The nurse ripped off the tape encircling Lace's elbow. "Your friend went home?" she asked.

Lace tasted the grit of her own dry tongue. "He's not my friend."

"Oh, yeah? He ripped up a quarter acre of Spanish broom to get you free."

And she'd kept her cousins from kicking his ass. It didn't make them friends.

What curse had he left on her? What *maldición* were her burns hiding?

She'd throw ice cubes at the next nurse who tried to tell her "that boy saved your life." They didn't know anything about the Corbeaus. If they did, they'd never let them past the town lines.

The knowledge that his hands had been on her kept clawing through her skin. Maybe her family would leave her here, like starlings abandoning a nest, the sky blue of their eggs tainted by a child's fingers.

Lace felt for the tips of her hair. They should have been at her waist. Instead, the ends bunched above her breasts. She was missing almost a foot of her hair.

The nurse drew a vial's contents into a syringe.

"What is that?" Lace asked.

"You'll thank me later," the nurse said.

Lace squinted against the sun. It crawled up, a blind at a time, sharpening the light, and she slept.

She woke to her mother and *Abuela* whispering. But she couldn't open her eyes, and they did not notice the twitch of her eyelashes.

"She'll heal," said her mother's voice.

"I can't put her back in the show," *Abuela* said. "Not looking like this."

"That's what you're thinking of?" Her mother huffed out a breath through her nose, like air wisping from a tire. "Whether you have your *sirena*?"

Abuela gripped a handful of Lace's hair, the smell of her perfume warm off her wrist. Even the slight pulling tugged at Lace's scalp, lighting up the roots.

"What will she do?" *Abuela* asked. "Wear a wig into the water?"

Pain fanned out through Lace's head, and the voices flickered to nothing, like a bulb burning out.

Lace opened her eyes to her father's hands leaving a clean dress folded on the bedside table. She recognized his hands without seeing his face, those calluses from soldering resistors at a *maquiladora* so he could save up enough money for school.

She tried to speak, tried to reach out to those hands. But her own hands were so heavy she could not lift them. He patted the dress, as though telling it not to go anywhere, kissed Lace's hair, and then was gone.

She woke up scratching at her own skin, dreaming of rain. She dragged her fingers over her arms, trying to get the drops off. But it kept falling, and took her under.

The next time she opened her eyes, *Tía* Lora stood over her, mouthing a prayer. Her tongue flashed between her teeth, like soap in the ring of a bubble wand.

Her hands clutched a ball of pink cloth. Every time her fingers tightened or loosened their grip, the fabric shimmered like the inside of a conch shell.

Lace couldn't move enough to cry, so the trembling stuck at the back of her throat. This poor woman. All she'd wanted was a child, and she'd lost two, each before they could be born. Both had slipped from her womb like water. Then the Corbeaus had killed her husband before they could try again. So *Tía* Lora made the younger Palomas her children. She taught Oscar to make foghorn sounds by blowing into empty soda bottles. She showed Reyna and Leti how to tweeze their eyebrows, not so much, so they wouldn't look surprised the way their mother always did.

And Lace. She had taught Lace to sew, to bead. To make corn and hot water and sugar into *atole* that made her younger cousins sleep. To love dry lightning as much as candles in glass jars. "Because for one second, all that light, you see everything. Maybe you don't know what you've seen, but you've seen it, and it goes with you."

*Los enemigos del hombre son los de
su propia casa.*

A man's enemies are those of his own house.

The girl in the car's side mirror looked both drowned and burned.

Lace raised her hand to her face. So did the girl. They both traced fingers over their foreheads and noses. Lips, and glue-stiff eyebrows. Left cheek, then right. The features were the same, shapes they both knew, but the feel had changed, some spots rough as salt, others smooth and raw.

She wanted to tell her father about the Corbeau boy touching her, so he could tell her it was alright, that after a week's worth of showers she wouldn't even remember. Her father never stood for superstitions. He had changed his last name only because his own meant something so hateful none of the Palomas would say it. He put little stock in *las patrañas y los cuentos de viejas*, the fairy stories and old wives' tales that ruled this family. To Barto Paloma, the Corbeaus' feathers and the Palomas' scales were just aberrations in biology, no different than an algae bloom lighting up the ocean like opals.

But the shame of *el gitano* holding her in his arms, taking her from the woods, her body against his chest, pressed down on her. She couldn't say it, not even to her father.

"Martha missed you," her father said. "She says a couple nights in that room alone is enough."

"A couple nights?" Lace asked. It had felt like a week, two.

Lace picked at a cut on her lower lip. So did the girl. The morphine wore off, and both Lace and the girl stared, each wondering how the other had gotten so ugly.

Her father parked the station wagon in the motel lot. Her family waited in the lobby. They all offered stiff hugs, hands only, space between their bodies. Except *Tía* Lora, who pulled her close and whispered, "You look beautiful, *mija*." And Martha, *la sirena anaranjada*, who combed her hands through Lace's hair and said, "Don't worry, I kept the boys out of fights for you." And Lace's mother, who gripped her so hard pain pulsed through her body. "You're fine," her mother whispered. "You're just fine."

Lace's younger cousins asked was it true that she'd gotten glued to the ground, and was it true that a ghost unstuck her. "People saw him," Reyna and Leti's little sister said. "But then he just disappeared," Emilia's five-year-old son said.

Lace shushed them, not wanting anyone to think too hard about how she'd gotten to the hospital.

When they thought she wasn't looking, her uncles shook their heads at the lobby carpet. Her aunts dabbed at their lower eyelids, as though she'd died.

Their pity filled her arms and made her tired. She carried it back to her and Martha's room, wavering under the weight.

Lace took off her dress and caught her reflection in the turned-off television. In the dark glass, she almost looked the same. Her mother's nose, her father's straight brow bone, her middle aunt's sloped shoulders.

She turned. Even in the dim glass, her back looked covered with brandy rose petals, crushed and half-withered. But a handful of clean, pale coins still arced across her lower back. *Las escamas.* The scales that marked her as a mermaid.

She went to the bathroom mirror, turning her back to the glass. The birthmarks shined in the overhead light. Almost iridescent. The burning rain had left them raw and a little pink, but no scars crossed them.

They'd been spared, as though *Apanchanej*'s own fingers had shielded them. The rain should have burned her *escamas* as badly as her cheek. But they were still on her, whole and unmarred, proof that she would live and swim, reach her hands through the sheets of light that floated through the river, turn her body in the same spring as *Abuela*.

The air in the room felt cool and thick as water. It rushed around her, clothed her like kelp ribbons. She touched her hair to check if it was floating. She felt the weight of shells and river pearls holding her breasts. By refusing to be burned away, those *escamas* had written these things onto her body. They were new birthmarks, unseen but true.

Salt stung the wound on her cheek. She pressed the pads of her fingers to the tear's path. The Corbeau boy had touched her. The rain had scalded her. But nothing in those drops or in his fingers could take the name Paloma from her.

She put her dress back on and threw the door open. She called for her mother and her father and *Abuela* and *Tía* Lora. Aunts, uncles, and cousins cracked their doors and peered out.

Apanchanej had given her a sign she would be healed. The garnet would fall from her cheek like flecks of mica. The crushed roses on her back and breasts would turn to skin again. She would swim. She would still be *la sirena rosa*.

"What is it, *mija?*" her mother asked, shaking painkillers from a bottle. Lace held her hand out to stop her.

Her fingers froze before they reached her mother's. A dark wisp of a mark on her forearm made her still. A burn, deep and red as a crushed blackberry, fanned in the shape of a feather, the barbs as clear as scratches of ink.

She'd missed that feather. Maybe the reddening and swelling had hidden it. Or she'd dismissed it as dried blood. Or the burn on her cheek kept her staring into the mirror instead of looking down.

But she saw it now.

Her mother saw it too. The pills and bottle fell from her hand.

Lace's aunts whispered prayers. Her cousins drew back, as though Lace had cut her hands on the thorns of *la Virgen Morena*'s roses. They all saw it, the messy, fluffy barbs seared into her arm.

The Corbeau boy's feather had scarred her. It had fallen from him and branded her. Now she wore the mark of the family who'd killed *Tía* Lora's husband. The net the Corbeau boy left for her would not let her go.

If the feather's imprint had been light, the pearled skin of a healed scar or the family's birthmarks, her aunts and uncles might not have drawn back. Her mother might not have hovered a nervous hand in front of her mouth. But this was the enemy family's mark. They knew it as well as if a thousand obsidian feathers had fallen from the sky.

Lace's father stepped between them all. "*¡Santo cielo!*" He took Lace's arm. "It's just a feather. You don't know it's theirs."

But to the rest of them, it was currency, true as salt and silver. Lace felt the poison seeping into her blood. She should have noticed it before, felt the sting of that family's venom.

Her father watched her. *Abuela* watched her. Her mother stepped back toward the yellowing wallpaper. The rest of the family fringed the hallway.

Abuela turned her back to them all. She went to the door of her room. One glance told Lace to follow.

"Lace," her father said, his assurance that, once, just once, she did not have to do as *Abuela* told her.

Lace's calves pulsed, fighting her moving. *Don't go,* her muscles crackled out. *You know how this will end. Don't go.*

But she shook off the feeling biting up her legs and followed.

The rest of the family let out a shared breath. When *Abuela* gave an order, any Paloma girl who did not want to become another Licha obeyed.

A quien dices tus secretos, das tu libertad.
To whom you tell your secrets,
you give your freedom.

Lace closed the door behind her, shutting out the hallway murmurs.

Abuela faced the window, back to Lace. "At the hospital the nurses talk about how some *gitano* boy pulled a girl from the woods. But I said not my granddaughter."

"*Abuela*," Lace said.

"I said my granddaughter is *una niña buena*. If my granddaughter had been touched by one of them, she would have told us. She would have let us help her."

"Help me?" A laugh pressed up from under the two strained words. "What would you have done?" *Exorcismo?* Brought her to a *bruja* who would push the breath out of her?

"Was that you with the *gitano* boy?" *Abuela* asked.

"He didn't know who I was," Lace said.

"Was that you?" *Abuela* asked again.

Lace would not say yes. *Abuela* already knew. She just wanted to make her say it.

"Those people killed my big brother," *Abuela* said.

The words dragged Lace's gaze to the floor. So often she thought of the Paloma who died that night as *Tía* Lora's husband, the man who made Lace's great-aunt a Paloma. She sometimes forgot he was also *Abuela*'s brother. When the lake flooded its shores, and he drowned, he was lost not only to *Tía* Lora but to *Abuela*.

Her grandmother turned from the window. The scent of her reached out to Lace. For more than half a century, she'd worn the same perfume her mother gave her on her sixteenth birthday. Her mother had scraped together enough for a tiny bottle, no bigger than a jar of saffron, and *Abuela* had saved up for a new one each year ever since. *Cream Lace*. Lace's mother had named her for that perfume, a gift to *Abuela*, a sign that Lace belonged as much to *Abuela* as to her mother and father.

The powdery smell of violets and almond sugar curled around Lace's shoulders. Such a sweet scent, shy and young. How did it stand up to *Abuela*'s wrists and neck?

Now *Abuela*'s face was soft as that scent, and almost as sad. "Pack your things, *mija*."

The words were the slap Lace had expected. She'd braced for them. They jolted her anyway.

Lace turned her forearm, letting the light glaze over the burn. If she fought *Abuela* on this, everyone would know she had been touched. *Abuela* would tell them all. She would be the cursed thing, a burr hooking its teeth into this family.

Abuela had only just let her be seen. *La sirena rosa* had come to shore for one night, and then had slipped back into the water. Now she could bring a plague on her family, sure as crows making chil- dren sick. It didn't matter that *Apanchanej* had spared her scales. She had let a Corbeau touch her.

A flush of shame gripped her, strong as the Corbeau boy's hands.

"Don't tell them," Lace said.

"They saw it already."

"Don't tell them how I got it."

Her grandmother said nothing.

Lace had obeyed. Her whole life, she'd obeyed. She'd done makeup for all the *sirenas*, even when it meant she couldn't finish her own. She'd hidden her *escamas* even though they were the part of her body she loved most, all because *Abuela* was sure people would call her and her cousins *los monstruos* if their scales ever showed.

Lace kept her feet flat on the carpet. If she didn't steady her own weight, she'd waver and sound desperate. *Abuela* would stick a knife through any break in her voice.

"What have you ever asked me to do that I haven't done?" Lace asked.

Abuela tipped her eyes to the curtains, studying the mismatched panels.

"If you don't tell them how I got it, I'll do what you want, I'll go," Lace said. Not a question. An equation, sure and immutable as the ones on her father's worksheets.

Abuela turned her head, half-shutting her eyes. She knew what Lace meant. *Listen to me, or I will make this messy. I will be a pain in your ass.*

"My dad will go against you on this," Lace said. "You know that. If you promise you won't tell them, I'll convince him. He'll let me go."

Abuela kept her laugh behind her lips. "You can take him with you. He has the name for it."

Lace flinched. *Abuela* had never forgiven Lace's father for being born with the last name Cuervo, even after he let it go, changed it, endured the taunting of other men for taking his wife's name.

She shrugged it away. She needed *Abuela*'s word. She could not have her mother and her father, and Martha and Matías, and the other *sirenas*, knowing she'd had *gitano* hands on her.

"If he goes with me, so will my mother," Lace said.

Abuela lifted her chin.

"Don't tell them," Lace said. Even if her father took her side, and her mother took his, her mother would never look at her the same way. She would see the feather on her arm as a mark of her sin, *un testamento* of what she had let the gypsy boy do. Maybe she'd even think Lace wanted it, wanted him.

Abuela didn't know about the net. If Lace told her now, it would sound like something she'd made up, a lie to explain why she was still out in the woods when the sky fell. To cover that she was meeting the Corbeau boy in the woods, letting him touch her, not knowing his last name. Or worse, knowing it, letting him put his hands on her anyway.

"Please," Lace said.

Her grandmother said nothing.

"Please," Lace said again, desperation spreading through the word like a stain.

"Fine," *Abuela* said, startled.

"What will you tell them?"

"That one of the feathers found you. Is this good enough for you, *princesa?*"

"Thank you," Lace said.

Her father caught her outside *Abuela's* door. "Lace." He stopped her, a hand over her forearm, like covering the mark would make it mean nothing. Like the rest of the family were children who would forget what they could not see.

He already knew what *Abuela* had said. The tightness in his face told her.

"Your *mamá* and I will go with you," he said.

It was easy for him. The show was nothing. He could shake it all away like sand from a rug. He'd married Lace's mother to be her husband, not to be a Paloma.

Lace wished it could be so easy for her, that she could shed the feather burn like he had shed his name.

Lace held the truth cupped tight in her palms. It fought and fluttered like a moth, but she would not part her fingers enough to let it out.

"You didn't want me in the show forever." She searched the words for wavering, smoothed them out with her hands like an iron. "I have my GED. I can register at any of the county colleges."

"Then I'll go with you," her father said. "*No me importa nada. Screw this family.*"

If Lace let that happen, *Abuela* would lay out the full story. How much did *Abuela* know? That there'd been nothing left of her dress but scraps of fabric? That the Corbeau boy hadn't had a shirt on, that Lace's skin had been on his?

Lace stood close enough to her father so he could hear her whisper. "If you go with me, none of my cousins will learn anything."

A wince flashed across his face. It was cruel, striking at the thing he cared about most.

"Half of them need summer school," she said. "You're the one who teaches them." Her father took on the bulk of the homeschooling. Without him, no one would get a GED. "If you don't stay, they won't learn."

Sadness weighted his eyebrows. He would never win against *Abuela*, or Lace's mother, who had said her piece by saying nothing. Now her mother stood at the other end of the hall, her sisters and cousins keeping close as sepals around an anemone.

They were already backing away from the girl with the feather. She was a wounded thing. If they kept her, her blood would draw more of the Corbeaus' *magia negra*.

"And where will you go?" her father asked.

Guilt flared through her burns, the feeling of getting too near a radiator. "Martha's friends in Tulare County," she said. "I can stay with them."

"You're better than this," he said. "Don't let *las supersticiones* force you to do anything."

"Nobody's forcing me," Lace whispered, the lie stinging her tongue. "I'm getting out like you always wanted."

Hesitation deepened the wrinkles around his mouth.

But he said, "Good," loud enough to make sure everyone heard.

So he let her go, and the truth of why he was letting her go pressed into the back of her neck. He had never wanted this life for her. Motel rooms strung together like beads. School squeezed in between sewing costumes. *Abuela*'s tongue, heavy as a gavel.

La sirena rosa was not her name, not to him. Her dreams of Weeki Wachee were only good enough to him because *Abuela* was not in Florida, telling her maybe she was spending too much time with her math books.

If this was how he could make her more than the fabric and beads of her tail, he would do it. She didn't know how to tell him that she'd loved her tail as much as her own skin and hair.

She went back to her room and found Martha sitting on the bed, waiting. "You're not really gonna go stay with my friends in Terra Bella, are you?"

Lace cleared her clothes from the middle drawer.

"Where are you gonna go?" Martha asked.

"You think we're the only mermaids?" Lace said. "They've got shows like us in Vegas, Atlantic City. Not just Florida."

"Vegas?" Martha laughed. "What are you gonna do, steal my driver's license? You couldn't even get into a casino."

"What about those dives in the middle of the desert?" Lace asked. They'd passed one last summer. A woman caked with waterproof foundation flipped and turned in an oversized fish tank, her plastic tail glittering. The family had stopped because they were hungry, but *Abuela* took one look in the door and wouldn't go in. She said she wouldn't sit and watch some old, fat fish-woman swimming around.

"If I can hold my breath and twirl around in a tank, I can get a job," Lace said.

The wildflowers from her hospital nightstand sat on the dresser, half-withered.

Palomas only brought flowers to hospitals when someone either had a baby or was so close to death the priest was on his way.

"Did you all give me up for dead?" Lace asked.

"Of course not," Martha said. "Why?"

Lace picked up the milk bottle. "Then why these?"

"We didn't bring you those," Martha said.

"You didn't?"

"Should we have?" Martha looked hard at Lace's middle. "Are you pregnant?"

"No." Lace set the bottle back on the dresser. "If you didn't bring them, who did?"

"The nurse said the guy who brought you in, but I don't know. I never saw him."

The feeling of the Corbeau boy's hands rushed over Lace's body. It whipped against her like blown sand.

The cornflowers. Outside the liquor store, he'd had one on his vest. It came unpinned and fell when her cousin hit him.

Wild roses. Red blossoms. The orange-haired Corbeau girl Lace had seen by the river wore them on her head. They grew wild on the Corbeaus' side of the woods, those undaunted blooms that carpeted the abandoned campground.

El gitano. The gypsy boy brought her the wildflowers.

He didn't know the girl he'd taken out of the woods was a *sirena* he'd set a trap for. He didn't know when he was freeing her from the brush that she'd just escaped his net. All he knew was that he'd saved her life, and she'd called him names. He'd brought her flowers, and she'd chased him out of the room.

Now he was angry with her. This was no different than Justin and

Alexia and her brother stealing the Camargue and being cursed with the skittishness of young horses.

She had to get the Corbeau boy's forgiveness, like returning that stolen colt.

A soft knock clicked against the door. Lace left her clothes on the bed and answered it.

Tía Lora stood in the hall, hands full of fabric pink as a grapefruit, the cloth she'd brought with her to the hospital. It glinted, sagging with the weight of glass beads.

A new *cola de sirena*, a mermaid tail made to replace the one that had been lost.

Lace wondered if shreds of her old one still clung to that colander, the current pulling them like streamers.

This one was finer than the lost one, the beading more intricate, the embroidery on the fin tighter, more delicate. A sign of *Tía* Lora's faith that she would swim again.

"You will come back," *Tía* Lora said.

Lace had to find the *gitano* boy.

Tía Lora set the tail's weight in her palms, the thread still warm from her hands.

Lace took it. "Yes," she said. "I will."

Un tiens vaut mieux que deux tu l'auras.

One that you hold is better than two you will have.

*C*luck braced his hands on the worktable. Half the wings still needed fixing. Alula feathers had gotten knocked out of place. Primary remiges had come loose, secondaries had fallen out. Wires had gotten bent or snapped; they'd snagged on branches when his cousins came down from the trees. Some the chemical rain had ruined.

Cluck watched from the trailer window as a woman in a skirt suit met his mother at the back door.

He knew why the woman was there. He could tell by the chamber of commerce pin on her lapel. The Almendro Blackberry Festival would go on. Calling off those days of farm stands and crafters' booths would be the same as a white flag, a sign that the town had curled up in its corner of the Central Valley to die.

Now she'd come to find out if Nicole Corbeau felt the same way.

His mother kissed the air next to the woman's cheek.

Cluck rolled his eyes. His mother did that with anyone they

needed to issue them permits. It always charmed them, made them walk away a little lighter, feeling sophisticated, unbearably French.

Great. Not only were they staying in this town, now the Palomas would too.

They should've just moved on to Madera County a couple of weeks early. Or scheduled a stop on the Monterey Peninsula, where slices of the ocean showed between the trees.

But his mother wasn't willing to burn bridges. No more than she was willing to let the Palomas win.

Cluck couldn't wait to save up enough money for community college, for an apartment that didn't move. He'd study like his grandfather had. He'd get a job anywhere but Almendro. He'd get a house he and *Pépère* could live in, and *Pépère* wouldn't have to go around with the show anymore. They'd be *les célibataires*, two bachelors in a house with a lemon tree.

Eugenie came in without knocking. Cluck let her get at the old mirror against the wall so she could check her feathers. Some Corbeaus, like Dax, pulled all theirs out. Most, like Eugenie, just checked for loose ones before each show. They never wanted the audience to sees feathers fall from their heads.

"You didn't go see that girl again, did you?" Eugenie asked.

"Right. Because she was so thrilled to see me last time."

Eugenie ran her fingers through her hair. "What was she so upset about?"

"I don't know." Probably him. A lot of people got upset about him.

"Did you tell her what happened?" Eugenie asked.

He cleaned the adhesive off a set of wire cutters.

"Do you know her?" Eugenie asked.

He straightened a few bent wires.

"Who is she?" she asked.

He threw down the wire. "I don't want to talk about this, Eugenie."

Eugenie pulled a last feather. "You're cranky today, *n'est-ce pas?*"

"You think?" Cluck called after her, waving a hand at the wings he was piecing back together. A few were so stripped of feathers, he could only save the frames.

Cluck couldn't even use the family's feathers, shed or plucked. He'd tried it once, weaving a few in among the peacock feathers. His mother found out before his grandfather realized what he was doing. "These are not spare parts to use for show," she had said. The bruise Dax left him with took two weeks to fade. But if they strapped feathers to their bodies, Cluck wondered, why shouldn't they be their own?

His grandfather had told him, "We put ourselves on show enough for the *gadje*," and Cluck understood. It was the same reason the blond Corbeaus coated their dark feathers in flour, to hide them. The show was all costumes and peacock feathers, lights hung in trees, tightrope walking. *La magie* of their bodies did not belong to the *gadje*, the people who were not like them.

His grandfather came in and tossed a paper bag on the worktable. "I bought you something." The bag fell over, its contents sliding out. A folded pair of brown corduroy pants, and a long-sleeved crewneck shirt the red of wet cranberries.

Not this again. Since Cluck turned eighteen, his grandfather had been trying to get him into Levi's. Last month, *Pépère* bought him a T-shirt the gray of a wet stone. In April, he'd left a jean jacket on Cluck's bed.

But Cluck liked wearing *Pépère's* old clothes, and the feeling that they might make him like his grandfather. The things that made Alain Corbeau would soak into Cluck's skin.

This new shirt wouldn't. The red was so close to the shade streaking Cluck's feathers that he didn't like looking at it. It made him blink first.

"One day I will die and you will have to burn my things," *Pépère* said. "Then what will you wear?"

Pépère had told Cluck what his family back in *le Midi* did with the possessions of their dead. Nothing that belonged to the deceased was sold, especially not to anyone else Romani, who would never want to buy it anyway. Little was kept, only a few valuables given to family members. The rest was burned, especially clothes and sheets. Anything death had made *mochadi*, unclean.

"I don't think we do that anymore, *Pépère*," Cluck said.

"We did it where I come from, and one day you will do it for me. What will you do then, wear nothing?" His grandfather pushed the bag toward him. "If you don't want to wear them, it's your business. But you will keep them."

Stubborn. That was the other thing wearing *Pépère*'s clothes might make him.

His grandfather coughed into his handkerchief.

Cluck could hear the force tearing the back of his throat. *"Pépère?"*

In the days since the mixing tank blew, his cough had gotten worse. The chemicals in the air irritated his smoke-worn lungs. He wouldn't say so, but Cluck knew. The adhesive had settled, but the vapor still thickened the air. One more reason Cluck made sure his grandfather slept inside, not in the trailers that stayed hot at night and chilled in the morning.

"And those geniuses think they know how to run a chemical plant," Cluck said.

"It wouldn't be the worst they've done," his grandfather said between coughs.

"What?" Cluck asked.

"T'inquiète." His grandfather folded the linen square. "It must be time for another cigarette, *n'est-ce pas?"*

Pépère paused as he reached for the pack, his eyes following Cluck's hands.

Pépère took hold of Cluck's forearms. He turned Cluck's wrists, showing the burns on his palms. "What's happened here?"

Cluck kept his head down. The girl shooing him out of the room, calling him *gitano*, had stuck him with the feeling that taking her from the woods was some awful thing he'd done. He didn't want *Pépère* knowing about any of it.

"It's from getting my shirt off," Cluck said. He didn't have to lift his head to know his grandfather's stare was on him. He felt it like a draft through a window. "The reaction with the cotton."

Pépère gripped his forearm tighter. "I have never in your life given you reason to lie to me."

Cluck felt the words on his shoulders, sure as hands. His grandfather had taught him everything about feathers. Remiges for flight, retrices for balance. And it was thanks to *Pépère* that Cluck had learned to work with the fingers he had. Nine years ago, his left hand had been so broken, he couldn't do anything with it. He learned to use his right, buttoned his shirts with it, forced out messy writing. It felt backward as putting a shoe on the wrong foot, but he did it. His fingers healed into a half-fist and grew restless, charged like the static on a metal knob. They wanted to work. But under Dax's eye, and his mother's, he couldn't let them.

When *Pépère* found him in the Airstream one night, his right fingers fighting with a needle and thread, he set a hand on his shoulder and said, "Use your left, boy." Cluck had hesitated, sure it was a trick, but his grandfather took the needle from his right hand and slipped it between his left thumb and forefinger, the only two digits on his left hand that weren't stuck curled under. *"Notre secret,"* *Pépère* had said, shutting the trailer door. *Our secret.*

Cluck had no right to lie to the man who kept his secrets.

"There was this girl," Cluck said. "She was out there."

Pépère let go of his forearms. "A girl."

"She had on a cotton dress. My hands made it out better than she did."

Pépère's eyes looked dark as palm ash. "You took off her dress?"

"As much as I could, yeah."

His grandfather let out a breath and put a hand to his temple. "The people here, they think things about us."

Cluck didn't need reminding. It was enough that they were performers, that they traveled from town to town. But a few of them, like Cluck and *Pépère*, stood out worse, a different kind of dark than the people around here were used to.

"If you touch a girl in this town," *Pépère* said, "it doesn't matter why, people will talk."

"You think I should have left her there?" Cluck asked.

"I think you should have told me. Then at least I'd know what you'd gotten yourself into."

"I haven't gotten into anything," Cluck said.

But *Pépère* was already halfway out the door.

Cluck's stomach felt tight as a coil of wire. His grandfather was the one person he couldn't take disappointing. To everyone but *Pépère*, Cluck was nothing more than the red-streaked semiplumes that grew under his hair. A poor substitute for flight feathers. Dax was a primary remex, long, straight, showing. Cluck was a lesser covert feather, hidden, structural. Or an afterfeather, the downy offshoot branching from the central vane.

Needed but easy to forget.

Boca de miel, corazón de hiel.
Mouth of honey, bitter heart.

*T*he other *sirenas* would say not to go, that she'd get herself killed. That family would peck Lace to death like the crows they were, or turn her whole body to black feathers.

But the only way to escape the exile of the *gitano* boy's hands was to face them. Justin, Alexia, and her brother had made their apology, broken free of the curse that stolen Camargue colt brought on them. As long as the Corbeau boy didn't realize she was a Paloma, she could do the same.

The feather burn wouldn't heal on its own. She couldn't wait it out. She needed the boy who'd made it. She needed to show enough remorse, enough fear and reverence for the strength of his family's *magia negra*, that he'd forgive her, and use that same *gitano* magic to lift the feather from her arm.

First she needed an offering, a sign of her contrition, the way a maize farmer's daughter who had ignored the goddess *Chicomecoatl* might have brought her flowers during a famine. So Lace walked the dirt-dusted roads to the outdoor market where her aunts sent her cousins for tomatoes and Casaba melon.

People tried not to stare. Their eyes flashed toward the red heart on her cheek, pity passing over their faces. Their sympathy prodded her. Lace held her throat tight, to stop herself from screaming at them. *You think this thing on my cheek is the worst I got that night? Go ask the boy with the wrecked hand what he gave me.*

She clutched the coins and dollar bills in her dress pocket. "What's good right now?" she asked a woman at a fruit stand.

The woman sucked air in through her teeth and touched her own cheek, like looking at Lace might make her grow an identical wound.

"Chin up," the woman said. "You're lucky. Three of our men died that night."

Lucky. It was a word Almendro held close. Those alive were *lucky.* The town, still alive, was *lucky.* But Lace knew better. Almendro seethed with the fallout. Any man in a suit collected a set of glares whenever he crossed a street. Some plant workers' wives, her father told her, protested outside the plant's fence the last few mornings, but most of them had jobs too, and children, so the picketing dissipated as one after another left for their shifts.

Lucky was the word this town pinned to its shirt collar, a good-luck charm. It helped them ignore the tension, between wanting to know what had happened, and hoping half their jobs would not be gone by the time the trees shed their marred bark and ruined leaves.

Lace paid for a flat of peaches and the strangest watermelon she'd ever seen. Midnight violet, almost black, speckled with dandelion yellow, and one gold spot the size and color of a Meyer lemon. Moon-and-Stars, the paper sign said.

She stepped out from the awning, and a mist of rain dotted the paper sack, the drizzle so light Lace couldn't hear it. She kept still, two steps from the fruit stand's edge. The drops hit her skin. They clung to the fine hairs on her arms. She picked at each water bead, pulling at the thin shields of scabbing grown over her burns.

The memory of sirens bore into her temples. The dusk turned to night, quick as a cloth torn off a table. The clouds overhead swirled and the rain turned hot. It stuck to her, turning her clothes to ash. It would streak through her body until she was nothing but a rib cage and a rain-seared heart. She had to get them off. Every drop. She dug her nails in to rake them away.

Little threads of blood showed.

She stepped back under the awning, her pulse shuddering in her neck. Her hands trembled, the threads of blood vibrating like river grass underwater.

"You okay?" the woman asked.

Lace nodded, keeping her back to the woman. She gaped at the air, getting her breath back, waiting out the rain.

A few days earlier, she'd thought of rain as little different than the spray off a river. It was all the same, wasn't it? All water. But now she knew better. She wasn't willing to offer the sky her blind trust that the drops coming down were water and not poison.

Yes, all the clean, venomless storms she'd run through, all the sudden showers and downpours, told her that this rain, and every one after, should be plain water. But she wouldn't count on it. She'd never give the sky that faith again. In place of that faith now lived her suspicion that all rain was hiding some secret she wouldn't know until she found it burning into her skin.

She should have known all along not to trust the sky. It was where the crows lived.

Eso es harina de otro costal.

That is wheat from a different bag.

*The closer Lace got to the Corbeaus' side of the woods, the more the scent of feathers pushed up through the trees' smells. The rain had let up, leaving the air clean and woody like damp bark, but that scent still hovered.

Lace caught a thread of it every time those black feathers blew to the Palomas' side of town, and here it was strong as *Abuela*'s perfume. A dull earth smell. Something waxy like crayons. A sweetness like powdered honey that Lace might have liked if she didn't know where it came from.

Lace set her suitcase at the base of a cottonwood tree. She buried it under wet leaves. *Los gitanos* couldn't steal it if they didn't know it was there.

She held the bag of peaches in one arm, Moon-and-Stars in the other. The sight of the old Craftsman house made an unsteady feeling jitter down her arms. But she reminded herself that the Corbeau boy couldn't have known she was a Paloma, that if he had, he would have left her to turn to smoke, and that stilled her.

From far off, the Corbeaus' camp looked like children's toys. Lace had heard rumors about the travel trailers, but until tonight, she'd never seen them. They were primary-colored like alphabet blocks— clover green, weed daisy yellow, apple red, crayon blue. One was plain aluminum. Another pink with tail fins like a jet. Strings of globe lights hung between them.

The wings on the performers' backs towered over their heads and spread out past their shoulders. Lace had never seen so much teal and bronze. Feathers brushed when one passed another.

The men wore no shirts, nothing but the flesh-colored bands that held their wings on. Lace tried not to laugh at the shine of their chests, wondering if they used Vaseline or vitamin oil. Women in antique dresses sat at outdoor vanities, rows of lightbulbs illuminating the mirrors. Their enormous wings filled the glass. They fixed their hair in soft waves and pinned curls, trailing under flower crowns.

One who didn't have her wings on noticed Lace, a flash of movement in her mirror.

She caught Lace's eye in the reflection. "You are early, and lost." She patted her hair and turned around. "The show doesn't start for an hour. You buy the tickets down the road."

Recognition pressed into Lace's collarbone. She knew this narrow frame, the copper hair, the sleepy flirtation in the woman's eyes. Lace had met her in the woods.

But nothing registered on the woman's face. Lace didn't have on her stage makeup, only lipstick, and base that did a poor job hiding the burn on her cheek. She didn't have on her tail, and her hair wasn't wet. She looked nothing like *la sirena rosa*.

"*Qu'est-ce que c'est que ça?*" The woman pulled back the edge of the paper sack with her forefinger. "Are you from the grocery store?"

Lace shifted the bag so their arms wouldn't touch. "No. I'm looking for someone."

"Who?" the woman asked.

Lace tried holding her hand above her head to show the Corbeau boy's height, but she didn't know his height. She just knew he was taller than she was. "Dark hair, longish," she said, hovering a flat hand over her shoulder. "He has"—Lace closed and opened her fist, thinking of his left fingers, curled under—"a hand."

"Two, I'd guess," the woman said.

"He wears old-timey clothes."

"You mean Cluck."

"His name's Cluck?"

"He answers to it." The woman gestured for Lace to follow. She stopped at a blue and white teardrop trailer. "Cluck." She banged her palm on the siding.

The door flew open. Lace put up a hand to keep it from hitting her. The boy in the old-fashioned clothes stepped down from the trailer.

He had his hair rubber-banded in a low ponytail, but it was a little too short to stay pulled back. A few pieces had fallen out and gotten in his face.

She'd only ever seen him in the dull neon of the liquor store or through the cloud of what the nurses had put in her IV. Now he looked different. His eyebrows, low-arched, dark as his hair, gave him a serious look she'd never seen when he was talking. The way his eyelashes screened his irises when he looked down made him seem a little sad. The inner curve of his lower lip had a lavender tint that should've made him look sick or cold, but it just added to that sadness that started around his eyes.

He held a pair of peacock-feather wings. The breeze stroked the feathers, and the gold and sea glass colors shimmered.

Lace caught the shine of bright aqua, the same blue as the nylon net, and her stomach clenched. She tried to forget that she'd come to apologize to the Corbeau who'd probably left that net for her, the boy who'd had no reason to be on the Palomas' side of the woods except to put those nylon threads in the water.

Cluck didn't see her in the door's shadow.

"*As-tu fini?*" the woman asked.

He turned her around by her shoulders and tied the satin ribbons to her torso, crossing them over her front so they looked like part of her dress.

The woman slid her thumbs under the ribbons, checking that they'd hold. They were the same bluish purple as the bodice, and almost vanished against the chiffon. "*Tu as de la visite.*" She pushed the trailer door shut, throwing light on Lace.

Cluck jumped when he saw her. He pulled off the rubber band and shook a hand through his hair. Not like he cared what he looked like but quick, out of habit, like taking his hat off before going into a church.

The woman skipped off. Her wings twitched as she ran. The plumes all moved together like a field of oats, wind-rippled.

"Here to take another shot?" Cluck asked. Sadness tinged his expression. She couldn't have hurt his feelings. The Corbeaus didn't bother with any opinions but each other's. As far as he knew, she was just some girl from Almendro. What did he care what she said about him?

She pulled her eyes down from his face so she wouldn't have to see that look.

He had his sleeves cuffed up to the elbow. A thread of blue vein ran along the muscle in his forearms, like an irrigation ditch snaking through a field. It gave Lace an idea of what the rest of his body must have been like under the loose fit of those old clothes, the kind of thin muscle that made him strong but not as big as the other men.

Abuela would murder her for thinking about a Corbeau with his shirt off. Lace tried to make herself stop, sure that *Abuela* would sense the thought from across town. But the more she tried to force it aside, the more the thought came floating back, like a balloon bobbing up after being held underwater. It was like the game she and her cousins tormented each other with. *Don't think of a Christmas tree. Don't think of an alpaca.* And then all they could think about for the rest of the day would be a whole herd of alpaca, or a pine forest big enough for every Christmas tree in the world.

She shoved the watermelon and the bag of peaches into his arms and flicked away the memory of that net. She pushed down the knowledge that he put into the water something that almost killed Magdalena, and could have killed her.

"I'm sorry," she said. "For what I said. For how I acted. I'm sorry."

"Heavily medicated?" he asked.

"Something like that," she said. "I just came to say thank you for what you did."

"Anytime," he said. "Well, not anytime. Never again, I hope."

"So we're okay?" she asked. The sooner he forgave her, the sooner the feather would heal. Her apology was the same as her cousins returning that Camargue colt.

Something behind Lace got Cluck's attention. "Great." He stopped a girl who looked about his age, wings on her back. He said something to her in French and set the paper bag and watermelon into her arms.

The girl eyed the watermelon. "I don't think it's ripe. It's purple."

"It's supposed to be purple," Lace said.

The girl startled, realizing Lace was there. Were they all this jumpy whenever anyone who was not a Corbeau came near the Craftsman house?

The girl eyed Lace, then took the fruit toward the house.

Cluck sprang toward one of the vanity mirrors, where the red-haired woman leaned over a pale-haired one, dotting color on her eyelids. The red blossoms on her flower crown almost touched the vanilla roses on the other woman's head.

"Eugenie," he said. "What are you doing?"

Eugenie paused her fingers. Her free hand was full of makeup brushes, the bristles color-drenched.

Cluck grabbed the brushes out of her hands. "Where's Margaux?"

"She never showed."

"Again?"

"She has a new boyfriend. I don't think she's coming back. Not this run anyway."

Lace followed him. She needed his word, for him to pronounce her forgiven, like a priest.

He felt her shadow cut across the light. "Sorry," he said, half looking over his shoulder. "My flake cousin flaked again." From across the yard, the sound of ripping fabric distracted him. It sounded thin, like the shantung or dupioni her mother wore to church on Easter Sunday. Old or expensive.

"Here." He shoved the bouquet of makeup brushes into Lace's hands. "Hold these for a minute, will ya?" He took off toward the Craftsman house.

With a bare foot, the pale-haired woman pushed a vinyl stool toward Lace. The sole was brown, like it had been painted. It was the only thing dark about the woman. She had a pinkish forehead, and hair blond as bean sprouts. Half the women here looked like her. Where had their *gitana* blood gone? Had they cast it out like *el Diablo*?

The other women, except for the redhead called Eugenie, had hair as black as Cluck's. But even some of them were pale as whipped-up egg whites. Same with the men.

Cluck was one of the darker ones, his forearms like the lightest peels of jacaranda bark. It almost made her sorry for him. He had that wrecked hand, and he didn't match his relatives. Even Lace's family teased Leti and Reyna for being light-haired *güeras.*

"Do you want to sit?" the woman asked, her consonants sharpened by a French accent. Lace wondered if it was real or put-on. The Corbeaus had been in this country as long as the Palomas, cursing them and stealing their business.

She sat down. The vanity was crowded with pots of color and powder compacts. Blue and green glass bottles, clusters of pastel rhinestones, and canning jars of cotton balls filled any extra space.

An open bag of cake flour leaned against the mirror. Lace didn't ask.

The makeup brushes looked like they hadn't been cleaned since spring. Pastels tipped the eye shadow brushes. Face powder and blush stained the bigger ones. The smallest ones had been dyed red with lip color and violet with eyeliner.

Her hands opened and closed, wanting to fix them. Lace cleaned her own brushes after making up one cousin and before starting the next. Were these people trying to make each other sick? One eye infection, and the whole show would have it.

Lace dampened a few tissues with an open bottle of alcohol, and rubbed the makeup from each brush. Yes, these things had touched Corbeau skin, but they weren't Corbeaus themselves. If she had to look at those stained brushes any longer, she'd throw them at somebody.

She turned each one over, pressing the color out until it wiped clean. The lip and eyeliner brushes were always the worst. She squeezed the color from the base of the bristles up through the tips, and her shoulders felt heavy with missing the other *sirenas.* These were things she did for them. Cleaning brushes. Rubbing color from bristles. Seeing each shade come off on the tissue like a streak of paint.

The blond woman looked over at the color-striped tissues. "You do makeup," she said, not a question.

"No." Lace put down the brushes.

"This is what you do, *n'est-ce pas?*"

"Not anymore," Lace said.

"But you did."

"But not anymore."

The woman closed her eyes, showing Lace her face. "Will you paint me?"

"Do your makeup?" Lace asked.

The woman nodded, eyes still closed.

"You don't know if I'm any good," Lace said, stalling, trying to figure out if there were enough brushes and sponges here that she could fix the woman's face without touching her skin. "What about Margaux?"

"My sister? She has her boyfriends, she forgets we have our shows." The woman hair-sprayed a loose curl. "She will marry one of them soon and have five hundred babies. The beauties always do."

She said "beauties" like she wasn't one.

"If you don't," the woman said, "I'll have to go on tonight looking washed-out, and it'll be your fault."

"My fault?" Lace splashed alcohol on another tissue, and wiped the color stains from her fingers. "Your sister's the one who didn't show up."

"But who knows where she is?" The woman opened her eyes. "And you're here."

Lace folded her arms, hiding the feather burn. She couldn't keep saying no without the woman wondering why.

It couldn't be harder than putting waterproof color on the other *sirenas*. She just couldn't use her fingers.

"What do you need?" Lace asked.

"Base, blush, lip color." The woman gestured at her temples, holding her pinched thumbs and forefingers at the corners of her eyes, opening them as she moved her hands out. "The eyes are more difficult. Liner, highlighter, shadow."

Lace remembered the wings of color on Eugenie. The lilac pink had fanned across the bridge of her nose, all the way to her hairline, the color dotted with press-on jewels. "I think I know what you mean."

She sponged foundation on the woman's face, then powder, then concealer, then more powder. She brushed color onto her cheeks, and picked a green cream eye shadow that matched the woman's dress.

A man stopped at the vanity as Lace was gluing on rhinestones. One of the winged men, his hair neat and gelled, good-looking enough to be a festival queen's older boyfriend.

If not for his size, Lace might have laughed at his bare chest and his costume. That the Corbeaus put their men into their shows made her family trust them even less. Men shouldn't display themselves like quetzals.

Justin and Oscar never got tired of the jokes. Male fairies. *Maricas. Reinonas.*

But Lace couldn't laugh. His wings made his muscled frame even bigger. He was the kind of man Lace had feared meeting in the woods the night she first saw Eugenie.

"What is this?" he asked, his voice a little like Cluck's, but edged with irritation.

Her spine felt tight and hard as the barrel of her father's Winchester. Her pulse beat against the raw skin on her back, like a moth in a jar.

The woman opened her eyes. "The locals are friendly here, *non?*"

"She'd better be the only local you're getting friendly with." He left, the shadow of his wings following.

The moth under Lace's skin shook itself off, and slept.

"Dax." The woman stuck out her chin and laughed. "He sees to it we children follow all the rules." She shut her eyes again.

Lace finished the color and added mascara.

A thread of black showed at the back of the woman's neck. At first it looked like a few strands of black hair mixed in with the blond. The woman moved, and a few more threads flashed dark, like the veins on a leaf.

Lace dabbed a sponge over the woman's eyelids, pretending she was still working so she could look. She made out the vane of a feather, the thick central shaft. The barbs looked like enormous eyelashes, spiny with too much mascara, then dusted with the palest face powder.

She blew gently on the woman's eyelid, to seem like she was helping her mascara dry. But she moved so her breath skimmed past the woman's temple, and down toward the hair against her neck.

A mist of white powder broke loose. It smelled like raw bread dough.

Flour. The open bag of cake flour was for covering their feathers.

Lace reached out a brush to the plume, letting a little flour frost the bristles. She held the brush so lightly the woman wouldn't feel it. The feather gave, and the hair around it parted, showing the root.

The feather's dark shaft vanished into the woman's head like a vein. It was growing out of her skin.

Lace looked around at the wings on the Corbeaus' backs, searching for black feathers. She couldn't find any. Not where one wing met the other. Not at the edges. Not flashing dark between the eyespots.

Those wings, all peacock feathers, no black, left her lost in dark water, trying to make out the trail of her own air bubbles to show her the way to the surface.

The black feathers the wind brought the Palomas didn't come from their wings. They came from the Corbeaus' bodies. The stories her family told their children were as much truth as warning.

Lace's heart felt dry as a pomegranate shell, all the fruit picked away. Her fingers worried at her sleeve, wanting to scratch the feather burn off even if it left her bleeding.

The only thing that stopped her was the truth, sliding its fingers onto her throat.

Unless the Corbeau boy declared her forgiven, she could dig her nails into her arm all she wanted. The wound would heal, and the mark would show up again, like a feather growing back among his hair.

Faute de grives, on mange des merles.

In want of thrushes, one eats blackbirds.

*E*ugenie followed Cluck, wiping blush and eye shadow off her hands. "You don't think I can help?"

"You've never done it before," Cluck said.

"Fine. You can do it."

Cluck couldn't have made up one of the performers to save his life, and Eugenie knew it. The only time he'd ever handled makeup was to cover a bruise Dax gave him, and even that he'd done badly.

"*Et alors?*" Eugenie stood in front of him. "What are we going to do?"

"I don't know," he said. "What happened to Margaux?"

"She just left a message. She said she's going to see some friends in Hanford."

"Great," Cluck said.

"So what now?" Eugenie said.

Cluck dug his fingers into his hairline. "Just let me think, okay?"

Eugenie glanced past him, toward the girl he'd left holding the makeup brushes. "You're distracted." Her words ended in a laugh, teasing, not reprimanding.

He didn't look where Eugenie was looking, not wanting to prove his cousin's point. And if he looked at Lace again, her face thin and tired, he'd think too much about her and too little about the performers with their unpainted faces. He'd want to turn her over to his youngest aunt, who was always trying to feed people, or let her sleep in the blue and white trailer until the pale, dull film of IV medications fell away.

But there was a kind of intensity in her eyes, a look like she'd pinched herself until she came out from under the morphine. It gave him hope that her coming here was about more than an apology held in that paper bag and watermelon rind. This hope, that she was here not to explain herself but for him, slid into his hand like a found penny.

The place where his feathers touched the back of his neck felt hot. "I am not distracted," he said. He'd turned his back to that girl so he wouldn't look at her, so the way her dress brushed the back of her knees wouldn't make him forget how little time he had until the show started. "I'm thinking."

"I doubt it." Eugenie's smile was pinched and smug. "Not with your *petite copine* here."

"I do not have *une petite copine*, here or anywhere else. I'm trying to figure out how we're gonna get through tonight."

Eugenie nodded once, looking past him again. "How about her?"

"Clémentine?" he asked. His cousin was good with color. Meticulous. But that made her slow. If he let her do the makeup, they'd have to start the show at midnight. "You're kidding, right?"

"No." Eugenie pushed on his shoulder until he faced where she looked. "*Regarde.*"

The girl stood where he'd left her, hands still full of brushes. But instead of just holding them, she leaned over his cousin, sweeping eye shadow onto her brow bone.

She'd called him *gitano* like it was a curse, like she would never go near him or his family for their Romani blood. But now she'd planted herself among all the noise and the lights, and with every move of her hands she looked more like she belonged here.

Dios los cría y ellos se juntan.

Birds of a feather, fly together.

"Have you made me beautiful?" the woman asked.

Lace added a last dusting of loose powder. "You're done."

The woman turned to the mirror. Lace had evened out her skin tone, flushed her cheeks, painted her eyes mint green to match her dress.

"*Magnifique.*" The woman tried to put her cheek to Lace's. Lace's pulling away didn't discourage her. The woman kept little more than an inch of space between their faces, and kissed the air.

Lace flinched away. She shook off the scent of the flower crown, the clean smell of wet marjoram.

Cluck stood in front of them both, arms crossed. "Clémentine." He looked at the pale-haired woman.

"She's very good, *non?*" the woman said.

He looked at Lace.

Clémentine got up and crossed the yard, her feet imprinting the damp earth. She was almost as tall as Cluck. When she was sitting,

Lace couldn't tell. Now that she was walking, Lace saw her wide, rounded shoulders supporting those wings. She looked made of white sand clay, the statue of some lost goddess.

The hollow space in Lace's stomach grew hot and tight. She didn't like how many forms this family took. The boy her cousins called *chucho*. One woman, red-haired and small, and another, solid and pretty as a vinyl-bodied doll. All growing those black feathers.

Her mother had warned her about that. "You can never tell," she said. "None of them look the same because they mate with anything."

"Do you want a job?" Cluck asked.

That snapped her away from watching Clémentine. "What?" she asked.

"Do you already have a job?" he asked. "Or school? Some of the schools here run year-round, right?"

"No. I mean, no, I'm not in school, but . . ."

"Then do you want a job?"

"Doing what?"

"What you just did," he said. "Six nights and weekend afternoons. Eight shows a week. Replace my flake cousin."

"I'm not part of your family," Lace said.

"And?" He dropped his hands, slid them into his pockets.

She studied the shape of his fingers in the pocket lining. In this light, standing like he was, he looked like an old sepia photograph, with his brown hair and eyes, his white shirt and brown pants. It made him seem printed instead of real, like Lace could reach out and crumple him, let the wind take him. But then she'd wear his mark forever.

"I thought you only hired family," she said.

"Who told you that?"

She stopped herself. The Palomas knew more about the Corbeaus than anyone except the Corbeaus themselves. If Lace wanted to pass herself off as a local, she'd have to forget anything she knew that an Almendro girl wouldn't.

"You come through every summer," she said. "People talk."

"It's mostly family, but not everybody. There's Théo. He fixes the trailers. And Yvette. She homeschools the kids." Cluck looked over his shoulder. "And Alexander's around here somewhere." He looked back at Lace. "So what do you say?"

This was what he wanted? Her apology wasn't enough, so he wanted her hands for Corbeau work?

"We're not as unforgiving as I seem right now," he said. "This is probably the tenth time my cousin's bailed in two seasons."

If she did this for him, he'd have to take the mark off her. If she stayed long enough, maybe she could make this boy owe her a little more than she owed him, make the Corbeaus owe the Palomas. Maybe it would be enough to demand they stay out of her family's way. *Abuela* would have to let her back then. Lace could come back clean, safe to touch.

All she had to do was keep brushes and sponge pads between her fingers and the Corbeaus. If her skin did not touch theirs, she would survive this.

"Okay," Lace said.

"Great." He shoved makeup brushes into her hands. "You start now."

"Then sit down," she said.

"Excuse me?" he asked.

"You're here. I might as well start with you."

"Huh?"

"Don't you need your base put on?" she asked. He wasn't even in costume yet.

"Why would I?"

The men must have worn makeup too. Not all the color that went on the women, but foundation, pressed powder.

"Aren't you in the show?" she asked.

"Do I look like I'm in the show?" He showed her his hand, those last three fingers curled under. "*M'sieurs-dames,*" he called out, and the others watched him. "This is the new Margaux. She'll be doing your makeup." Then he left her holding the brushes, half the show standing around her.

The lights, the colors, and the wings swirled like a soap bubble's surface. Her cheek stung like it was still bleeding. If she was going to make up a whole show's worth of performers, she'd need a few more ibuprofen from her suitcase.

"I'll be right back." She set the brushes down and slipped into the woods.

Clémentine glided out from behind a tree, first the tip of a wing, then the rest of her. "Looking for this?" She held up Lace's suitcase.

Lace's back tensed. If this woman had touched the new tail *Tía* Lora made her, Lace would rip the feathers from her wings. She may not have had a bra of fake pearls to hit her with, but she had her hands, her fingernails, her teeth. She'd shred that flower crown to potpourri.

"I took nothing," the woman said. "I did not even open it. *Je promets.*"

Lace held out her hand.

Clémentine moved the suitcase out of reach. "If you tell me where you are sleeping tonight, you can have it."

Lace's spine relaxed. This woman thought she was a runaway.

Her father had given her some money "to get to Terra Bella," though he didn't believe it any more than she did. At best, he thought she was going to stay with Licha.

But neither of them said so. Lace had just taken the folded bills, thanked him, and hidden the money in the lining of her suitcase.

"Ever heard of a motel?" Lace said.

"It's the weekend," Clémentine said. "They are already booked for this berry festival."

Lace hadn't thought of that.

Clémentine set the suitcase down between them. "If you work here, you stay here."

Lace left the suitcase where it was. She was no runaway, and the woman couldn't have been more than thirty. She wasn't old enough to play mother.

"No, thank you," Lace said.

"Dax won't like it. He likes to keep track of everyone." Clémentine looked over her shoulder, through the dip between her wings. "Is it the house you are afraid of?"

"A little," Lace said. The deep, weathered wood and age-darkened windows made it look like a place Cluck could seal her inside of, making her a thing that belonged to the Corbeaus.

"You can sleep where I sleep." Clémentine pointed to a yellow trailer. "Inside the house to wash, to cook. *Ça y est.*"

Sleeping in one of the Corbeaus' trailers, a few feet from a Corbeau woman.

If all this would lift the feather off her forearm, Lace would do it.

She picked up her suitcase.

"*Bien,*" the woman said.

A donde fueres, haz lo que vieres.

Wherever you go, do what you see.

he Corbeau show was nothing like Justin said.

They didn't just put on costumes and stand in the trees. They climbed the boughs like cats, moving as though the high branches were wide and solid. The hung lights showed the contours of the men's bodies, and made the women's dresses look like mint and peach milk. Their skirts trailed and billowed, the edges fluttering. Sometimes their curls came unpinned and spun loose against their shoulders.

The performers climbed with their wings folded down, leads tethered to their wrists so that when they reached the top, they could pull the wings open to their full span. Those cords gave them a way to bring the weight of their wings forward. But if they didn't hold themselves upright, a sudden gust could still make them fall. If one of the women stepped wrong, she could catch her dress, tearing the fabric and slipping on the organza.

The men moved with as much calm as if it was their own muscle and not the trees holding them up. They pulled themselves onto higher branches as though the wings helped them instead of getting in the way, but Lace could guess how heavy they were.

The women's flower crowns never came undone, the larkspur and paintbrush clinging to their heads like a swarm of butterflies. They danced like the branches were broad as a field. They arched their arms so softly they looked as though the wind moved them. One in a champagne-colored dress stood so far up on her toes and lifted a leg so high and close to her body she looked like a clock striking noon. A tall one wearing mauve did an arabesque and tilted her body so her pointed foot showed between her wings. Another in dusk blue spun along a bough in a row of turns, spotting with nothing but stars.

Now she knew why Justin said so little about the show. He didn't want to admit how beautiful their enemies looked as they danced. When one of the men lifted one of the women, the wind turned her skirt to water. When he set her down, she landed so softly the branches didn't bend.

The women leaped like they knew the branches would hold them, like the boughs whispered their reassurances as they flew. The men's jumps from higher branches to lower ones made the audience gasp, and then applaud. The wind streamed through those feathers, and they looked like they were flying.

Even with the weight of those wings, Lace never caught them stumbling or flailing their hands to keep from falling. Each of them had balance as constant and rooted as these trees. If they extended their arms, it was part of the dance.

These winged creatures, *las hadas*, kept rhythm with each other, with no music but the sound of chimes hung in the trees. No metal or wood, just pieces of polished glass, the same pastels as their dresses. If the wind died down, the performers touched them, and the glass gave off shimmers of sound. They made one chime answer another, then a few more answer that one, like the staggered song of night-birds.

When one *bada* stepped into the light, another faded into a bough's shadow. It looked random, an unplanned dance, charged with a romance that made the audience forget these people were relatives.

Lace could sense the choreography under their movements. The show had the same patterned feel as the mermaids' dance. The trick was making it look like no two nights were ever the same, so each performance brimmed with fleeting magic.

Sometimes a Corbeau woman opened her hand, releasing a shower of wildflowers, and girls who watched from the ground held up their palms to catch the cream petals. Lace could never spot the women filling their hands. They must have hidden the flowers, one *bada* gathering a handful when the audience was watching another.

Tourists stared up, their necks taut with the worry of watching tightrope walkers. Locals didn't gasp, used to these shows year after year, but they still watched, smiled. Children lifted their hands and pointed whenever they spotted another fairy in the trees. After the show, the women offered children fairy stones, cheap glass pebbles full of glitter, and their small faces flooded with wonder.

Watching sowed a strange jealousy in Lace. It burrowed into her as she fell asleep on the floor of the yellow trailer. Her exile and her wounds kept her from the shutter click of families taking pictures for vacation scrapbooks. They kept her from daughters in bright dresses reaching out to touch her tail fin, wondering if it was real.

Did the women on those branches know how lucky they were to be beautiful? Lace had never been their kind of beautiful, but she'd faked it. The less stunning of the Corbeau women faked it too, now with Lace's help.

She woke up scratching at herself, dreaming of rain. Her nails left thread-thin trails of blood, like razor cuts. Waking broke her out of the feeling that the rain was eating through her.

In the morning, Lace found another of Cluck's feathers. It had settled into the folds of the blanket Clémentine had lent her.

Lace clutched its stem. She turned it, and red streaks showed among the black.

She thought of burning it. Instead, she tucked it into the lining of her suitcase. If she kept the ones she found, collected them, owned a little of this boy, it might give her power over him.

Her back ached as she got dressed, not from the mattress on the trailer floor, but from turning over, trying to find a way to sleep that didn't hurt her raw skin.

She listened outside the blue and white trailer. Cluck was already throwing things around, fixing costumes. She moved to look through the cracked door. He hunched over a table, trousers on but shirtless, his hair wet. She turned away as soon as she saw his back.

As long as she could help it, she wouldn't enter the house when he was there. She wouldn't let him trap her inside like a firefly in a jar. It was dangerous enough being in those walls with any Corbeau.

She let herself in the back door of the house, toothbrush and makeup bag in hand. Clémentine stood at the stove in bare feet, frying an egg. Lace passed behind her.

A woman sat in the heavy-curtained dining room, her posture straight as the lines of her shoulders. She looked around forty, age softly puckering the skin at the corners of her eyes. Her hair was pulled back into a neat bun that looked better fit for a catalog than a schoolroom, but her plain linen dress had the clean, bland shape Lace would expect on a mayor's wife.

She wrote in a heavy leather book, but did not bend over the page. She kept up straight, as though her dress was embroidered to the chair back.

"You are our new makeup girl," the woman said, not looking up.

Lace thought of putting down her toothbrush to show respect. She didn't know who the woman was, but if she kept the books, Lace shouldn't cross her.

Lace just nodded.

The woman finished writing, and raised her eyes to Lace. She didn't hide her study of the wine-colored burn on Lace's cheek, or her uneven eyebrows; adhesive had left them in patches.

The woman's face, her inspection, asked the question without her having to speak it. *You look like this and we should trust you to make us beautiful?*

Lace pressed her tongue to the back of her teeth. If she got angry, this woman might hear the sound of her uncles' *zampoñas* under her breath, betraying how little she belonged beneath a canopy of glass chimes.

"Makeup doesn't cure ugly," Lace said. She took her things toward the downstairs bathroom.

"There are no ugly women," the woman said. "Only lazy ones."

Lace stopped, laughing softly. *Abuela* threw the same quote at her and her cousins, when she pointed out that Lace was getting a little fat, or that Martha's modest dresses made her look dowdy, or the flare of acne reddening Emilia's cheek.

Lace turned around. "Helena Rubinstein."

The woman nodded once. A little light from between curtains crossed her face. "*Très bien.*" She motioned to a chair. "Come."

Lace sat down, the chair legs creaking as she shifted her weight. How did the woman's chair stay so quiet?

The table looked like an estate sale leftover. Once it must have been dark-polished wood, shining like still water. But it had been nicked and dulled so many years, it looked no grander than a wine cork. No wonder the owners left it to be rented out with the house.

"*Je m'appelle* Nicole," the woman said.

"Lace."

So this was Nicole Corbeau, *Abuela*'s rival.

Nicole reached for Lace's makeup bag. *"Puis-je?"* she asked.

Lace nodded. She had nothing to hide in there. Her tail was in her suitcase, locked, and her skirt and blouse covered her scales.

"Are you one of the performers?" Lace asked.

Nicole laughed a curt laugh, neat as her chignon. "I was." Her fingers searched the pouch's contents. "Now I keep the books. Dax is my son. So is *le cygnon.*"

"Who?" Lace asked.

"It's a nickname. His cousins call him Cluck."

"Dax and Cluck are brothers?"

The woman laughed again.

Lace bit the knuckle of her forefinger. She hadn't meant to sound so surprised. They had similar voices, but didn't look much alike. Though Cluck wasn't small, his brother's shadow would have swallowed him whole.

"La vérité sort de la bouche des enfants," the woman said.

Lace didn't ask what that meant. If the woman wanted her to know, she'd have said it in English.

Nicole set out Lace's foundation, concealer, and powder. "This is what you use?"

"It's what I used to use."

"And now?"

Lace had tried. The covering up only drew attention, made the burn look like a deep patch of scar tissue. The reddening on her arms would fade. The dead skin would peel back and fall away. But her shoulder had pressed her sleeve hard against her face that night, quickening the reaction. Even once the burn on her cheek healed, it would leave a bad scar, hard to hide.

"It makes it look worse," she said.

Nicole opened the powder compact, turning it so the mirror caught Lace's reflection. "Show me what you are doing."

This was all vinegar, having to be polite to a woman who stared at her marred face. But Lace did it, spread on a good layer of foundation and concealer, finished with powder. Not for *Abuela*, but for her father and *Tía* Lora.

Lace set the powder brush down. She lifted her chin to show the woman her face, her right cheek rough and mottled.

"Je comprends," the woman said. "Now wash your face."

"Excuse me?" Lace asked.

"I will show you how to fix it."

"I know how to do makeup."

"No," Nicole said. "You know how to do show makeup. It won't help you with your own. And if you cannot do your own face, how will they trust your hands?"

None of them seemed to mind the night before. They'd all sat down one at a time and let her put on their bases and colors.

"Your work is good for the shows," Nicole said. "But for you, for daylight, it is too heavy. Wash your face."

It was easier to do it than argue. Lace scrubbed off the makeup at the downstairs sink, gritting her teeth against the soap.

She came back with her face heat-reddened, and sat down, her thin scarf tied to her arm to hide the feather burn.

Nicole sponged a little foundation over her face, then concealer. She brushed the lightest layer of powder over Lace's cheeks and forehead, then a little more base, then powder again. "Better to use a light hand many times than a heavy hand once."

Lace clenched her back teeth to keep from wincing, her skin still raw enough that bristles and foam pads stung.

Nicole swirled blush onto her cheeks, swept on eye shadow with a few flicks of a brush, handed her a lipstick. Lace dabbed it onto her mouth and rubbed her lips together.

Nicole set the compact mirror into Lace's hands. *"Regarde."*

Lace opened her eyes. The coral on her cheeks and lips stood out. Her eyelashes looked pure black against the cream shadow.

The burn on her cheek was still there, still visible. Just fainter, a little discoloration under a veil of sand. In the right light, if Lace wore her hair down, it might go unnoticed. In the dusk and globe lights, she could pass for almost pretty.

"How'd you do that?" Lace asked.

"A light hand, and patience," Nicole said. "You teach people what to see."

Ne réveillez pas le chat qui dort.
Don't wake the cat who sleeps.

*C*luck watched his mother standing at the kitchen counter, picking lavender from a dish of *herbes de Provence*. Every time she bought a jar, she never noticed the violet buds until she got home, when she cursed in French as though it were her first language.

Years ago Cluck used to do this. His mother and Dax figured out that telling six-year-old Cluck to pick out all those tiny buds would keep him out of the way for a couple of hours. "Look, we have found a way for you to be useful to this family," she'd say.

Cluck leaned on the door frame, thinking of how different Lace looked now that his mother had gotten ahold of her. Still pretty, but painted. Her skin looked made of powder and blush.

"Did you have to do that to her?" he asked.

She flicked the lavender into another bowl. If Clémentine didn't ask for it, she'd throw it out. "Do what to who?"

"Lace," he said. "All that makeup. She looks like a pageant contestant."

"You hired a girl to do makeup, and you don't like that she wears it?"

His mother couldn't act like she didn't have a hand in this. He'd seen that same look on half the girls in this family.

"I know your work," he said.

"And she thanked me." She shook the dish. "Now she looks us in the eye. This is a good thing in the girl we trust with our faces."

He'd liked seeing Lace the way she was the night before, without anything covering her face, her lipstick almost the same deep red as the patch on her cheek. Nothing between that wound and the air it needed to heal.

If she had to scrub off all that makeup every night, her burn would take twice as long to scar over.

"Three days ago, she was in a hospital," he said. "She doesn't need someone telling her to cover up something that just happened to her."

"Girls need what they need to feel pretty," his mother said.

"She's pretty without it," he said.

His mother lifted her eyes from the counter, catching him in her peripheral vision.

He crossed his arms. This way his mother had of looking down at him even though he was taller than she was made him want to take up as little space as possible.

"Careful," she said.

There were only a handful of people with the show who weren't Corbeaus by blood or marriage. And everyone, not just Cluck, had to follow one simple rule: don't touch them.

But there were more rules for Cluck. Cluck was everything bad about his father, and Dax was everything good, chaff and wheat like the verse in Matthew. When Dax asked about their father, aunts burst with stories about how handsome and tall he was, how when he played the euphonium it sounded like the breath of *un séraphin*. When

Cluck asked, they looked at him as if he'd been the one to make their father leave. They reminded him that the man had left so completely after Cluck was born that they did not even know for sure what county he was in now. Inyo, they guessed? Monterey maybe?

Cluck, the bad son, was only allowed to talk to girls Dax and his mother chose for him. Girls they met at churches they would never bring Cluck to. Girls they thought would grow into women who might make him something less dangerous than he was.

Lace was not one of them. And now Lace worked for the show. He couldn't have found a girl more off-limits to him in Saint Mary's Convent.

"*Cygnon*," his mother said as he was leaving.

The nickname stopped Cluck in the door frame. Until Eugenie came up with "Cluck," for the way the fingers on his left hand looked like a rooster's claw, Dax got all the cousins to call him *le cygnon*, for having no more contour feathers than a young swan, gray and ugly.

Dax and his mother still called Cluck *cygnon* sometimes, Dax's way of pointing out that all the other Corbeaus had feathers that were stiff and neat, narrow on the leading edge and wider along the inner vane. And they were the true black of forest crows, not red-streaked like Cluck's. Cluck's hadn't changed as much from when he was small, when his first feathers grew in fluffy and short. They weren't natal fluff anymore, but they'd only developed into semiplumes, a cross between a cygnet's fuzz and a flight feather.

Cluck turned around.

His mother kept picking out lavender. "Your brother would like to talk to you."

Cluck slid his hands into his pockets, hiding his wrecked fingers in the lining.

This wasn't an order to go find his brother.

Dax would find him.

Cría cuervos y te sacarán los ojos.

Raise crows and they will peck your eyes out.

*L*ace held an eye shadow brush under the bathroom tap, flooding out the color she couldn't get with rubbing alcohol the night before. Lilac-tinted water swirled down the drain.

One of the Corbeau women pushed on the half-open door. Lace couldn't remember her name. Only that the dress she wore for the show was yellow as a pear.

"Excuse-moi." She reached past Lace for a bottle of perfume all the Corbeau girls shared.

Lace nodded to the woman's reflection. At first she'd kept the door closed, but cleaning the brushes took so long that every few minutes a Corbeau woman knocked, wanting the mirror so she could fix her lipstick on her way out to the Blackberry Festival. After the second time, Lace gave up and just left the bathroom door open.

She'd wondered what about those booths and fruit stands thrilled them so much until Eugenie sighed and said, "So many farmers' sons," as she combed her hair.

The woman sprayed on a little perfume, and the room filled up with a warm, sweet smell like cardamom. All wrong for the weather, but if the Corbeau girls wanted to stand out among all the powdery flower perfumes, that was how to do it.

The woman rubbed one wrist against the other, eyeing the brushes. "How'd you get stuck with that job?"

"Someone has to." Lace pressed water out of the rinsed bristles. "And I don't mind."

"Better you than me." The woman set the bottle back on the counter. "Next time use the sink upstairs," she said on her way out. "Horrible little mirror. No one will bother you."

Forget it. Lace would rather do all this at two in the morning than go upstairs. Being in this house was bad enough.

Lace laid out the brushes to dry, the chatter of a few Corbeau girls rounding the side of the house and then moving too far away to hear.

A door slammed at the other end of the hall, and Lace jumped. So many Corbeaus had left the house in the last few hours—off on errands or enjoying the free hours before tonight's show—that she'd thought the whole downstairs was empty.

Even from the bathroom doorway, Lace could hear the muffled yelling. She patted her hands dry on her skirt and took slow steps to the other end of the hall, trying to keep the old wood quiet.

She stopped at the closed door, making out two voices she was just starting to learn, and the clipped sound of skin hitting skin.

"Who is this girl?" one voice asked. Dax, the man who'd stood over Lace and the blond woman.

"She's from around here," the second answered. Cluck.

Dax chuckled. "She's from around here. Well, that fixes everything, doesn't it?" Then came the thud of a body hitting a dresser or a wall. "We don't know enough about her. She could be a thief."

Lace pressed herself into the door, listening against the wood.

"That's what everyone thinks we are," Cluck said, his voice strained with trying to get his air back. "So I take that as a recommendation."

"You don't get to make that kind of decision on your own."

Guilt pinched at the back of Lace's neck. It crackled down her body, spreading through her *escamas*.

"Do you want me to fire her?" Cluck asked. "She's good. You saw her work."

"*Les mecs*," a voice behind Lace whispered, close enough to warm her shoulder.

Lace startled, tripping on the hallway carpet.

Nicole Corbeau passed by, shaking her head. "*Il faut que jeunesse se passe, n'est-ce pas?*" She rolled her eyes at Lace, ready for her to agree.

The alcohol and sharp floral scent of Nicole Corbeau's perfume slipped into Lace's open mouth and needled her throat.

This woman had given her back her face. She'd told Lace about dyeing Eugenie's hair red, teaching the blonder Corbeaus to coat their feathers in cake flour, showing Violette and Margaux how to bleach their freckles with salt and lemon juice. And now she kept on her way down the hall, taking out her earrings, gliding by the room where one of her sons was beating the other?

Lace waited for Nicole Corbeau to shut herself in her bedroom. Then she put her body back against the door, and listened.

"She's good," Cluck said. "She doesn't even use her fingers. Just brushes, sponges, Q-tips."

"So she's a germaphobe," Dax said. "Wonderful."

Lace's fingers worried the doorknob. She thought of opening the door, wondered if that would make things worse for Cluck later.

"You shouldn't have gone around me." Lace heard the snap of Dax's fist on Cluck's skin.

What was Cluck doing? It didn't sound like he was fighting back, but he was still talking. He took what Dax did to him, but did not let it make him silent.

"We were screwed," Cluck said. His words sounded wet, and Lace wondered if there was blood in his mouth. "We needed her."

"You should have asked me," Dax said. Again, the sound of Cluck's back against the wallpaper. "I would've given her a shot."

Lace could almost make out Cluck's breathing, faint as far-off rain.

"Then give her one," he said.

She heard a body hitting the floor. Older brother throwing the younger one down against the baseboard.

The guilt knocked around in her, a heavy bead inside a jewelry box, rubbing down the velvet lining.

Dax's footsteps made the floorboards whine, and Lace ran down the hallway.

She opened the refrigerator and stared in, showing Dax she'd been there all along, of course she hadn't been listening.

Dax passed her and said nothing.

She turned her head, checking on what she already knew. Dax wasn't bleeding. His hair looked neat as it had before last night's show.

Dax slammed the back door, and the window blinds rattled.

Lace took off her scarf, filled it with half a freezer tray of ice, carried it back down the hallway.

Cluck sat on the floor of that room, arms resting on his knees. A dot of blood broke the line of his bottom lip. Sweat stuck his hair to the back of his neck.

Lace stepped through the half-open door. The screech of the hinges made him look up.

She stood over him, offering the scarf full of ice.

He gave her a weak laugh. "Cute." He took it and held it to his cheek.

"You okay?" she asked.

"Well, I gotta let him win one every now and then. It's good for morale."

He didn't look at her. The flush in his jawline and neck showed his embarrassment. She should've gone back to Clémentine's trailer and pretended she hadn't heard anything.

Standing over him felt cruel, rubbing it in even if she didn't mean it that way. So she sat on the floor, a good five feet between them. "What happened?"

He retied the scarf. "Nothing. We were just talking."

"You were just talking?"

"This is kinda what it looks like when we talk."

No wonder he hadn't panicked when her cousins cornered him. He was used to it. His brother could hit him, and his mother wouldn't look up.

Cluck wasn't in his family's show. Whether he'd wanted to be or not, she doubted he'd had the choice. This family called him a name that suited a hen better than a man.

Her mother would tell her she must have a fever to feel sorry for a Corbeau. But this boy had all the *mal* in him of being a Corbeau when the Corbeaus didn't even like him.

"Could I ask you something?" she said.

He nodded and rested the back of his head against the wallpaper.

"That night," she said. "What were you doing out in that part of the woods?"

"I was trying to find Eugenie." No flinch of lying in his face. Only the tired look of remembering. "The mixing tank blew, and nobody knew where she was."

Maybe Cluck hadn't put the net in the water. Maybe he wasn't the reason Lace was late getting out of the river. All of that could not live inside his body. Enough malice to go trapping mermaids. Enough worry to keep track of his cousins. Enough fearlessness of the poison in that rain to help Lace when he did not know her.

"Thank you," she said.

"You said that already."

But this time she meant it.

"Don't worry." He turned his head, his temple against the wall. "We're good."

They weren't good. She owed him however long he'd make her stay, however many nights cleaning brushes and fixing eye shadow he wanted. She'd work off the feather scar, stop fighting against the debt and just pay it.

Cluck got up, smoothed out his shirt, held out his hand to help her up. Burns had reddened his palm, leaving his skin uneven as raw citrine.

That night outside the liquor store, she hadn't known his last name. The night of the accident, she'd seen the feather, but her skin was too covered in poison to fight. But right now, she had no excuse. Taking his hand would mean touching a Corbeau on purpose.

But taking his hand was less of a betrayal to her family than touching any other Corbeau. These people, Cluck's own family, hated him. They didn't say it but she felt it, like heat under the earth. His hand looked like it had gotten broken all at once, maybe slammed in a door, or crushed under a costume trunk. If these people loved him, they would've gotten him to a doctor in time to save his fingers.

If she hated him, she'd be like them, their scorn of Cluck Corbeau the same as a shared eye color. It would make her one of them.

But she could defy this family by touching him.

She shut her eyes, took his hand, let him pull her to standing. The grain of his burns gliding over hers stung. The heat of his hand radiated through her wrist. If she squeezed her eyes shut harder, she could hear *Abuela*'s gasp like the rush of the river's current.

But it didn't kill her. And it didn't make her father and *Tía* Lora feel any farther away.

"Nice work last night," Cluck said. "You're good. And fast. Where'd you learn?"

"Community theater on the weekends."

"How old are you?" he asked.

"Eighteen."

"Sure, you are."

"Seventeen."

The raise of his eyebrows showed the swelling along his temple. If he didn't keep ice on it, he'd get a bruise.

"In September," she said.

"Does your family know where you are?"

"No," she said.

"Are they looking?"

"Fat chance."

He shrugged, a look telling her he wouldn't push it. He kept the ice on his jaw and stepped into the hallway.

"Cluck?" she said.

He turned around.

"All those feathers," she said. "Do you kill peacocks for them?"

"Of course not," he said.

"Where do you get them?" she asked.

He thumbed a blood spot off his lip. "You really want to know?"

Il faut qu'une porte soit ouverte ou fermée.

A door must be open or shut.

❧

Cluck opened the Morris Cowley's passenger side. He watched Lace stare into the truck cab. The look on her face wasn't fear, the skittishness of a bitten animal, *un chat échaudé qui craint l'eau froide.* It was suspicion.

People always found something they didn't like about his family. They were Romani. They were French. They were show people. The traveling kind.

"Did you think we brought a flock with us everywhere?" he asked. "If you want to know where I get the feathers, we're gonna have to drive there."

"What's your real name?" she asked.

He laughed. He liked that she wanted to know that before she decided whether she was getting in the truck, but it didn't mean he was gonna tell her. Everyone called him Cluck. His real name wasn't any more of her business than her family was his.

"Sven," he said.

"No, really. What's your real name?"

"Rupert."

She shook her head and got in. "What's your real name?" she asked, a last try.

He didn't blame her. In the fairy tales Eugenie told Noe and Mason, the number three was a charm. Anything—kissing a lover to break a curse, piercing an enemy with a dagger—had to be tried three times before it worked.

But he wasn't a locked door or enchanted tree. He wasn't telling her his real name just because she kept asking.

"*Le bâtard,*" he said, the words slipping from his mouth before he could pull them back. This was what his older relatives called him when they thought he couldn't hear. Even when he was little, this was his name to them. *Le bâtard.* Bastard. It didn't matter that Dax and Cluck had the same father, that he had left them both without marrying their mother. Dax was fatherless, but Cluck was *le bâtard.*

"How do you spell that?" Lace asked.

"I'm kidding," he said.

It was fair. She didn't know his name. He didn't know why she wasn't with her family. It wasn't his business. He didn't care to add to the stories about *les Roms* stealing *gadje* children, but the flinch of her eyelashes made him think she was telling the truth, that nobody was looking for her.

"What happened to your hand?" she asked after he started the truck.

"Rogue rhinoceros," he said.

"What happened to your hand?" she asked again.

"Jousting accident."

She looked out the window as he pulled the truck onto the road. "It wasn't your dominant hand, was it?"

"No. It wasn't."

It was a lie and not a lie. He'd started out left-handed, still was when no one but his grandfather was watching. His family's French blood disapproved of left-handedness. Witches greeted Satan *avec la main gauche*, they said, so no Corbeau would write or stitch with his left hand. "We only see ghosts if we look to our left," warned one aunt. "*Le Diable* moves our left hand more easily than our right," added another. A third, "The Devil watches us over the left shoulder."

Mémère, according to *Pépère*, always called them superstitious old women and shooed them out of her kitchen when they started talking that way. Cluck would've liked to see that.

"You're lucky," Lace said. "It could've been the hand you used more."

"Yep. I'm lucky alright." He rolled down the window. Highway air rushed through the cab. It brought the smell of diesel fuel and wild sorrel, and the sharp green hint of onion fields.

He noticed Lace pinching the air, catching one of his feathers. She held it by the calamus and turned it between her fingers.

The back of his neck grew hot. He kept his eyes on the highway's white lines, pretending he hadn't noticed.

She held it in the wind, letting the air ruffle the downy barbs. He felt it, and the chill made him shiver.

When they got to Elida Park, Lace folded the feather she'd caught into her palm, and tucked it into her pocket.

He helped her down from the truck, and the sight of the cats and peacocks made her catch her breath in her chest. Calicoes and tabbies sprawled in patches of light, and the great birds strutted across the crabgrass.

"Where'd they all come from?" she asked.

"The cats come because the locals feed 'em," Cluck said. "The birds are here thanks to some idiot who ordered a cock and hen from a mail-order catalog ten years ago."

"Mail-order peacocks?" she asked. "Was this before or after the rogue rhinoceros?"

"It's true," he said. "His wife couldn't take the way they shriek, so he just left them here. Unfixed, so you know the rest."

An orange tabby sunned itself on the lower rung of a wooden fence. A young peacock swept by, its fan down.

Lace winced, waiting for one to attack the other.

"Don't worry," Cluck said. "They get along enough."

He picked up a shed feather, pulled garden shears from his back pocket and clipped it. He threw the lower half to an adolescent tortoiseshell cat. It chewed on the hollow shaft, back feet kicking the feather barbs.

"How do you get enough feathers if you pick them up one at a time?" Lace asked.

"I don't. They're not shedding much now, but come the end of summer, they'll molt." The feathers would half-carpet the ground, like *la couleur* of fruit blossom petals turning the ground pink in spring.

A gasp parted Lace's lips, one breath away from a laugh.

Cluck knew why before he looked up.

They both watched the white peacock shake itself out of the tall grasses. The bird took one slow step, then another, his body so covered in white Cluck always expected it to dust the ground like powdered sugar.

Cluck crouched so he'd look smaller. It made the birds shed their skittishness like molted feathers. He didn't ask Lace to. She wasn't much taller than the peacock's upright tail fan.

The peacock took one step into the sun, like toeing cold water. In full light, he looked made of the fringe off white bearded irises.

He dropped a single tail feather, long as Cluck's arm, and left to follow after a peahen with eyes like black marbles.

Cluck lifted the plume off the grass, cradling it so the stem wouldn't bend, and clipped the hollow shaft of the calamus.

"You're gonna touch that?" Lace asked.

"I'm not gonna catch anything."

"No," she said. "I mean because it's white."

He got up from his crouch. "And?"

"I don't know. I thought since yours are black."

He laughed. "I have black feathers, so I won't touch white ones? No." Was that one of the rumors going around Almendro? Just because the name of that other family meant "dove"? None of them despised the Palomas for their name, or even for the white scales that showed up on their bodies. It had never been about doves or birthmarks.

It had always been about what they'd done.

He handed Lace the eyespot. "If you look close, it's not all white."

She held it in the light, tilting the left side down, then the right. Most of the feather was pale as bleached linen, but from different angles, the iridescence on the eyespot showed tints of color. Pollen-dust yellow. Traces of blue, like bits of sky and robin's eggs. Dusk colors, violet blue and bluish lavender. A pink that matched Lace's mouth when her lipstick wore off.

Now she laughed, light as the colors on the eyespot.

"It's because of the white," he said.

"Because white has every color," Lace said.

Pépère would like her for knowing things like that.

They stood there as the light fell, watching until the peacocks scattered.

Having her there made him look at the birds a little less. When she was watching, he could watch her. He could study how her skin and her eyes and hair were all gradations of the same color, lighter to darker. The only parts of her face that broke the sequence was the pink on her lips and the deep red on her cheek, like crushed raspberries. If he stopped thinking of how much it must have hurt her, that patch on her cheek was beautiful.

"You hungry?" Cluck asked when he started the Morris Cowley. "Or do you always wait until the middle of the night to eat?"

She reached over the gearshift and shoved his upper arm.

"Oh, good," he said. "You're becoming a Corbeau."

Her eyes opened a little wider.

"I was kidding," he said.

The park disappeared into the rearview.

"It's not catching, I promise," he said. "You're not gonna grow feathers from being around us."

She nodded and looked out the window. She may or may not have believed him.

Dime con quién andas y te diré quién eres.

Tell me who you're with and I'll tell you who you are.

Before she and Cluck left the roadhouse where they'd stopped, Lace bought two postcards. One showed a field of wild poppies, the other a pasture flecked with cows. Both smelled of syrup and fryer grease.

She set them on the dashboard and filled in the River Fork's address, the truck's speed making her pen wobble. If she and Cluck stopped before the county line, they'd have Tulare postmarks.

Cluck glanced across the front seat. "Who're you writing to?"

"My family," she said.

On both, she wrote "Greetings from Terra Bella, *con cariño*," and then the four curled letters of her signature.

"I thought they didn't care where you were," he said.

"I never said they didn't care." She added *Tía* Lora's name and room number to the poppies, then her father's to the cows. First names only, in case Cluck had good enough vision to read her handwriting. "I said they weren't looking."

The latch on the passenger side door clicked, and it swung open. The pavement rushed past like white water, and Lace choked on her own gasp. Fields flew by, speed turning them to liquid. The scent of new onions stung her throat.

"Dammit," Cluck said, like he'd cut himself or touched the handle of a hot pan.

The wind ripped the postcards off the dashboard. They twirled like leaves and flew out toward the road. They shrank to two white flecks against the sky, and then vanished.

Lace's body felt insubstantial, untethered. She grabbed at the door, but couldn't reach.

Cluck pulled her toward the middle of the front seat and set her hand on the steering wheel. "Hold this."

She gripped the wheel so they didn't swerve. It didn't take much to make the truck drift, but a lot of tug on the wheel to get it straight again. The truck's weight pulled on the steering column.

"Cluck," she said, but he was already leaning behind her, reaching for the door.

He tried to keep one foot over the brake. Cluck's side grazed her back, her hip against his, his hair brushing her arm.

Cluck clicked the latch back into place and swung the door shut, one hand on the back of the seat to steady himself. She shifted her weight to move out of the way, and ended up half on his lap. Their bodies tangled like roots as they got back to where they'd been.

She wouldn't have caught Cluck's laughs if she hadn't been so close to him. They were short, quiet, the same low pitch as the air pulling past the cab. They intertwined with Lace's, her hands still sparking with the feeling of him giving her the wheel like she knew how to hold it.

The truck streaked off the highway and through town, and they pulled onto the Corbeaus' rented land.

"Sorry," Cluck said. "That happens sometimes."

"You could've told me," Lace said, the breath of a laugh still under her words. "I would've held onto the door."

"No one's ever in this thing who doesn't already know." He down-shifted. "Besides, it's never happened before when the truck's not speeding."

"You *were* speeding."

He set it into park. "Really?"

"By about ten miles," she said. "Why didn't you just pull over?"

"It was a soft shoulder. We would've gone straight into a ditch."

"Then get the door fixed."

He leaned over her and opened the passenger side. "It's a problem with the striker." His fingers followed the latch's grooves. "It's a tough part to find." He turned his head, and then flinched, like he hadn't realized how close he was to her.

The idea fluttered along her rib cage that if she touched him again, she would turn to dust or fire. She lifted her hand to his face, wanting to know if it was true.

But the whispers from the other side of town stilled her. The wind carried the call of reed pipes. River kelp wrapped around her, pulling her down. It would take her under until water filled her, and she did not breathe. Those voices whispered their assurances. *Better you drown than touch him.*

So she didn't touch his cheek like she meant to. Didn't follow the shape of his temple down to his jawline. She took a lock of his hair between her fingers. It felt slick as the barbs of a feather, smooth, ready for rain. He shut his eyes as though he felt it, like the blue-black of his hair was living, as full of blood and nerves as his skin.

His look toward her mouth was quick, like she might not notice if he was fast enough. Then he lifted his eyes back up to hers. Even in daylight, his irises made her think of wet earth.

"Sorry about your postcards," he said.

"It's okay," she said. "If it's windy enough, maybe they'll get where they're going."

She tilted her head enough to tell him she wanted it, but didn't move so much that those voices could say she started it. He was close enough that she could have traced his lower lip with her tongue.

The sound of laughing came from the back of the house, and he broke away. He raised his head, looking past Lace out the truck window. He mumbled something that may or may not have been French, and got out on the driver's side.

Lace glanced around the truck. The laughing wasn't close enough to be at them. She jumped down from the cab and went after him.

Dax and a couple of the other Corbeau men clustered behind a trailer. Cluck joined them, his back to Lace. Even through his shirt, she could make out the tension in his shoulders.

Cluck shifted his weight, and Lace saw the thing in Dax's hands. She stopped, and her feet skidded against the ground.

She knew those scraps of beaded fabric as well as her own body. The small stitches. The bursts of glass beads. Her old tail, the grapefruit pink now dulled to peach. The current must have pulled it loose from that ball of roots. The silt and river water had left it dirty, drying stiff.

Something deep red had splattered it. The color, close to new blood, pressed into Lace's collarbone. Then she saw the jar of blackberry jam, dark as wine, in a cousin's hands.

Dax holding her old tail made her feel his hands on her lower back, her hips, her thighs. Everywhere Cluck had touched cooled, leaving room for the pinch of Dax's grip.

"What the hell are you doing?" Cluck asked.

"What does it look like?" Dax asked. "We're gonna make a delivery."

"Where did you get this?" Cluck grabbed the fin, balling it in his hands. The sense of his fingers on Lace's ankle, while Dax still held the rest of her, almost made her kneel.

"It washed up," said one of the cousins, flicking more of the blackberry jam over the fabric. "One of the fish must've lost it." Red stained his fingers, and Dax's. It stained all their hands.

Lace had made her peace with losing that tail to the river. The water would swallow it and keep it. Like a communion *hostia*, it would dissolve on the current's tongue.

But now the Corbeaus had it.

If she saved it from their hands, they'd know, and she'd have to run. The feather burn would stay on her forever, this family's hate searing it deeper into her skin.

If she did nothing, they would stain it, leave it outside the motel for *Abuela* or Martha or worse, her great-aunt, whose skilled, tired hands had worked so many nights to make it. *Tía* Lora would take it as a sign that Lace had died or would soon.

The one with the jar held it out to Cluck, offering him a turn.

Cluck stood close to his brother. "Stop."

Dax laughed and splashed a little more blackberry jam on the tail. Lace felt it, sharp as cuts.

Cluck ripped the tail out of Dax's hands. Flecks of red sprayed both their shirts.

The cousins froze. One stepped back.

Lace folded her tongue and bit down. The relief of her tail going from Dax's hands to Cluck's was so sharp it was almost pain.

"You really want to go over there and make this worse?" Cluck asked, his voice low enough that Lace could barely hear it, the words meant just for his brother. He shrugged his shoulder toward their cousins. "You want to see one of them die this year?"

A few Corbeau women came outside. Clémentine. Eugenie. A couple others Lace had done makeup on. One screamed at the sight of all the red, but one of the cousins rushed to show her the blackberry jam jar.

Dax thumbed a spot off his chin and stared his brother down. "You hate them as much as I do."

"More." Cluck tightened his grip on the fabric. "But we are not doing this."

Dax glanced over his shoulder, sensing the women watching.

He looked back at Cluck. "You just used your one free pass." He took a handful of the tail and shoved it at Cluck's chest, staining his shirt worse.

Cluck balled the tail up in his hands and took it into the costume trailer.

Lace followed him.

He folded the tail like an antique dress or a lace tablecloth. "Sorry you had to see that."

She shut the trailer door.

"We're not crazy, just so you know," he said, but didn't look at her. "There are reasons we feel how we feel."

Right then, she didn't care what he thought of her family, what he would think of her if he knew her full name. She cared that her old tail wasn't in Dax's hands, on its way to *Tía* Lora.

"What are you gonna do with it?" she asked.

"I don't know." He set it down on the counter. "If I throw it out here, Dax'll find it. I could throw it out in town." He ran his fingers over the beading, and Lace shivered. "But it just doesn't seem right."

"What doesn't?" she asked.

"I don't know." He looked a little sad, a half-frown creasing the corner of his mouth. "It's just good work, that's all."

The sting of Dax's hands faded, and the feeling of Cluck's came back. Cluck may have hated the name Paloma, but he recognized the art in those stitches and beads. To him, seeing them stained and torn must have been a little like finding a pair of peacock-feather wings ripped apart.

Her last name may not have been safe on his tongue, but this fabric and these beads, this part of her the water had sealed to her body like skin, was safe in his hands.

"If I bring it to the other family, it's gonna look like a threat," he said.

"Then let me do it," Lace said. "They don't know who I am." She could get it to Martha, who'd hide it in with the dresses *Abuela* didn't like her wearing.

"No," Cluck said. "I don't want you anywhere near that family."

That family. Her mouth grew hot with wanting to tell him whatever he thought he knew, whatever he thought about her family, he had heard wrong, been told wrong.

He was the one good one out of all these crows.

"I have an idea," she said.

She brought him to the river, the ruined tail in her arms. This way it would be out of the Corbeaus' hands, and her great-aunt would never see the stains.

She gathered handfuls of small stones, worn smooth by the current, and stuffed them through a hole in a fin seam. When enough stones weighted down the bottom edge of the fin, she gave it back to the water.

The dull pink sank and vanished. Quiet fell over her, the slow joy of finding the sun on a cold day. Those stones would hold her ruined tail at the river bottom.

The relief was so perfect it made her *escamas* sore. It bubbled up through her, spilling out of her, making her kiss Cluck's cheek.

He ignored it, took it as the same kind of teasing as her shoving his arm. So she kissed him on the mouth to make him understand, lightly, just enough to feel the fine grain of his lips, a little chapped by dust and wind. He accepted it, not pulling away. But he didn't deepen it. He didn't take her tongue or give her his. He took it like she meant it. More than a greeting, less than it would have been in the cab of his grandfather's truck.

When she pulled away, he did too.

He opened his eyes. "What was that for?"

"For what you did," she said.

He squinted enough that his eyelashes almost met. "What do you care? This isn't your fight."

"It *is* my fight." She said it without thinking. But it slipped into lies she'd already told, easily as her old tail sinking into the river. "This town's too small for a war," she said, like this town, not the war, belonged to her.

He watched the corner of the fin flick up and then go under. Then he started back toward the house.

A few steps away, he realized she wasn't behind him, and looked over his shoulder. "You coming?"

She searched the river for a flush of peach, but the water had folded it into the dark.

They walked back to the old Craftsman. She went in with him, and the breath of the Paloma women followed. Those *voces* tried to tell her that him holding the door wasn't a polite thing. He could turn himself into a crow with knives for feathers, and she wouldn't see in time to run.

Petit à petit, l'oiseau fait son nid.

Little by little, the bird builds its nest.

*C*luck held his hands under the kitchen tap, washing the blackberry off his fingers.

He watched Lace pat her hands dry on a dish towel.

"Take off your shirt," she said.

The water jumped from warm to hot, prickling his fingers. "You getting ideas?"

She shoved him. "It's stained. I can get those out."

Cluck unbuttoned the cuffs. "I know how to wash a shirt."

"Do you know how to get Almendro blackberry out? Because I do." She cut open a lemon from the fruit bowl and found a half-flat bottle of soda water in the fridge. "My younger cousins always got this stuff on their good clothes."

He unbuttoned the front, and slipped out of it.

She rubbed the lemon and soda water into the stains and ran them under the kitchen tap. The flecks faded and disappeared.

"Hey, that actually works," Cluck said. "I thought I was gonna have to figure out what to wear with a pink shirt."

"Why not just wear stuff you can throw in a washer?" she asked.

"My clothes used to be my grandfather's," he said. "I like wearing what he wore."

"Why?"

"I don't know, I guess it makes me feel like I could be like him." He thought of the Alain Corbeau-ness flooding into him.

She scrubbed at a stain. Even watching her profile, he could see a little bit of a smile at the corner of her mouth.

"You doing okay here so far?" he asked.

"Yeah. They trust me to make them look good, believe it or not."

"Why wouldn't they?" he asked.

She turned her head, and that smile turned sad and patient, bearing with the question.

She meant the burn on her cheek. Even his mother, piling loose powder on her like layers of *une millefeuille*, couldn't make her forget it. That burn kept her from seeing how her hair was the deep brown of black mustard seeds, or that her eyelashes looked like the smallest feathers.

"You're beautiful," he said.

Her lips parted a little. She looked as likely to tell him to go screw himself as she did to say thank you.

"You don't have to say that," she said.

He needed to shut up. The older Corbeaus always taught the younger ones how to talk to girls, but nobody had taught him. At eighteen, he was too old to be outright forbidden from talking to girls, but he was still *le petit démon*. His uncles' glares whenever they saw him so much as ask a local girl for directions was enough to put him off trying altogether.

But he couldn't let Lace think he was talking about some version of her from before the accident. She had the same face. It just had a bloom of red on it.

"I know I don't have to say it," he said. He stopped himself from saying the word "beautiful" again. "It's just true."

She stared at him. Her hands stayed still, holding his shirt. The wet fabric dripped into the metal sink.

He shouldn't have said it at all. Saying it with his shirt off just made it worse. Why not unbutton his fly while he was at it?

He grabbed for something to change the subject to, but everything he landed on made it worse. The pattern on her dress. How the ends of her hair had gotten in the way, and were wet from the tap. Her hands working the fabric of his shirt in a way that made him wish he was still in it.

She wrung out his shirt and handed it to him. "Just hang it up. It should be good." She put the club soda and the other half of the lemon in the fridge. The citrus smell made the air feel thin and clean.

He had to leave. Standing there with the wet shirt in his hands would make him look even more *comme un con* than he already felt.

You're beautiful. It's just true. His own words hovered in the air like dragonflies. Even when he went out the back door to hang up his shirt, he could hear the humming of their wings. He had no way of knowing if she wanted to swat them away or open her hands to let them land.

Pájaro viejo no entra en jaula.

An old bird is difficult to catch.

*L*ace."

Lace woke first to Clémentine's voice, then to the pain in her arms.

"Lace."

Clémentine held her hands, stopping her from clawing her own skin.

Lace sat up. She remembered the dream of that cotton-candy sky, how it fell, scalding everything.

"You've scratched yourself open," Clémentine said.

A few dots of blood speckled Lace's sleeves. Clémentine tried to roll them up, but Lace pulled her hands away.

"You should clean those." Clémentine handed Lace the things she needed to shower.

Hot water still hurt. It drummed heat into Lace's back, scratched at her cheek. It came on like the sting of touching dry ice. It made her brace her hands on the wall tile.

So she flipped the shower to cold and shivered under the tap. Beads of water clung to her body, icing her back and her breasts. The chill stayed, her lungs and heart cooling like fruit in the *aguas frescas*.

The sound of the water made her think of Cluck's voice, him saying, "You're beautiful" under the soft rush of the kitchen faucet. She wished, as hard as she wished for her skin to heal and close, that she'd been looking at him when he said it. His face would've told her what those words meant. If he felt sorry for her, or if wondering what might have happened in the front seat of the truck, absent his cousins' laughter, bothered him as much as it bothered her.

A shudder rattled through her as she dried off and pulled on her clothes. Dresses only, as long as she was here. No more skirts and tops. If her shirt rode up in the back, her *escamas* might show.

She did her makeup the way Nicole taught her. A thin layer, then another. Then blush, lip color. Her hair soaked the back of her dress, sticking it to her skin. She balled it up to pin it on her way down the hall.

The sound of coughing startled her. Her hands opened, and whips of her wet hair hit her back.

She followed the sound farther into the hall. It had the deep, hollow echo of a hard cough. She could hear it starting and ending in the lungs, pinching the heart and pressing against the rib cage.

Lace found the room the coughing came from. The wooden door was cracked, letting her see the old man standing among the mismatched furniture. A plain bed and a dresser with vine-shaped carvings along the edges. Yellowing doilies on everything. A wooden bead rosary dripped off the nightstand.

He held a white handkerchief to his mouth, the cough shaking his body.

Lace had exchanged few words with Cluck's grandfather. The night she'd started with the show, Eugenie had introduced her to

Alain Corbeau, who'd made a "Hmm" sound that was not quite a greeting but not quite disapproval either.

The strings of globe lights hadn't shown how much Cluck took after him. But now, with daylight filling this room, she would've bet her new tail that Cluck would look just like him in fifty years. They both had the same tint to their forearms, brown, but not like Lace's family. That brown had the gray thread of an ashwood tree, more silver than olive.

Both had that same dark hair too, worn a little long. Gray streaks lightened the old man's, but he still had plenty of black left.

The old man lowered the handkerchief from his mouth. The linen came away blood-speckled, like the flecks of brown on a robin's egg.

The difference between Cluck and the old man was more than age. It was the way, when the old man realized Lace was there, his eyes caught the light a little more sharply.

"Are you okay?" Lace asked.

"This is the last time I let my daughter give me one of her sleeping pills," he said. "This morning I was so foggy I tried to brush my teeth with my razor." He forced a smile. It started out kind, then twisted, wry and wary, when Lace didn't return it.

Mixing up his razor and his toothbrush. It was so strange she almost believed it. But he'd made a little too much of a point of showing the blood-dotted handkerchief while he said it. For how unimportant she was, he cared a little too much about her taking his explanation as truth.

"And you?" he asked. "Why are you here?"

"I do the makeup now," she said.

"I know what you do. Why are you doing it here?"

His eyes drifted toward the feather burn on her arm. She'd covered it the same way Nicole Corbeau had taught her to do her face, layers of foundation and powder as thin as the dried husks of tomatillos.

To anyone except Lace, it wasn't there. But the old man studied the patch on her arm like he could see it.

He knew.

He met her eyes. She read the bargain in his face, the offer, an exchange of silences. *Don't tell, and I won't tell.*

She shut the door and pressed her back to the hallway wall. The sound of his coughing stabbed into her forehead. Maybe this man was the Corbeaus' version of her father, skeptical of *las supersticiones.* As long as she didn't make trouble for him, he'd let her stay.

If she told, she'd lose any chance of getting the scar lifted, along with this small, feathered thing growing between her and the boy called Cluck.

But the sound of the kitchen faucet came back to her, this time with the things Cluck had said about his clothes. They'd belonged to this man, coughing a mist of blood into his handkerchief. This man Cluck wanted to be like so badly he wore collared shirts in the heat of a Central Valley summer, hoping the invisible things that made his grandfather who he was would rub off like a scent.

If Cluck could lose him, he needed to know.

Lace heard Cluck's voice upstairs. She stood in the front of the wooden staircase and looked up at the second floor. She could've called his name, but then Cluck's grandfather would hear her. He could tell her secret in a few words. The Corbeaus would trap her in this house, and she'd never have the chance to tell Cluck that his grandfather had a secret of his own.

She took a breath in and ran up the stairs, quick as *las sirenas* slid into a cold river.

The second floor barely looked different from the first. A few closed doors. A few open. An unscreened window at the end of the hall. But even with the hardwood under her feet, she felt the distance to the ground. The third and fourth floors of motels had never bothered her, but here, she was sure a coin tossed out a window would fall forever. This house may not have belonged to the Corbeaus, but by renting and staying in it they'd filled it with their reckless love of heights. They made their living by not fearing falling.

Cluck stood at the end of the hall, talking to another Corbeau about lights and cables. She took a few steps down the hall as fast as she'd taken the stairs and put her palm to Cluck's shoulder blade.

He turned around. "What's wrong?" His eyes flashed over her face.

"There's something I have to tell you," she whispered.

Cluck said something in French, and the other man nodded and left.

"What happened?" Cluck asked.

She dragged the words off her tongue. The coughing. The blood. The handkerchief.

Cluck did not flinch. He got on the phone and didn't put it down until he found a doctor three towns over who could take a last-minute appointment.

"How do you know he'll go?" Lace asked.

"I'll tell him the appointment's for me," Cluck said. "I'll say I want the company."

That bought Lace time. Cluck's grandfather wouldn't know she'd told, not for sure, until they got to the doctor's office. That gave her a chance to run.

"What if he doesn't believe you?" Lace asked.

"He will." Cluck's eyes ticked toward his hands, scarred from pulling at the cotton of her dress. "I can't believe this. How many years working at the plant? And he acts like all those chemicals are just dye and water."

The floor wavered under Lace. "Your grandfather worked at the plant?" she asked.

"Yeah," Cluck said. "For most of his career."

Lace didn't know any of the Corbeaus had done anything outside of this show.

Cluck pulled on a blazer, soft with half a century of wear. "You know where the thread is. If someone tears a dress, you think you can handle it?"

"Yes," she said. She'd do everything they expected tonight, painting all their faces. If she left them, took off without doing her job, it would be one more wrong against Cluck. One more stolen Camargue horse. She might wake up with a feather on her other arm, her back, her neck.

But once the show started, she'd run.

Cluck set a hand on her upper arm. "I'm glad you told me."

She nodded, bit the inside of her cheek, kept her face from telling him that when he came back, she'd be gone.

Celui qui veut être jeune quand il est vieux,
doit être vieux quand il est jeune.

He who wants to be young when he is old,
must be old when he is young.

Pépère barely acknowledged the nurse who took his pulse and blood pressure. When she told him the doctor would be right in, he looked out the window like he was waiting for a bus.

The nurse flashed Cluck and his grandfather a smile, bright as the flowers on her scrubs, and shut the door behind her.

Pépère nodded at her, his mouth in the same pinched smile he gave children. Cluck knew that look. His grandfather gave it to Dax and to Cluck's cousins when they were small. How Cluck escaped it, he didn't know. Probably because his hand bothered the rest of them so much they didn't want to be near him. *Pépère* took their disdain as a recommendation.

"I don't like that *gadji*," *Pépère* said.

Cluck leaned against the sink and flipped through an old copy of *Popular Mechanics*. "The nurse?"

"Your new makeup girl."

"You don't like her for telling me about the blood on your *mouchoir*."

"You let her follow you around like she is your little sister."

Cluck cringed. Yes, that was exactly how he wanted to think of Lace.

"I understand," his grandfather said. "You saved her life. She has nowhere to go. You want to care for her like she is some stray cat."

Cluck turned the page. "So which is it, *Pépère*, is she my sister or my cat?"

The doctor came in, asked *Pépère* a few more questions, told him, "You should stop smoking."

"I've told him that my whole life," Cluck said. A waitress from Calais had gotten *Pépère* started on cigarettes before he left *le Midi* for the United States.

"Yes, it is the smoking." *Pépère* stood and shook the man's hand. "Thank you for your help, Doctor." His way of ending an appointment he hadn't wanted. Feign repentance of his half-century cigarette habit, and be on his way. This was why Cluck's mother didn't drag him to doctors anymore.

Cluck hadn't even told his grandfather the appointment was for him until they'd parked and gone in. He'd said he was going in to see someone about his hands, still spotted the pinks and reds of worn brick. Only *Pépère's* pity had kept him from suspecting on the drive over.

Like Cluck cared what his hands looked like, as long as they worked enough to make the wings. His guilt felt like an elbow jabbing his ribs. But if he hadn't lied, *Pépère* never would have come.

The doctor scrawled on a prescription pad. Wrinkles softened the skin around his mouth. His hair had more gray than *Pépère's*. *Pépère* must have been hoping for a resident. They were always pleased thinking they'd converted a smoker. Easier to con.

"I'm writing you a script." The doctor tore off the sheet and held it out to *Pépère*. "For antibiotics. The way you've weakened your lungs, they can't fight off infection the way we'd like."

Pépère wouldn't take the prescription. He pretended not to see the paper flapping in the man's hand.

Cluck reached over for it. "Thank you."

The doctor left.

"I'll meet you in the lobby," Cluck told his grandfather.

Pépère rolled down his shirtsleeves. "Where are you going?"

"To apologize for you." Cluck followed the doctor into the hallway. "Do you have a minute?"

The doctor looked up from a chart.

Cluck checked the hallway, in case his words might bring out a risk manager. "What about the accident? Could that have anything to do with it?"

The doctor hesitated, his mouth half-open.

"Please," Cluck said. "I just want to know."

The doctor lowered his voice. "With what the smoking's already done to his lungs, and now with everything that might or might not be floating around in the air . . ."

"Might or might not?" Cluck asked.

"They won't tell us anything. We know there was some kind of ECA or MCA, but we don't know what else. They're calling it 'trade secrets.' That means there's only so much we can do."

Cluck's eyes stuck on the hallway carpet.

"But it means the same thing," the doctor said. "He's probably a lot more open to infection than he would be."

Cluck folded the prescription paper. "So get him to take the pills?" he asked.

The doctor nodded. "Get him to take the pills."

Bonne chance; il en aurait besoin. Cluck would have to crush them up and ask Clémentine to slip them into his food.

De la vista, nace el amor.

From what you see, you love.

❧

*C*luck had told Lace that he and his grandfather wouldn't be back until late. But now she heard the Morris Cowley's tires crunching the leaves, an hour earlier than she'd expected.

The truck parked outside. Alain Corbeau would have told Cluck by now. They would come for her.

She got the trailer's back window open, ready to climb out into the dark, a borrowed kitchen knife in her hand. But Cluck and the old man's steps led away from the trailers. Away from the yellow Shasta.

If she wasn't gone by the time they came back, they'd kill her. The Paloma among the Corbeaus. When she was little she had nightmares about them all turning to crows, the spears of their beaks poking a thousand holes in her.

She pressed her suitcase shut.

The door flew open, and Eugenie stumbled in.

Lace's ribs felt sharp, jabbing at her lungs. She backed toward the trailer wall, gripping the suitcase and the kitchen knife. She could knock Eugenie down with one swing of that suitcase. Anyone else she'd wave the knife at.

Clémentine appeared in the doorway, still in a show dress like Eugenie. Only their wings were off. Wouldn't they want them on to kill her? Wouldn't they want the last thing she saw to be the cover of those enormous wings?

"What are you doing?" Clémentine asked.

They hadn't turned to crows. No black feathers sprouted from their arms. They looked at her not like they planned to kill her and scavenge her body, but like they'd caught her undressing.

They didn't know. The old man hadn't told him.

"I think I broke the lock," Lace said. "I'm trying to get it open."

"With a steak knife? You'll kill yourself." Clémentine pulled a pin from her hair. "Here."

Lace set the suitcase down and pretended to fiddle with the lock.

"What's the matter?" Eugenie asked.

Lace turned the suitcase so they couldn't see the lock, and kept moving the hairpin. Her heart felt squeezed tight, giving off blood like juice from a plum. Maybe the old man had told only Cluck, and would leave her to him.

"I shouldn't have said anything about Alain," Lace said.

Clémentine sat on the built-in bed. "Alain Corbeau's an old mule. If he felt a heart attack coming on, he'd say he was too busy, could it come back next week."

Lace jerked the hairpin like it had done the trick. "Thank you." She handed it back to Clémentine.

Eugenie hopped up on a counter. "If it makes you feel better, he's angrier with Cluck than he is with you."

Lace dropped her shoulders, the tension swimming down her back. Maybe Alain Corbeau hadn't told Cluck. But his stare told her it was not her place to interfere. *Entre dos muelas cordales nunca pon-*

gas tus pulgares, her uncles would say. Don't put your thumbs between two wisdom teeth.

The old man's face would never tell her anything. She wanted to look at Cluck and find out what he knew.

"Where's Cluck?" Lace asked.

"He's at his tree," Eugenie said.

"His tree?"

Clémentine swiped a cotton pad over her face, rubbing off her eye makeup. "Every place we stop, he has his tree."

Eugenie gave Lace vague directions to the cottonwood. But Lace did not go there first. She found Cluck's grandfather leaning against the Morris Cowley, a half-burned-down cigarette between his fingers.

He took the pack out of his shirt pocket and held it out to her.

"No, thanks," she said. "I'm trying to quit."

He hummed a quick laugh and put the pack away.

She wanted to ask why he hadn't told Cluck who she was, but bit back the question in case she'd been wrong. If Alain Corbeau hadn't recognized the Paloma in her, hadn't seen the feather on her arm, she wasn't telling.

"I'm sorry," she said. "But Cluck had to know."

"It made the boy feel better," the old man said. "And it was nothing to me. Doctors are *les crétins*. They can't make me do what I don't care to."

The end of his cigarette glowed against the dark, a flake off a harvest moon.

Lace tried not to touch the burn on her cheek. "You used to work at the plant?" she asked.

"Years ago." He put out his cigarette and went inside.

Lace followed the clean, honey scent of wild roses through the trees. It drifted over the old campground, heavier and sweeter at night, like gardenia.

She spotted the white of Cluck's shirt and the pale soles of his bare feet, moon-brightened. In the dark, they were all of him that stood out. The black of his hair, his dark trousers, the light brown of his face and hands faded into the tree.

"Well." He saw her and climbed down, hands and feet gripping the branches. "If it isn't the only person my grandfather likes less than me right now."

"That's not how Eugenie tells it," she said.

Cluck got down from the lowest bough. "She's probably right." He gave her a worn-out smile.

"You okay?" she asked.

"Yeah," he said. "Just angry."

"Why?"

"He doesn't take care of himself. Never has."

She set her hand on the trunk and looked up. "How do you climb without shoes?"

"I'm not sure I could climb *with* shoes. I've been doing it without since I was five."

"What do you do up that high?"

"I just like being up there. It's quiet."

No one in her family liked heights. They'd never understood why anyone put themselves somewhere they could fall from. But now she wondered if being up high was a little bit like swimming, when the shelf of a lakeshore dropped out to the water's full depth. The light thinned out before it reached the bottom. The distance to the lake bed felt endless as the night sky.

The difference was gravity. There was no falling to the lake bed. If she stopped swimming, she drifted toward the light.

"Looks dangerous," she said.

"You can't avoid everything dangerous."

"I try."

"Oh yeah? How's that going?"

She slapped his upper arm, pulling her hand back as soon as she touched him. The last time she'd done that, he'd said it meant she was a Corbeau. She felt the words like a stain.

He grabbed her hand before she let it fall to her side. "Thank you," he said. "For telling me. If you didn't, nobody would."

She held onto his. She never got to see his wrecked hand this well. It was always doing something with wires and feathers.

She guided his thumb against her palm. "Does that hurt?" She touched his curved-under fingers.

When he slow-blinked, his eyelashes looked blue-black, like the river at night.

"No," he said.

Their hands weren't crossing the space between them, her right to his right. His left hand held her right hand. Nothing between their bodies.

He'd reached out for her with his left hand. Without thinking, he used his left hand.

"Are you left-handed?" she asked.

He pulled his hand away. "No."

"But you just . . ."

"I work with both. It makes you ambidextrous."

"No, it doesn't." Lace had been sewing since she could hold a needle, and that had never happened, not even when she broke her right wrist jumping into a shallow pond.

"What happened to your hand?" she asked.

"I told you. Bull fighting."

The more she asked the same questions, the more he lied. It made her own lies smaller, easier to stuff into her suitcase with her tail, pink as *agua de sandía*.

"So what's special about this tree?" she asked. It was a plain cottonwood, dull brown, the leaves full but the ordinary green of a Bubble Up bottle.

"This, I'll have you know, is a perfect climbing tree." He set his palm against the bark. "It's got a good trunk. You can't climb a tree if the trunk's skinnier than you are. It's got to be at least two, three times as thick as you." He touched one of the lower boughs, twisted and hanging down. "It's got branches low enough to reach. You can't get up there if you can't get on the first branch. The branches are close enough together to climb, and they're sturdy. They don't have to be as strong as the trunk, but they have to be pretty solid." He stared up into the tangle of boughs. "You want to see?"

"Sure."

He got onto the lowest branch and held out his hand to her.

"What are you doing?" she asked.

"You want to know what's special about this tree," he said. "I'll show you."

"I don't climb trees."

He looked at her like she'd said she didn't eat, or didn't own a Bible. "You've never climbed a tree?"

Her mother kept her out of trees. No *damita* dirtied her dress on maple boughs or fiddle-leaf figs. *Abuela* kept Lace's male cousins on the ground too. Branches were where the crows lived, she told them.

"If I do, will you tell me your real name?" Lace asked. If she knew his name, she could fold it into the same place she hid his fallen feathers.

"Sure," he said.

"Really?"

"I promise." He took her hand and pulled her up, showing her where to brace her heel on the trunk.

"See?" he asked when she'd gotten her footing. "Easy, right?"

She pressed her back against the trunk.

"Stop looking down," he said. "I'm not gonna let you fall. If I did, I'd have to find a replacement by call time tomorrow."

"Very funny."

She set her hands and feet where he told her to, pulling herself up. He went with her, following after on some branches, going ahead of her on others to help her up.

Her arms liked the work. They'd missed fighting the river's current. Now they snapped awake.

The wind raked the branches, and she laughed at the leaves brushing her hair.

"See," Cluck said. A branch blew between them, and he held it aside. "You're a natural."

"I'm up here," she said. "Now what's your real name?"

"It's Luc," he said.

"Really?"

"Really."

"What's so embarrassing about that?"

"I never said I had an embarrassing name. I just like people calling me Cluck."

"Why?" she asked.

"Because my brother hates it."

"That's mature."

He picked a leaf out of her hair. "My mother likes him better."

"You don't know that."

He laughed. "Yeah, I do."

She pulled a scrap of twig off his shirt collar.

"I gotta hand it to my mother though," he said. "None of that 'I love my kids the same' stuff. I appreciate the honesty. It's refreshing."

"Nobody loves their children the same." *Abuela* had always liked Lace's mother best. She had the spirit and spine to tell *Abuela* off, but not the nerve to go against her. Justin, Oscar, and Rey's mother loved Justin a little more, because he had realized, before he had words for it, that his place as the oldest brother would have to spread and grow to fill the space their father left. If Lace had brothers or sisters, she was sure she'd be her father's favorite, and sure she wouldn't be her mother's.

A black, red-streaked feather settled between Cluck's neck and shirt collar. He didn't seem to feel it. Maybe he'd gotten so used to the downy barbs against the back of his neck, he didn't notice them any more than Lace did her own stray hairs.

She picked the feather out. Her fingers grazed his neck, and he shivered.

"Why do you do that?" he asked.

"What?"

"Save those things."

"Do you want me not to?" she asked.

"I just want to know why."

She held it up to the sky. The moon brightened the red. "I like them."

"You're alone there."

She slipped it into the pocket of her jean jacket. She felt it through the fabric, hot against her rib cage. One more feather for the collection in her suitcase.

The wind brushed another one from his hair. It swirled down, settling on a lower bough. She climbed down after it, from one branch onto the one under it.

She let go of the higher branch, and her right foot slipped. Then the dark looked like she'd imagined, the same as the deepest lakes on bright days, the light reaching down and then vanishing.

Cluck's arm hit the small of her back. His hand gripped her side, and her *escamas* glowed like a fever. "Put a little of your weight down before you put all of it down." He held her up, tight enough that the feather in her pocket burned into her. "Shift too fast, and that's what makes you feel like you're falling. If you think you're falling, it's more likely you will."

His mouth almost brushed hers. The way he held her made her stand on her toes, sharpening the feeling that the ground underneath them was the same endless depth as those lakes.

He didn't stop her pressing her fingers into him. She didn't stop him when he took her top lip between his. Her hand found the feathers under his hair, soft and thick as river grass, and she kissed him back. She opened her mouth to his and pretended the sky was water.

Quien no tiene, perder no puede.

He who has nothing, loses nothing.

When Lace passed Cluck in the hallway the next morning, he nodded in greeting but didn't make eye contact. The minute he walked into the kitchen that afternoon, Lace left, Eugenie in midsentence. They did that until call time, him not looking at her, her leaving any space he entered, and she took it as a shared understanding that what happened last night would stay in the trees.

Then the sun turned from gold to copper, the slight change in light that came just before it went down. If how he kissed her was something that had to stay in those branches, she wanted to know if it also had to stay in the night before. Or, if tonight, once the show was done and the sky was dark, they'd do it again.

She made up an excuse to stop by the blue and white Shasta, something about costumes.

She forgot it as soon as she shut the trailer door behind her.

Cluck's dress shirt had been flung onto the built-in bed, and he worked in his undershirt.

He saw her and set down a wire cutter.

The feeling of his mouth still glowed hot on hers from the night before.

He put his hands in the pockets of his dress pants. Odd, considering how much she knew he had to do and how little time they had before the show. Then his eyes flicked down, and she realized his hands might have been in his pockets because he wasn't sure whether to put them on her.

She caught his eyes as he looked back up, and held them. He took one step toward her. He didn't take another one, but it was enough to tell her he was in if she was.

She kissed him as hard as when they were in the cottonwood. He held her waist, felt her body through her clothes. She held him against the trailer wall, and he shoved the empty wire frame of a pair of wings out of the way. It rattled against an age-spotted mirror.

He slid a hand under her shirt and onto the small of her back, his palm half on her bare skin, half on the waistband of her skirt. A skirt she thought she would not wear as long as she was among the Corbeaus. His fingers pressed against her *escamas*. As long as he didn't look, he wouldn't see the birthmarks. The texture of her healing body would hide them.

It hurt, his hands on her burns. It stung like a hot shower, pins of water and steam stabbing in. She was ready for it. The sting reminded her she was a body knitting itself back together. It was why she liked his hands on her. His wrecked fingers knew how to handle something ruined.

He kissed her like her lips were not chapped and scarring. Ran his tongue over the curve of her lower lip like it was soft. Like the rose and lemon oil she spread on her mouth at night made a difference. Maybe he did not feel it because his were just as rough. He and Lace were sewn of similar fabric, the raw edges of their families' cloth.

Her mouth left a smudge of lipstick on his. She rubbed it away. He closed his eyes and held her hand there, kissed her thumb and took it lightly between his teeth, holding onto it. It trembled the veins that held her heart, that feeling of his teeth on her thumb pad and fingernail.

The feather on her forearm flared with heat.

She kissed him so hard he kept his breath still on his tongue. He left the taste of black salt on her mouth. The woody flavor of charcoal. The sugar and acid of citrus peel. The soft metal of iron.

A knock rattled the trailer latch.

"Cluck?" said Eugenie.

Lace ducked down behind a counter.

"What are you doing?" Cluck asked.

"She's gonna wonder why I'm in here."

"She's gonna wonder why you're on the floor. Just say you're helping me fix something." He opened the door.

Lace stayed down.

Eugenie handed him a few rolls of satin ribbon. "Closest match I could get."

Cluck held the tail of one against another spool of ribbon. "Good enough."

Eugenie's eyes wandered over to the counter, her feet following. She stood over Lace, hands on her hips. She already had on a dusk-blue dress, but Lace hadn't done her face yet.

"I lost a needle," Lace said.

Eugenie shrugged and left her to it.

Lace tried to follow her out. Cluck shut the door behind Eugenie and held his arm to the small of Lace's back, the same as he had in the tree last night.

He wore his loneliness like his scar. Most of the time his sleeves covered it, but when she cuffed them back, he couldn't hide it. She wanted to tell him she was not afraid of what he was, this red-streaked thing in all the pure, perfect black. But the words dissolved between their lips like ice crystals.

She pulled her mouth off his. "I still have to put makeup on half of them."

"You're fast."

"Later," she said.

She stepped down from the trailer and left Cluck to the wings, the taste of violet-black salt still under her tongue. She made up the last of the performers, and the Corbeaus drained toward the woods like sand through fingers. Lace put away the powders and colors, cleaned the brushes, swept the flour off the wood.

A small shadow broke the light. Lace turned her head. A girl no older than five or six stood near the vanity. She had hair dark and coarse as Cluck's, but eyes pale as dishwater.

She sipped from a plastic cup. "Will you do me next?" she asked.

Next? Who was ahead of her? The performers had gone, and no one was out here. Cluck's grandfather was inside. Yvette had Eugenie's younger brothers and the rest of the children in the house, cutting construction paper with craft scissors. Georgette, thanks to a heavy dose of cough syrup, was sleeping off a cold. "She chooses now to be sick," Nicole Corbeau had said.

Lace pulled out a chair. "*Bien sûr,*" she said, one of two or three French phrases she'd picked up.

The girl set her cup down and closed her eyes, letting Lace give her a dusting of powder. She swung her legs, her shoes brushing Lace's skirt. "When I'm in the show I'm going to wear a purple dress, like Violette's."

That told Lace what color eye shadow to use. She washed on the lightest tint of lavender.

The girl reached out for her cup, eyes still squeezed shut. Before Lace could help her get it, the girl's small hand knocked it over. Grape juice splashed across the desk and onto Lace's skirt and top.

The girl's eyes snapped open. She took in the mess, and her face scrunched up. Lace knew that look from her younger cousins. It meant she had about five seconds until the wailing started.

"It's okay." Lace mopped up the spill. "I've done it a hundred times."

The sugar soaked through Lace's skirt, stinging the burns on her thighs.

"In fact," Lace whispered. "How about we don't tell anyone? I spill stuff so much, if we tell, they'll think I did it, and I'll get in trouble. So we won't tell, okay?"

The girl nodded, a smile showing her baby teeth.

Lace breathed out, her shoulders relaxing. The last thing she needed was Yvette and the girl's mother wondering what she'd done to make her cry.

She blotted the juice from her skirt, but the sugar still stung. "I'll be right back, okay?"

The little girl nodded.

Lace went to get a clean dress from her suitcase.

The sound of *arundo* reed pipes echoed through the yellow trailer. They reached out from the other side of the woods like fingers. She wondered if the girl had heard them. She wouldn't have known what they were. But they might have sounded enough like the cry of far-off wolves to startle her into tipping over the cup.

Lace peeled off the blouse and skirt, and splashed water over the stains. *Happy?* she wanted to call back to the *arundo* sounds. They'd quieted now that she was out of her skirt and top, her foolish choice. She'd put on a dress that would hide her *escamas*.

The trailer latch clicked, and the door opened.

She couldn't grab her dress fast enough.

Cluck stood in the doorway. His eyes found her lower back, where the arc of white birthmarks crossed her skin. No paillettes hid her *escamas* now. She felt them glow under his stare.

He stepped down from the trailer. "Go inside, okay, Jacqueline?" Lace heard him tell the little girl.

The little girl skipped inside. The house's back door fell shut behind her.

Lace pulled on her dress and followed Cluck into the trees.

"Son of a bitch." He let out a curt laugh. "When you said you did a lot of swimming, you meant it."

She buttoned her dress, trotting to keep up with him. "Cluck."

He stopped. "Did your family send you?"

"No," she said.

"Are you here to sabotage us? Or just to spy?"

"My family doesn't know where I am."

"Right." He kept walking.

She got in front of him. "It's your fault I'm here."

"What are you talking about?"

"This." She held her forearm to his face, letting him see the garnet-colored scar. "You did this to me. You put this on me, and now my family doesn't want me."

"I didn't do that to you. The plant did that to you."

She blocked his way. "It's because of your feathers."

"They're part of my hair. They can't do anything to you."

He knew. He had to know.

"If you thought I did this to you, why were you keeping my feathers?" he asked.

"I thought it would give me something on you," she said.

"Something on me," he said. "So when you came here, it was to try to get me to fix that." Not a question.

He looked at her, and the truth sank through her, a stone through a river. He'd thought she'd come here because she wanted him.

The night she first came here, she was so quick to hold down thinking of him that way. Now something ticked inside her, an urgency to tell him that yes, she came here about the scar, but she had already wanted him that night. She should've come here for no reason other than that she wanted him.

If she'd known how his hands would feel as they spread over her body, or how his mouth tasted like black salt, or that he was beautiful in ways that made him ugly to his family, she would have. She would've left the hospital still in her blue gown and gone looking for him.

But she could see the last few days crossing his face. The two of them scrambling over each other in the front seat of his grandfather's truck. Her fingers catching in the feathers under his hair. Him holding her in the high branches, and her letting him, giving him her body so completely that she would've fallen if he'd let go.

"Cluck," she said.

"This was all because you thought I could take that off you?" he asked. "Wow, you really know how to commit, don't you?"

The place where his hands had slid over the small of her back went cold. Now he thought she'd kissed him, cupped each of his red-striped feathers in her palms, for no other reason than that she wanted the mark off her arm.

"Luc," she said, calling him his real name without thinking, some wild grasp at getting to him.

All he gave her back was a hurt smile that said he thought it was cheap for her to try it, and almost funny that she thought it would work.

"You and your family," he said. "You really think I have nothing better to do than curse you? What kind of old wives' tales do you all tell each other?"

"Our old wives' tales? You're one to talk. You won't even admit you're left-handed."

"I'm not." He almost yelled it.

She picked up a pinecone and threw it at him. He caught it with his left hand, his thumb and index finger gripping the scales.

He hurled it at the ground.

"If you don't believe me," Lace said, "ask my family why I'm not with them."

He gave that same dry laugh. "Sure. Why don't I just stop by? I'll bring a salad."

"They don't know who you are," she said. "My cousins sure didn't."

"Your cousins?" Then it registered. "The guys at the liquor store. Those were your cousins."

"You really think I'm here to spy? Go ask my family where the pink mermaid went. They'll tell you I'm not with them anymore. Or they'll pretend I'm dead, or I never existed, I don't know. Go ask them."

Water glinted at the inner corners of his eyes. His jaw grew hard, eyes stuck on the pinecone. "I think I know enough, thanks."

He took a step away from her.

"Cluck." She reached out and clasped the curved-under fingers on his left hand.

"Don't." He pulled his hand away, not rough but decisive. Final.

Her guilt over hurting him drained away, and the empty place filled up with anger. He took every time their lips brushed, her body up against his, and threw it all out like scraps of ribbon.

"I don't want to see you around here again," he said.

"Or what?" Lace asked. "You'll get the shotgun and take care of me?"

"No. That's *your* family, remember?"

The burn on her forearm pulsed. He'd seen the dead crows. He knew about her uncles with the Winchester. She dug her nails into her palms, thinking of Cluck finding one of those birds, eyes dull as black beach glass.

"At least we've never killed anyone in your family," she said.

"What are you talking about?" he asked.

"Twenty years ago."

"You're kidding, right? Why would my family sink the trees they were performing in?"

"I'm guessing they didn't mean to, and whatever they meant to do went wrong."

"Like what?"

"Like drown everyone in our show," she said. "The flooding at the lake messed up our part of the river. It was calm, and then halfway through the show it was white water. It could've killed half my family."

"And the next time my family turned around, all of you had taken over the lakefront. You perform where a member of my family died. And a member of yours. You perform in your own family's grave-yard. You get that, right?"

"There wouldn't be a graveyard if it weren't for all of you. You killed my great-aunt's husband. Did you know that?"

"Did you ever think your great-aunt's husband was the one who did it?" Cluck asked. "What other reason did he have for being there?"

"The same reason your brother knew exactly what our tails looked like. He spied on us. Just like my great-uncle spied on all of you."

Cluck dropped his hands. "I'm so glad you have it all figured out."

Sadness crept back into his face. The feeling of wanting to kiss him struck her, hard and sudden. To show him that her touching him had been in defiance of her own family, and she had not cared. To slip back into the rhythm of her mouth and fingers responding to his.

She was hollow with the knowledge that if she had any other last name, he would've let her.

"For the record," Cluck said. "Every burn you have, you can thank your family."

"What's that supposed to mean?" she asked.

"My grandfather worked for the plant until your family got him fired," he said. "If he'd been there, this wouldn't have happened. He would've pushed for the damn overfill pipe. That was his job. To keep things like that from happening. You want to blame someone for that scar, blame your family. Because they did this to you before you were born."

"My family's not the one who put the net in the river," she said.

One slow blink, and the anger in his face fell away. "What?"

Lace thought of Magdalena, fighting the nylon net, and Lace fighting one of her own, a string of their last air bubbles floating across the eight years between their half-drownings.

"The night you found me," Lace said. "I'd gotten caught in a net. If I hadn't, I would've gotten out of the water a lot faster. I could've gotten home."

"How do you know it was a net?" he asked.

"Last time I checked, blue nylon doesn't grow in rivers."

His eyes went over the ground, like he was looking for those bright threads among the leaves.

"But don't take my word for it," she said. "We're all liars anyway, right?"

The corners of his eyes tensed, the anger coming back.

When he left she didn't follow him. The feather burn vibrated on her forearm, searing into her, claiming its place on her skin.

Qui se fait brebis le loup le mange.

He who makes himself a ewe, the wolf eats.

He got out all the white peacock feathers. The ones he'd hidden in trunks, under the mattress, under the false bottom of a wooden drawer. He'd burn them all. They'd be nothing but ash. The next time he went to Elida Park, he'd leave the leucistic peacock's eyespots where they fell.

Nothing settled. Nothing stayed still.

He'd brought a Paloma into his family. He'd let her sleep in the same trailer with Clémentine. He'd held her body against his, her mouth on his.

And he couldn't count on Dax doing what their mother said. Sure, Dax never listened to Cluck, not nine years ago, and not now, but he listened to their mother.

Just not this time. The Palomas coating the branches with Vaseline, Camille's fall. These were reasons Dax must have felt justified giving some younger cousins the go-ahead to set another one of those nets. They wouldn't have gone after the Palomas without Dax's blessing. Dax would have told them something about how he couldn't give permission for that, not anymore, and it was too bad he couldn't. They would've known what that meant. *Do it. Do it and don't get caught, because if you get caught, I'll deny you ever brought this to me.*

How stupid did Lace have to be? Hadn't she seen what his cousins wanted to do with the mermaid tail? If she was smart, she'd run. Not just back to her side of Almendro. Farther. He didn't want his cousins finding out and getting at her. If they hurt her, it would just make things worse with the Palomas. The fighting would take anyone who got in the way. If Clémentine or Eugenie or her younger brothers got hurt, the guilt would dig through him, wear a hole in him.

He didn't want Lace Paloma dead.

He just wanted her gone.

The scent of her clung to him. The smell of citrus peel. The perfume of roses growing fast as weeds, their brambles twisting around new tree roots. That perfume had seeped into him, and he felt the thorns snagging.

Dax threw the trailer door open. It banged against the siding.

"I can't believe you did this." Dax slammed the door shut. "Paul or Bertrand, sure. But you? I taught you better than this."

Cluck put a few feathers down. "What?"

"You and that girl." He shoved Cluck against the counter.

The edge hit Cluck's lower back.

"Everyone in the house heard you arguing," Dax said.

The pain echoed up Cluck's spine. He should've been careful. If he'd wanted to have it out with Lace Paloma, he should've gone deeper into the woods. Now they all knew. Dax knew. Cluck had hired a Paloma. And if they let him live, it'd be no less of a miracle than if *Sara-la-Kali* had appeared to him. His Romani blood meant she should protect him, but he was the last Corbeau a saint would ever show herself to.

Maybe they'd throw him to the water spirits who combed their fingers through the river's depths. Maybe they'd decide that if *Sara-la-Kali* didn't save him, he deserved to die.

Dax's face reddened even through his stage makeup. "We have what, five women here who aren't related to you? You managed to keep your hands off four of them, so what happened with her?"

"I didn't do anything," Cluck said.

"What, you're gonna lie to me now? Tell me you're just friends?" Dax grabbed his shirt collar. "Friends don't fight like that."

The weeds growing in Cluck's rib cage let him take a breath. Maybe Yvette had seen them yelling, but she might not have caught what they were saying.

This was about him and Lace arguing the way a boyfriend and a girlfriend did.

"I thought you cared about this family," Dax said.

"I do."

"Then why did you do it?" Dax threw him down.

Cluck hit his lip as he fell. The Formica split it open, and blood trailed to his chin, hot as honey.

He slumped against the wall, holding his temples. He could have fought back, but didn't. It always made it worse. Fighting back turned one bruise to four.

"You think we have rules for the hell of it?" Dax asked. "This, this kind of stuff is why we don't date anyone who works for us. Because we don't need anyone getting into some little *prise de bec* when we're trying to run a show."

Relief settled into Cluck's chest. Dax didn't know anything. He wouldn't go after Lace. He'd smack Cluck around a little more and consider his point made. Clémentine and Eugenie and this family's children would stay as safe as they could be.

"You slept with her, didn't you?" Dax's voice vibrated through the trailer.

Cluck wiped at the blood on his lip. Right thumb. Around Dax, he'd gotten used to using only his right hand. "That's what you think?"

Dax crouched down and grabbed his hand. The blood seeped into Cluck's thumbprint.

Just stay still. It was all Cluck had to do, and it'd be over. Dax would get bored with him, and leave.

"Why her?" Dax asked. "You could have gone after some girl in town. Why did you have to go after one who works for us?"

Some girl in town. Cluck knew what that meant. In each town where they stopped, he overheard his mother and her sisters make fun of girls with silly, hopeful smiles and too-short jean skirts. "She looks like a nice one," his aunts would say. "You could give *le cygnon* to her." His mother didn't even bother checking if he was in earshot.

It was half-joking, half-planning. One day he'd be too old not to talk to girls, and when he was, his mother, no doubt with Dax's help, would steer him toward one who would treat him like a thing to be tamed, controlled, contained. His family wanted him with a woman who would pet him and keep him from biting anyone. A girl with a drawer full of pink lipstick and a heart for some blue-eyed local who hadn't liked her back. She'd get as bored with Cluck as Cluck would get with her.

Lace hadn't bored him or gotten bored.

Dax jerked Cluck's right hand. "Why her?"

Because it was hard to make her laugh, and hard to scare her.

"Why do you hate us?" Dax asked, sadness pulling at the corners of his eyes. Pity that Cluck had been born the thing he was. Frustration that he hadn't fixed Cluck. "Why do you hate this family?"

"I don't," Cluck said.

Dax held Cluck's hand open.

Cluck tried to pull it away. "Don't do this."

Dax held onto it.

This couldn't happen again. As far as Dax knew, he'd broken him like a colt, made him right-handed. What else did he want?

Where's the net, cygnon? The question from nine years ago knocked around in Cluck's head. The nickname Dax tried to make stick.

Nine years ago Cluck had found a net hidden under his brother's bed, bright blue nylon. His cousins had been leaving rope nets in the lake and river for years, and the Palomas always found them. But in the water, the nylon would be invisible. A mermaid could get caught in it, and drown.

It may have been the Palomas, but it was still killing. So Cluck took it, hid it. As soon as Dax found it gone, he knew. He threw Cluck into a wall to try to get him to say where he'd put it.

What did you do with the net, cygnon?

Cluck wouldn't tell. He wasn't letting there be blood on his family's hands. The next blood drawn might be Eugenie's, or his grandfather's, or his younger cousins'.

But Dax had caught him fidgeting with a loose button, passing it between his left fingers. *What are you doing using this hand? You're supposed to use your right,* crétin.

Now Dax spread out Cluck's right fingers. "Which one did you touch her with?"

"I didn't," Cluck said.

Dax pinched his third finger. "This one?"

Cluck looked away and didn't answer.

Dax grabbed a needle and shoved it into Cluck's right hand. Without thinking, Cluck gripped it with his thumb, index, and third finger.

His older brother was nothing if not practical. Even nine years ago, he didn't go for the fingers Cluck needed most to help their grandfather with the costumes.

Right hand this time, because Dax thought Cluck had learned. *Pépère* had kept the secret, so everyone thought Cluck only held needles with his right fingers now.

Cluck didn't fight. Fighting would just lose him use of more of his hand.

Dax took the needle and held Cluck's ring finger. He bent it back, the pressure building at the joint. Cluck felt himself getting smaller, the edges of him pulling in, until he was half his age again. Folding his tongue, pressing it against the roof of his mouth, clenching his back teeth to keep from crying, because if he started crying, Dax would think he had him, and he'd break every one of his fingers until he gave him what he wanted.

A tear found the cut on Cluck's lower lip, the salt stinging. It wasn't the pain coming. It was all the lies after. *I closed my hand in a door. I fell. I got my fingers caught in the wire.* Trying them on like his grandfather's old clothes, seeing which one fit. Coming up with one good enough that even *Pépère* would believe it. And the fear of what his mother would do to him if she knew he'd stolen something from Dax.

It was *Pépère* arguing with his mother about why she hadn't taken Cluck to a doctor. His mother screaming that—*Nom de Dieu!*—she hadn't known anything was wrong with the boy's hand. *Pépère* yelling that it was her fault for not watching her sons, that now he'd watch Cluck since clearly she didn't, that now the doctors couldn't do anything unless they had the money to get his fingers broken again and reset. The knowledge that Cluck had done it wrong, curling his fingers under to protect them when he should have set them straight.

That one tear soaked into the cracks on his lips. Then there was just the taste of salt. The memory of nine years ago, of Dax bending back the fingers on his left hand. *Where'd you put the net?* But Cluck wouldn't tell. Dax snapped his pinkie to show he wasn't kidding, but Cluck wouldn't tell. Surprise shot across Dax's face. Then he broke Cluck's ring finger. *Tell me what you did with the net.* Cluck still wouldn't say. An almost-fear had flared in Dax's eyes, the clean, new knowledge that even though Cluck was small, and ugly, and stupid, he would not talk when hit.

Dax had broken Cluck's third finger anyway.

This time Dax had his right hand, his right ring finger. This time shutting up wasn't a way to get half his hand broken.

It was how to survive this.

But a question had gotten into Cluck. It'd been burrowing in since he walked away from Lace. And he wasn't as good at keeping quiet as he was nine years ago.

He looked up at Dax. "Did you let them put another net in the water?"

Dax held Cluck's hand still, the pressure steady for that one second, not easing up, not pushing harder.

"Did you?" Cluck asked. Pain got around the words, strangling the sound out of them.

Dax wrenched Cluck's finger, and the bone cracked like ice in hot water. Cluck clenched his teeth to keep himself quiet. They cut his tongue, and blood spread through his mouth.

The pain tore through his arm up to his shoulder. This was Dax's flight call to Cluck, the stab of a new bone break, something that hurt enough to make him remember.

It would remind him to stay with the flock.

Dax dropped his hand.

They shared a breath out.

Dax left, slamming the trailer door. The vibration splintered through Cluck's finger. He gritted his teeth against the pain. That feeling of cracking ice, bound around his finger like a ring, pulled every other feeling from his body. The memory of his mouth on Lace's. The warmth of her under his hands. The grain of cottonwood bark on his palms and the soles of his feet.

Dax must not have checked the yellow trailer. He hadn't seen Lace had already left. Her things were already gone.

Qui ne risque rien n'a rien.

He who risks nothing has nothing.

"Where are you going?" Eugenie asked.

Cluck kept his hand at his side so she wouldn't notice his finger, bent out of place.

"We need milk," he said. They always needed something. Bread. A crate of peaches or strawberries. Eggs, bought a flat at a time. The least *le bâtard* could do was make himself useful.

He taped his ring finger to his middle one, three bands to hold them together. If he'd known to do this when he was nine, if he'd had enough unbroken fingers to pair them up, maybe he'd still be Luc. Not *cygnon*. Not Cluck.

The bones in his finger wouldn't settle. He'd lost the feeling of his veins and muscle holding him together. He'd burnt out into pieces, like firewood gone dark. The wind breathed on the few live embers left, keeping them lit. The little knives stabbing into his ring finger every time he moved his right hand. The cut on his tongue. The wet salt of blood, drying on his lower lip. Where Lace had set the glow of her mouth, a burn's left-behind heat. The rest of him was as broken as wood crumbling into ash.

He scratched at his lower lip. The cut opened again, and he tasted the salt in his blood.

He wasn't going after her. If she was there, he didn't want to see her. He just wanted to know how much of a liar she was, if she believed that *conte de bonne femme*. Some story about the scar she'd gotten when one of his feathers stuck to her arm.

Keeping his head down worked. The woman at the lakeside took his money, told him to enjoy the show.

The audience gathered on a low cliffside, just high enough to see down into the water. His grandfather told him that before the lake took those trees, there'd been a wide beach between the drop and the waterline.

Cluck stood behind everybody else who spread blankets on the rough grass and rocky ground. The sun had gotten low enough to make the lake glow. The blue-green was translucent as a dragonfly's wings. He could see straight down to those sunken trees, bare of leaves, an always-winter. Those reaching branches made him shudder, the stark look of dead things.

An old man stood on the bank, holding a pan flute as long as his torso. His fingers, dark and wrinkled as a shelled chestnut, gripped the woven band. He blew a first note, wide and empty as the sky. The first mermaid, a purple one, took her cue and swam in. A few more bars, and another came, bright yellow like a nectarine. Another couple of minutes, and they'd all gathered. Turquoise and indigo. The mint green of tarnished copper.

They moved like kelp, the shapes of their bodies rippling like a current. They didn't fight their costumes. Instead they looked like they'd gone their whole lives with their legs sealed in the shimmer of beads and sequins. They bent backward and touched their own fins. They joined hands, and the sheer fabric trailing from their tails became the points of enormous stars. Pairs of mermaids touched their fins and arched their backs to form hearts.

They gathered and then dispersed like damselflies. They swam together and then staggered. Like his family's show, it had the magic of seeming unplanned. The truth was probably that it took weeks of rehearsal. Every time they set up in a new place, they would've had to relearn the current of rivers, the depths of lakes, how fast to move, how far down to go.

He never saw them come up for air. They must have swum to the edges of the lake, taking their breaths behind rocks. He never saw them scramble either. They moved quickly, easily. They didn't startle or scatter when the sky flashed, dry lightning that bleached the deepening blue.

The shells and pearls dotting their hair made them look crowned with their own small coral reefs. Light blinked off their bodies like fish scales speckled their skin. Some illusion faked with sequins or paint. The Palomas' scales didn't shine like that, not like the sheen of plastic. He knew that now.

The mermaids wove in and out of the sunken trees. They'd turned the drowned branches into their kelp forest. He couldn't understand it, how the Paloma mermaids swam where two people had drowned. Even if they hated his family, the water had taken a man from theirs too. Their show was no different than if Cluck's cousins had danced in the trees above a cemetery.

This was where a Corbeau died, a woman who took the name through marriage and who flitted in the trees so well her new family could not believe she wasn't one of their own. He could almost see her walking those trees that now made up this drowned forest, flowers crowning her head. The sound of the river emptying into the lake was a little like glass chimes.

A mermaid flicked an orange-gold tail. He'd seen enough. Lace wasn't there. *Les sirènes* swam as though they didn't notice she was gone.

He walked along the river, following a path of candles burning in old glass jars. The mermaids must have found their way by these. By the time the show ended, they'd have nothing but the iris blue sky and the glow off these small candles.

"You're not supposed to be here," said a woman's voice.

He couldn't find her right away. The light that made the lake glow couldn't get down through the trees.

He spotted her sitting on a rock, her back straight as a birch trunk.

A loose-knit sweater hung off her. The way the waistband of her skirt cut across her body made her middle look soft. She had small eyes, round and shining like copper pennies. Her hair, thick as Cluck's wrist, was braided down her back. But she couldn't have been older than sixty, sixty-five at the most. Her wrinkles were thin and fine as the pleats of wild poppies.

Bright fabric covered her lap. A mermaid tail. She stitched beads on the fin, the moon winking off the needle. How did she sew in so little light? Maybe she worked by touch. The story in his family went that when *Mémère* had cataract surgery, she started crocheting a doily as soon as *Pépère* brought her home, bandages still on her eyes.

"Sorry," he said.

She kept sewing.

"I'm looking for the pink mermaid," he said, and cringed. It hadn't sounded that creepy in his head. Now he was some guy stalking one of their performers.

The woman pulled her face from a slat of light. "She's not with the show anymore."

"What happened to her?" he asked.

She tied off the thread. "It's not your business."

Pain shot down through his ring finger, so sharp he looked for sparking at the nail. The woman was right. It wasn't his business. If some tourist came asking where Margaux was, he'd tell him to get lost.

But Margaux had left them to go off with her boyfriend. The Palomas had thrown Lace out, made her an afterfeather like Cluck. Afterfeathers didn't follow the same grain as remiges. They were smaller and messier than flight and tail feathers. Made of downy barbs, they shot out in different directions, fluffy and unruly.

A few of his aunts had whispered their suspicions that Margaux's disrespect for the family business would turn her into a crow one day. They told stories of how it had happened before, years ago. A wayward son, a runaway sister, all turned to black-feathered things. But even they would never be afterfeathers. They were whole birds, not extra plumes that broke the line of their own wings.

"Sorry," Cluck said, this time for asking about the pink mermaid.

He put his hands in his pockets, not remembering his broken finger until it hit the lining seam. He held a grunt at the back of his throat.

The woman looked up. The pinch to her eyelids fell away. The way her stare moved over his hair, his face, his shirt, made him feel like she was cataloguing him, figuring out what specimen jar to put him in.

He stepped back, hands vibrating with the knowledge that he could not fight with his right hand now, or his left. Any second, the woman would scream to call the rest of the family, warning them that a Corbeau had crossed the woods.

She didn't. Her eyes settled on the collar of his shirt, where a few drops of blood had stained the white.

She shook her head, the light shifting over her face. "What did they do to you?"

"They didn't," he said. She probably thought Lace's cousins had gotten him, and he'd come to finish the fight.

She folded over the costume tail and got up.

He moved back a little slower than she moved forward. She reached him, taking his elbows in her palms. Her stare was so fixed, still even when a moth fluttered between them, that he didn't pull away.

She could kill him. Holding his elbows could spread the Palomas' poison through him.

But if he pulled away, if he startled her into thinking he was violent, she'd yell. Lace's cousins would come kill him themselves.

"You're a beautiful boy," the woman said, quiet as the click of the moth's wings.

She moved her palms to his forearms, and pulled his hands from his pockets. His wrists stiffened. She lightly clasped his fingers, and his muscles settled and stilled.

"You know this, don't you?" she asked. "That you're a beautiful boy?"

Her eyes were so round, like the blue spots on a peacock's tail fan, that for a second he believed it. That he was more than red-stained feathers and three broken fingers.

Four broken fingers. Three on the left, wrecked years ago. One on the right, the break new. The bones in his right ring finger floated like glass shards in water.

If Lace had told the truth, if this family had locked her out for that scar, this woman hadn't done it. If there was that kind of malice in her, he would have felt it in his finger. The weight would have ground down his knuckle joint.

She put her arms around him. He tensed. She held onto him, but didn't tighten her hold.

The scent of her pressed into him. She smelled like halved apples and the new metal of sewing needles and a little like cinnamon. Remembering *Mémère*'s picture, those watercolor eyes and light Alsatian braids, turned this woman's scent to lavender, the shells of pale green eggs, those doilies his grandmother crocheted from when she ten until she died.

Mémère would have hugged him this way, if he'd been born soon enough to know her. But she'd died years before, so all he had was guessing.

The tension didn't leave, but it shrank, pulled its branches back into its heartwood. He shut his eyes.

His finger hurt so much he bit down, and his lip opened again.

He pulled away. The woman let him.

"Thank you," he said.

The woman pressed her lips together, and went back to her sewing.

He left looking over his shoulder. The woman didn't look at him. She stared into the dark, moving her needle without watching it.

He still had to get the milk. Without it, there'd be questions about where he'd gone. He couldn't go by the liquor mart again. That left the grocery store. So he walked to the wide parking lot it shared with a twenty-four-hour donut shop and a boarded-up storefront that once sold vacuums.

The thought of the grocery store's fluorescents made him cringe. He'd feel their hum and buzz in his broken ring finger. But he walked, and the crackling in that small bone faded.

He peeled off the three rings of white tape on his right hand.

He curled his right fingers into a fist. He folded them down, and spread them out. His ring finger came with the rest, closing until his fingertips met his palm. Then it opened with them, stretched out straight as the woman's needle.

The three wrecked fingers on his left hand stayed curled under, stuck closed. But the right one worked like Dax had never touched it.

Cluck could still feel *la magie noire* from the Paloma woman's hands. It shivered from his healed finger to the rest of his body. He could feel his blood carrying it to every part of him, turning him into something even darker and more dangerous than what he'd been born.

De noche, todos los gatos son pardos.

At night, all cats are black.

A woman stuck her head out of the donut shop door. "You want to come in?"

"Thanks," Lace said. "I'm okay."

The woman stepped out onto the sidewalk. "Come on. Four times out of five the bus is late. No reason to stand out here." She tilted her head toward the few tables inside. "They don't mind."

Lace came in and sat down. The girl at the register kept looking over at her. She glanced up after wiping down the counter, then after taking down her hair and fixing it up again.

It might have been a look for not buying anything. But Lace didn't think she could stomach the coffee, so strong she could taste it in the air, or the few donuts left at this time of night, each with a sheen of hours-old grease. So she went up to the register and bought two coffee refills, one for the woman and another for the man she was sitting with. They both thanked her, whispered *my goodness, what a nice girl.*

The cashier kept looking over. She consolidated almost-empty bakery trays, and eyed Lace. She took apart a ballpoint pen that wouldn't write, and looked over again.

Lace looked back at her. She found the girl's face open and wide, the pink of a favorite prom dress.

This wasn't mean staring. The girl couldn't help it. Lace had forgotten the red on her cheek, deep and wet as pomegranate seeds.

The couple couldn't help it either. They whispered between glances over to Lace's table.

Then, around the time the cashier started drawing on napkins, the couple stopped whispering.

"You're one of the mermaids," the woman said.

Lace uncrossed her arms.

"We brought our granddaughter to see your show," the man said. "We took her picture with you."

"I don't think so," Lace said. She'd been in plenty of shows this summer, but had only taken pictures with the tourists once, the one night *Abuela* had promoted her. The night of the accident. The one time little girls studied the fin of her tail, wondering if it felt like a fish's scales.

"You were the pink one, weren't you?" The woman rested an elbow on the table, her hand in the smoke blue of her perm. "She said you were the prettiest mermaid."

It never had anything to do with how pretty Lace or her cousins were. It was always about what tail they wore. Pink must have been their granddaughter's favorite color. If a girl liked orange or gold, she called Martha the best mermaid. If she liked blue-green, it would be Emilia, with all those sea-colored pearls glittering in her hair.

The little girl Lace put makeup on had declared she'd wear a purple dress when she grew up and joined the show, so she would've picked Alexia, for that tail as purple as field milkwort.

Lace said thank you anyway. Moving her mouth knocked tears from the corners of her eyes. Twin drops fell, one from each lash line.

The first traced a smooth trail. The other caught on the raw skin of her burn. The salt seared her cheek.

The man and woman's kindness hurt. It made her hunch her shoulders and round her back.

She'd had one night as a mermaid close enough for posed pictures. At least someone would remember it. The little girl wouldn't. She was too young. But her grandparents would. One day they'd pull the snapshot from an old album and remind her of when they took her to see mermaids.

Maybe they'd gone to see the fairies too. Lace didn't ask.

She ran her fingers over her forearm, feeling the change in texture when they crossed the feather burn. For now it felt rougher, sand-coated. It would heal smooth, like dried amber. She held it to her mouth and kissed it, stroked it with her thumb. She clutched it against her body, let it spark through her. It kept her heart charged and alive.

The bus rolled into the parking lot. The groan of the brakes finished so high that Lace, the couple, and the cashier all flinched.

"That's yours," the cashier said. She smiled at them, even Lace, no shame from staring. Maybe she didn't realize she had been. Lace was a junk thing on a road. A lost hubcap, or one of the strips of tire tread her father called *los cocodrilos.*

Lace got the door for the couple and their rolling suitcases, and then followed.

Clouds had turned the sky to pewter. A mist of water hit her skin.

She stopped, felt the drops sticking to her, dissolving her dress, turning her to wet silt.

The distance to the bus opened. It wasn't the graded shelf of a lake where the sun reached the mud. It was a steep drop-off, where everything floated into the dark.

She backed toward the donut shop.

The woman caught her arm. "Don't worry, just a little water. If my hair can take it, so can yours."

Lace tried pulling away.

They had to feel it, the rain searing them. The woman's blouse, printed with flowers big as hydrangeas, must have been some kind of cotton. Those flowers would fall to pieces, burning her skin underneath.

The woman tightened her grip. "They won't wait," she warned. "This town's a nothing little stop to them. We had to make noise for them to keep it on their route."

The man put a hand on Lace's back. "Come on," he said, and she remembered his voice, him talking to his granddaughter. *Stand right there. Smile, Sierra.*

Lace tried pulling on the woman's arm. "We have to go," she said, her voice not breaking a whisper. "We have to run."

"Nobody's running," the woman said. "They know we're coming. But if you go back inside, they'll leave without you."

Lace put her whole throat behind her voice. *We have to run.* But nothing came out this time, not even that weak whisper.

They'd all melt, like painted faces on wet canvas. This was no plain summer storm. It had teeth, and breath hot as a gas flame.

Pain flared through Lace's body, like sandpaper rubbing the new skin on her burns.

She forced the sound stuck in her throat. It came out not in words, but in screaming. She screamed into the sky, looking for that spreading cloud. She wrenched herself out of the woman's hold, but the man set his hands on her shoulders to lead her forward. She listened for the plant sirens under her own screaming, but there were only those two voices, telling her to calm down, there was no reason to get so upset.

The rain picked at her skin, peeling it back like old wallpaper. Sobbing punctured her screaming. They would all die here, because no one had turned the sirens on this time.

Her screaming pulled a crowd from the grocery store. They would die too, because of her, because she couldn't turn the sound to words.

Palms spread across her back. Not the woman's or her husband's, but hands Lace knew. They carried the violet and ash scent of black salt. The wax and powder down of feathers. They came with a voice that told the man and the woman, "It's okay, I know her, she's with me."

He held her against him, one hand in her hair, the other gripping her waist, and she couldn't feel the rain anymore. She screamed into his shirt, sending the rage of unmade words into him. It vibrated through him to her hands on his back. The rain on her dress and his shirt would stick them to each other, dissolve the skin between them, until their veins tangled like roots, and they breathed together, one scaled and dark-feathered thing.

Les fruits défendus sont les plus doux.
Forbidden fruit is the sweetest.

He'd gotten her back to the trailer. More because she wanted to get away from the bus stop than because she wanted to go with him, but he'd take it.

He set water on the stove. He couldn't stay mad at her. If she'd seemed mad at him, he could've kept it going. But she just sat on the built-in bed, wearing one of his shirts, crying into the sleeves that hung past her hands.

She stopped for a minute, saw the makeup stains her eyes had left on the cuffs, and started crying again.

"Don't worry," he said. "It'll come out."

Then she just held the heels of her hands to her eyes, pressing her front into her knees. "Everyone in this town thinks I'm crazy now, don't they?"

By morning the whole town would probably hear about the girl who snapped while waiting for a bus.

"You want me to lie to you?" he asked.

"So that's a yes."

"If they know you're from a show family, then believe me, they thought you were crazy already." He poured hot water over lavender buds, thyme leaves, lemon peel, the way his grandfather told him *Mémère* used to for her sisters when they couldn't sleep, and then for *Pépère* and their children.

The lavender and lemon cut the scent of rain. It had stopped, but the metallic smell of clouds hung on.

"They really kicked you out, didn't they?" Cluck sat next to her on the built-in and set the cup in her hands. "Your family?"

She took it. "It's not that simple."

He rolled up one of the shirtsleeves, one slow cuffing-up at a time, in case she stopped him. She didn't.

He folded the cuff up to show the semiplume imprint. "You thought I gave you this?"

"It's your feather," she said.

The truth pinched at him. It did look like one of his feathers, its shadow caught and made still.

"Maybe," he said. "But I didn't put it there. I promise. It's a burn. It'll heal, and it'll either scar or it won't."

It wasn't Cluck's choice whether it stayed, but he wanted it to. He wanted that mark on her, the copy of one of his feathers. The shame of it pushed up against his anger about Dax signing off that net.

"How'd you get out of that thing?" Cluck asked. "The night the mixing tank blew."

"How do you think?" she asked. "I ripped my costume."

He remembered putting the fabric and beading into the river, watching the water take it. "That was your tail Dax had, wasn't it?"

She nodded.

That was why she'd kissed him, because he'd taken something that had once been part of her out of his brother's hands.

"Don't you hate me?" she asked.

"For not telling me? I can't blame you, seeing as how I took it so well."

"No, because you hate my family."

"I don't hate your family," he said. "I hate what they did."

"How do you know they did it?"

"I wasn't there, so I don't. But my best guess is that they did."

"Your best guess is wrong," she said.

He wasn't doing this again. Whatever happened twenty years ago, neither of them had been around to be part of it. Lace hadn't even been born when the Palomas got his grandfather laid off. It wasn't on her. Cluck was keeping the rest of their families outside the trailer door. There wasn't enough room for everybody.

"Does it matter?" he asked.

"You tell me. If you knew for sure you were right, would you still want me here?"

"If you knew for sure you were, would you want to be here?"

She brushed her thumb over the cut on his lip. The pad was hot from the cup.

"What happened to you?" she asked.

"You should see the other guy."

"It wasn't my cousins, was it?"

"No."

"Who was it?" she asked.

"I don't know. There aren't usually introductions." He got up from the built-in. "Drink that, okay?"

"Are you drugging me so you can go through my suitcase?" she asked. "I'll save you some trouble. Yes, my costume's in there. Not that I'll need it anytime soon."

"I'm sorry," he said.

She rubbed her thumb over a cuff button. "I'm sorry I didn't tell you."

"I'm not," he said. If he'd known, he wouldn't have wanted to know her. He'd never have known what it felt like to hold a girl with a fear of falling, to help her steady her weight on those high branches. He never would have met that woman who made him so sure what *Mémère* would have been like.

He listened for the back door of the house opening or closing. He shouldn't have had Lace in the blue and white trailer with him. But he was so far past "shouldn't." He'd held a Paloma girl close enough to feel the heat of her mouth through his shirt. He'd let a Paloma woman fix the splintered bone in his ring finger. If the Palomas' *magie noire* was poison, he had more than enough in him to kill him. And if it didn't, it meant there was so much in him it was turning him, his body folding it into its cells until he was immune.

Cluck wouldn't tell anyone about the Paloma who'd fixed his ring finger. They'd just call her *une sorcière*. He didn't even know how to tell Lace without sounding like he was calling the woman a witch.

"You want to come back to the show?" he asked her.

Lace watched the lavender spin in the cup.

"You're good at your job," he said. "No one wants to lose you."

She flicked the side of the cup with her forefinger, and the buds spun the other way.

"No one has to know," he said.

"Half your family must have heard us." She set the teacup down. "I think they already do."

"They didn't hear what we were saying. My brother. He just thinks we're, uh . . . You know."

She laughed and curled on her side, looking up at the trailer's water-stained ceiling. *Mémère's* dreamless cure was working.

"Why'd you come after me?" she asked.

"I didn't," he said. "I went out for milk."

She shut her eyes. "What happened to your hand?"

Even half-asleep, she kept trying.

"Car door," he said.

"Which one?"

"Which car?" he asked. "It was this old Ford. It barely ran. We don't have it anymore."

"Which hand, Cluck?"

A hollow place inside him grew hot and tight, like the neutron stars in *Pépère's* books. He checked his right ring finger. It bent and straightened. He flinched, wondering if *Mémère's* tea let Lace see things, places now healed but once broken.

Lace let her cheek fall against the mattress. "It's not fair. You know everything about me now."

"No, I don't."

"There's stuff I want to know about you, and there's nothing left you want to know about me."

"That's not true," he said. "There's plenty I want to know."

"Like what?"

"How you look in that tail."

She smiled, not making it all the way to a laugh, and slept.

The muscles in his right hand hummed, full of electricity as dry clouds. The bone knitting in his ring finger was new and restless. It wanted to act, to make something. So he collected the years of white peacock feathers off the floor, and took his wires and tools to the Airstream.

Thanks to Lace, a little of *la magie noire* ran through his blood. A trace of what made her a Paloma had gotten into him.

He liked it, that sense of something new and sharp and alive. If he forgot for a second that Lace and that woman who made him think of *Mémère* were Palomas, it made him feel safe and awake. Like when everyone was gone in the afternoon, and Cluck slept for that one quiet hour before call time, knowing Dax and his mother were far from the blue and white trailer. He'd wake up and splash cold water on his face, ready for all the evening's noise and little lights.

But just because he liked what Lace had done to him didn't mean he'd let it go one way.

It was time he returned the favor.

*Qui craint le danger ne doit pas
aller en mer.*

He who fears danger should not go to sea.

He didn't remember finishing, or falling asleep.

The sun came through the Airstream's curtains, needling his eyes. It lit up the worktable, and the hundreds of leucistic feathers wired into wings. They had the same frame as the other wings, bent metal standing in for humerus, ulna, radius. Carpals and metacarpals. The leucistic peacock's back coverts, molted each season, shaped the grain of the feathers.

The sun showed the faint washes on the eyespots. The sheer yellow of a lemon slice's inner curve. A blush of pink and violet. The blue and green of certain chickens' eggs.

He sat up and rubbed the back of his neck, stiff from falling asleep at the table. He hadn't been able to use the wire frame he'd salvaged after the accident. Those were for men's wings, too tall and broad for Lace's body.

He checked the blue and white trailer. "Lace?"

She wasn't there. She'd smoothed the sheet on the built-in, folded the blanket. Her suitcase was flopped closed but not locked.

A point of light winked from the floor. He picked it up, held it to the window. A plastic sequin, pink and translucent as a grapefruit segment.

He took off toward the woods. If that sequin had fallen off what he thought it had fallen off of, he had to find her before Dax did.

He ran toward the river, listening for the sound of her splashing over the soft rush of the current.

Through the reeds, he spotted the pink of her costume and the wet black of her hair. She turned in the water, the sun glinting off her body. It made the drops on her shoulders and arms glow. It glimmered through the beads and sequins on her costume. Her fin flicked the river, a petal off a tulip tree.

Her skin was healing. Though still dark as new blackberries, the heart on her cheek had grown small as an apricot. The burns on her back had lightened and started to scar over.

She dove down, staying under so long he thought of the colanders catching her tail.

"Lace?" He took off his shirt to go in after her.

She surfaced, blinking the sediment from her eyes. How did she tread with that tail on? Wet, with all the beading, it must've weighed ten pounds.

His family would tell him countless men had lost their lives this way. In stories, soldiers and travelers neared ponds and rivers, drawn by *les feux follets,* those luring lights, and the laughter and singing of water spirits. Some were like *Melusine,* the river spirit whose legs became fins every Saturday. If a mortal man caught her in her true form, she would turn to a serpent and kill him.

These were his family's bedtime stories, those evil women with scales on their bodies and fins for feet. Where other children were told not to play with fire, Cluck and his brother and cousins were warned off water. When Cluck was thirteen or fourteen, his grandfather cautioned him against the *nivasia,* mermaids who became pregnant by mortal men and then murdered them.

All those stories ended the same. She was beautiful. A man loved her. She killed him.

Lace saw him, but didn't startle.

"What are you doing?" he asked.

"You said you wanted to see it." She flicked her tail, and water sprayed his forearms. "I thought if I showed you, you'd tell me what happened to your hand."

"I never agreed to that."

The shape of her bare breasts showed, lighter brown than the rest of her. They floated like fallen oranges. He couldn't tell whether the accident had scarred them. The refraction through the water kept him from seeing.

The blue-black of the river made them look pale. They glowed like twin moons, turned gold from staying near the horizon.

Heat crawled up the back of his neck. "You're not wearing a top."

"What were you expecting? A couple of clam shells and a piece of string?"

"Don't give me that." He'd seen the show. The Paloma women wore costume pieces that looked like bras covered in sequins. "If you all performed topless, the chamber of commerce would have you arrested before your hair dried, and you know it. You've got to wear something."

"We do," she said. "And mine got ruined the night you found me."

She must have forgotten how much length her hair had lost that night. When she lifted her shoulders out of the water, the ends stuck to her breasts, but didn't cover them. He looked at them so hard he could almost feel their weight in his palms. He wondered if the water would leave them cool, or if they'd give off the warmth that lived under her skin. He thought of touching her until there was none of the river's cold left on her, just the heat of his hands.

Those thoughts stayed on him. He felt them sticking to him like his feathers stuck to the back of his neck when his hair was wet. That feeling, strong as the prickling of vanes and barbs, made him want to check his body for some mark she'd left on his skin. There had to be something on him that would tell her how much he wanted to touch her, a thing clear and dark as the imprint his feather had put on her.

"You're blushing," she said. "I thought you were French."

"Not that kind of French."

She flicked her tail again. The glass beads looked like the million bubbles of water just starting to boil.

If any of the family caught them, they'd have worse trouble than stories about *Melusine* and the *nivasia*.

"Get out of that thing before somebody sees you." He knelt on the bank. "Where's your dress?"

She went under again, staying close enough to the surface that he could make her out. Her hair was as dark and blue-black as the river until the sun lit it up and turned it red-brown. Her back looked like a sandbar glinting with mica. He couldn't tell the scarring from the rippled water.

Her tail reminded him of raw pink salt. As she moved, the light found the clusters of glass beads.

She surfaced. The sun on the water broke into pieces.

She swam up to the bank and rested her forearms on a rock. "You coming in?"

"I don't swim," he said.

"You don't know how?"

"I know how." He wasn't going to win any contests for holding his breath, but he knew how not to drown. How to get out of a colander and how to fight a current. His grandfather had taught him so he would keep safe around rivers, not so he could swim in them. "I just don't."

"Fine." She wrung out her hair and let it all fall to one side of her neck, leaving one of her breasts bare under the water. He hoped the distance between them was enough to hide where he was looking. "But I'm not getting out until you get in," she said.

Pépère didn't much care for water, so Cluck didn't either. It had to do with the Romani traditions, what parts of their bodies they could wash at which places in the river, how if a man didn't know the current, something clean could be made *mochadi*. Unclean.

But Cluck had never learned all the rules. His mother had told him he was too young to understand, and then, when he was older, too stupid. That he shouldn't worry about it because they were lucky enough to have running water. They didn't have to think about the Romani laws that ran in his grandfather's blood like silt in streams.

Lace brushed a hand over his thigh, leaving her wet fingerprints on his pants. "You coming in, or not?"

His shirt was already unbuttoned and off, from almost going in after her. So he pulled off his undershirt, his socks and shoes, but kept his trousers on. If his grandfather had worried over Cluck taking Lace's dress off the night of the accident, he'd have strong words about Cluck pulling off his pants to swim. Going shirtless was bad enough. If Cluck wore nothing but his boxers around a girl, *Pépère* would know. He'd just know, the same way he knew, years ago, that Cluck was lying about having made himself right-handed.

Cluck didn't jump or slide in. He found where the bank sloped instead of dropping off, and waded in one slow step at a time. The water soaked his ankles, then crept up his trouser legs.

If *Sara-la-Kali* and the Three Marys wanted to pull him back, he'd let them. But they didn't, so he let the *nivasi* near him.

Lace dove down again, too far for him to see her shape.

He waded in up to his chest, the water cooling his skin. "Lace?"

She grabbed him and pulled him down. He stumbled forward, and went under.

He opened his eyes and saw the colors of her. The black of her hair, her skin the brown of river alluvium, the rose salt of her tail. Light streamed through her like she was made of water.

He ran out of air fast. When he tried to get to the surface, she held him down. He fought her, and she held him tighter.

The muscles around his lungs tensed and then cramped. She was killing him. The truth that she was a Paloma, a *nivasi*, dug into his skull. She would murder him before she would love him. She would keep him under and drown him.

Water got into his throat, and he couldn't fight her anymore. She wrapped her arms around his chest, pulling him into the dark. Then she dragged him out of the water and up onto the bank.

The light stabbed into him. Air flooded into his lungs, shoving the water out.

She turned him onto his side and held a hand to his back. "Breathe."

He coughed up the water.

She held onto him. "Breathe."

He sat up and gasped to get his breath. "Are you trying to kill me?"

"I was trying to move you," she whispered. "Look." She turned his head.

The muscles near his lungs eased and then tightened again. Two figures showed through the tree cover. Two of the guys from the liquor store.

They threw pinecones into the river and pulled wild pomelos off a tree.

"What are they doing here?" He didn't have to try to keep his voice low. He didn't have the air to break to a whisper.

"Our families are closer together than you think," she said.

He hadn't thought about it since the accident. He'd gone out looking for Eugenie, and Eugenie never would've seen Lace if they didn't share a band of woods with the Palomas.

Lace's cousins found all the ripe pomelos, tugged down each yellow-green fruit. The tree seemed to straighten its shoulders, free from the extra weight. Lace's cousins moved on, toward the Palomas' side of the woods.

"What the hell can you do with those things?" Cluck asked. Pomelos were bitter as cough syrup, especially the wild ones.

"*Aguas frescas,*" Lace said. "With enough water and sugar, you can make anything drinkable."

She pulled herself up on the bank, her tail dragging through the mud. "I'm sorry I almost drowned you."

His breathing evened, but the guilt of thinking she was trying to kill him made the tensing of his lungs worse. "Better you than them."

She lay on her back, squinting into the sun, and covered her breasts with her palms. The sun shone off her wet hands.

"It's because I was hungry," she said, like he'd asked her a question.

"What?" he asked.

"The night we met. I was buying that much from the liquor store because I was hungry. I wouldn't eat all day because if I ate I looked fat in my tail. Then after the show I was really hungry, so I'd eat everything. Then I had to not eat the next day. Same thing every day, trying to fit into my tail."

He looked at how the tail clung to her hips and legs. "Seems like it fits to me."

"Thanks to hospital food." She patted her thigh through the fabric, her other hand sliding over so her arm covered her breast. "But these show everything."

She sounded like Clémentine and Violette with their honey and chili powder. The show's filmy dresses floated near their bodies, hiding a lot more than that tail. It didn't matter to them. They downed those chili powder mixes a few weeks before the show season started. *We don't want to be fat fairies*, n'est-ce pas?

It wasn't just the women. Before the shows, the men oiled their chests, and after, they argued over who the girls in the audience had looked at most. Cluck had given up competing early. His body was strong enough to do what it needed to do. He'd never be much to look at, and he'd never be as big as Dax, but he could do his work. *Pépère* had taught him that mattered more than how a man looked with his shirt off and wings strapped to his back.

"My grandmother was a mermaid in Florida," Lace said. "They swim with manatees and sea turtles there."

"Sure they do."

"It's true." She turned onto her stomach. The ends of her hair brushed the bank. The mud darkened the back of her tail. "I'm gonna get there one day. Be one of their mermaids."

If Florida was anything like his family's show, they'd throw her out by the time she turned thirty. Thirty-five if she was really good.

"Is that what you want?" he asked.

"It's what I've always wanted."

"Then you should do it. But you should know it's not all you can do."

"Sure." She turned over again. "I'll just get a job with my rocket science degree."

"I mean it," he said. "There aren't a lot of people I know for sure are smarter than I am." It didn't matter how bad or how ugly he was. *Pépère*, always asking for the wingspan of the snowy owl, or when cobalt chloride was pink and when it was blue, had made sure Cluck didn't grow up stupid. "My grandfather's one of them. You're one of them."

She squinted into the sun. "How do you know?"

"You fooled all of us, didn't you?" he asked. "You could do anything you want."

"I want to do something I'm good at," she said. "I was getting good at this."

"You're good at a lot of things."

She reached over for a black-red feather that had stuck to his collarbone.

Her fingers skimmed his chest, and he flinched.

Maybe this was how the peacocks felt at molting season, having him come around to pick up what they'd shed.

"Can't you collect somebody else's?" he asked.

"I like yours."

"But they grow in red." The reason sounded as weak as the idea that he would hate white birds. It sounded like a superstition with no more weight than *les contes de bonne femme,* the old wives' tales. He'd never needed to give it words. His family had always understood better than he had, and they did not tell strangers.

Lace held the feather up to the light and blew on it, fluffing the barbs. A slick of river water still shone on her mouth. He wondered if it would taste more like her or more like the river.

"Cuervo," she said, soft as breathing out.

"What?" he asked.

"My last name should have been Cuervo," she said. "It's my father's last name. But my grandmother made him change it to marry my mother."

"Why?"

"It means 'crow.'"

Cuervo. Corbeau.

Cluck knew what Lace meant, that they weren't so different, that the space between them was made only of names and colors. But the bitterness went into Cluck like the slip of a paring knife. He would have wanted the choice not to be a red-streaked thing among all his family's perfect black.

Now her father took aim at the black birds in the woods, shooting his own name.

Lace propped herself up on her elbows. A thin layer of silt coated her breasts.

The scales on her back caught the light. He counted five, each perfect, like the adhesive rain hadn't touched them. The reaction between the cyanoacrylate and the cotton of her dress should have burned them as much as the rest of her, hiding them. Instead they arced across the small of her back, smooth as coins of scar tissue, iridescent like the leucistic peacock's eyespots. She moved her hips, and a handful of colors showed.

The blade of that paring knife pulled back, the wound mending shut.

She moved, and the waist of her tail slipped down an inch.

He counted a sixth, a seventh, each iridescent as a blue mussel shell.

"There's something I want to show you," he said, counting them again, this constellation of moons glowing under her skin.

Árbol que nace torcido, jamás su tronco endereza.

A twisted tree will not grow straight.

🪶

Cluck took her right ankle in his hand. "It won't hurt. I promise." His hair was still wet with river water. It dampened his shirt collar, graying the white cloth.

Lace's soaked the back of her dress, turning the thin fabric cold. Her dress was a little like the one the adhesive rain ruined, off-white, saffron-colored flowers instead of blue. She was already forgetting the lost one. The details were falling away. How many petals the blue flowers had. Whether the *agua de jamaica* stain that stayed, stubborn, through so many washes was on the right sleeve or the left.

Tía Lora had made them both. Missing her clutched at Lace.

Now that she thought of her great-aunt, the act of showing herself to Cluck Corbeau in nothing but her tail felt like a betrayal. With her costume top gone, Lace hadn't known what to wear on top—a bra? The camisole she slept in? So she'd just worn the tail, and the way Cluck looked at her made her feel brave and sure, like his stare was covering her so no one else could see her.

Cluck soaked a brush in a dish of iodine. It smelled like nail polish remover, salt, balsamic vinegar left out too long. Lace's stomach tightened. Smells like that no longer reminded her of painting her nails, but of the solvents they used on her in the hospital, the morphine holding her under. The smell wrapped around her throat.

He ran the brush along the bottom of her foot. The feeling of bristles on her arch made her twitch.

"Sorry," he said. "You're ticklish, aren't you?"

The iodine soaked into her foot, darkening the sole so it was almost as brown as her hair. "What's this for?"

"It's good for climbing trees." He held her other ankle and painted the sole of her left foot. "It seals your skin. Keeps things from getting in, makes you less sensitive to the grain of the bark."

The night she found him in his tree, the soles of his feet had been pale as his palms, shades lighter than the rest of him. They stood out like the moon. "You don't use it."

"I've been climbing trees barefoot long enough I don't need to." He rinsed off the brush, twisted the iodine bottle shut. "My cousins all do it. It helps with the show."

The iodine dried, leaving the soles of her feet tight and leathery.

He pulled her to standing. "Close your eyes."

She did. "Why?"

His fingers brushed her shoulders and set a ribbon against her rib cage. The heel of his hand grazed her right breast, a band of thin satin following after.

Weight pulled on her back. A feather skimmed her neck.

She stopped his hands with hers. "Forget it. I'm not one of your fairies."

"Trust me, okay?"

"Are you trying to convert me?" She reached back and slapped at him, her hand hitting the thigh of his pants.

He gathered her hair and moved it to her left shoulder. "No." He fastened the ribbon between her shoulder blades, his fingers warm on her dress. He tied the bow and knotted it. He moved her, turning her waist to lead her. "You can open."

Even down, the wings filled the mirror's age-speckled glass. Her sudden breath in felt like taking air after surfacing.

At first the wings looked white as flour-covered feathers. Then the eyespots showed their colors, like the tints of a rainbow. Those after-storm skies were never as bright as children painted them. The light washes, so watered down, didn't live in crayon boxes. This was where to find them, on the eyes of white peacocks.

A wire wing frame leaned up against the corner of the mirror, clean and bare as a winter tree. This was what Cluck did, making these winter branches, filling them in like there was summer in his hands.

But he always covered them in bronze and blue and green, not the white of frost and the glint of color when the sun hit wet ice.

"Those things on your back are a lot like these feathers, you know," he said.

"How?" she asked.

"Iridescence." He kept his hands on her waist. "The way the colors look like they're changing depending on the angle. It's all directionality. Polarization of light." He moved her left hip a little forward, then her right, and the pale colors flashed like light through a prism. "Same as with the blue peacocks. Morpho butterflies, hummingbirds, fish."

His breath fell on the back of her neck. "The structures are hard to describe optically, because little adjustments to the angle of illumination change what you see." The wood and water scent he picked up from swimming displaced the vinegar smell of the iodine. "It's a pain in the ass to study, but it's the best thing about them."

She shut her eyes, and listened, her pulse clinging to the spot where his breath heated her neck. Her father's lessons never would've covered anything like this. To him, it wasn't worth the time. Smart girls didn't need to know what made some birds shimmer like soap bubbles.

Her father had taken her to the shore at night to look for sea sparkle, those algae blooms glowing like moonstones, but that was different. *Noctiluca scintillans* lived in the water. Her father taught her about sea sparkle for the same reason he taught her about undertows and wasp jellyfish. *Noctiluca scintillans* shimmered with its own light, but with the right depth and nutrients, it flared into red tide. She was *una sirena*, and she should know the water was full of beautiful things that were one moon phase from turning poisonous.

Cluck traced where the ribbons crossed. She didn't point out that he was using his left hand. If she did, he'd stop.

"Biologically speaking, it's more trouble than it's worth," he said. "Turning yourself all those colors. Especially if you don't have a lot of pigment, like white peacocks, or your scales. And you're more susceptible to damage afterward." His hand stopped over her *escamas*.

She opened her eyes and met his in the mirror. The sharp note of *arundo* reed reached across the woods, warning her that if her birthmarks were not for *turistas*, they were even less for a *gitano* boy.

"So my question is," Cluck said. "Why do you have them?"

His hair smelled like the wet leaves dotting the current.

"Why do you have your feathers?" she asked.

He dropped his eyes from the mirror, his half-smile sad. "You got me there."

She didn't mean why were his red instead of all black. She meant what had given his family their plumes, the same as his question about her family's *escamas*. They were both birthmarks. His feathers marked him as a Corbeau the way her *escamas* marked her as a Paloma. The things they wore on their bodies made them as distinct as water and sky.

"Come on." He took his hands off her back. "I'll show you how to open them."

He took her outside and guided her up his favorite cottonwood, holding smaller branches away so the folded wings didn't snag.

The coat of iodine let her feel the warmth of the ground and the bark but not the texture. When she lost her balance, the ball of her foot slid as Cluck caught her. She braced for the friction, but it didn't hurt.

Cluck picked a branch he liked, and they stayed. He tied a ribbon to each of her hands, slack loops around her wrists. He held her hands, guiding them away from her body, until the bent wires unfolded, and the wings opened. They cast a translucent shadow on the ground below, like a glass-winged butterfly.

He slid one hand between her back and the wings. "Wings aren't so different from arms." He touched her shoulder blades. "This is where the scapula connects to the rest of the body."

He pressed on her back just enough to ease her forward. She took a step, farther out on the bough. Cluck followed her, staying close enough to fill the space behind her.

The sheer silhouette of her wings crossed the lower branches. Cluck guided her so slowly she could not startle and run back toward the trunk. His touch helped her keep her balance, but he was not keeping her up. He just moved her, one slow step at a time, toward leaves and open sky.

He ran his hand down her upper arm. "This is where the secondary feathers attach." Then her forearm. "And the primaries." He put his fingers over hers. "And your thumb's a lot like the alula. It helps direct flight the same way your thumb helps you do things with your hands."

She turned her palms, interlocking her fingers with his. She wanted to tell him how much she liked the red in his feathers. But if she brought it up, it'd just make him quiet. He was quick to talk, and even quicker to stop, this boy who did not like water.

She pressed his left hand into her body, keeping her palm tight over the back of it so he couldn't pull it away. Her thumb found the hollow between his palm and his three curved-under fingers. If they would not open, she could find her way in.

With her next step forward, the branch felt narrower under her feet than she'd expected, and she faltered. Her hands flew out, reaching for leaves or clouds.

Cluck gripped her waist. "I've got you." He held her until she was still, and then lightened his touch enough to give her back the feeling of holding herself up. But his hands still stayed.

She turned enough to kiss him, fast enough that she felt a hitch in his throat when her mouth got to his. The sense of falling did not touch her, not as long as her body was between the hands of this boy who felt steadier in the air than on the ground.

But he must not have felt in his palms how anchored and still he made her. He left the smallest space between their lips and whispered again, "I've got you," like he thought she might not know.

Entre dos muelas cordales nunca
pongas tus pulgares.

Don't put your thumbs between two wisdom teeth.

⟡

Jt's your turn to go buy fruit." Clémentine shoved money into
Lace's hand. "Get the same kind of peaches. And another
purple watermelon."

Lace tried to hand it back. "I don't want anyone seeing me. Even
with makeup they all stare."

That wasn't the whole truth though. If her mother or aunts had
stopped by for strawberries or Meyer lemons, they'd have more questions than Lace had lies. The day she left, she could've pretended she
was on her way out of town, to stay with her cousin or Martha's
friends. But if they saw her today, they'd wonder what she was still
doing in Almendro, and if word got back to *Abuela*, she'd know, the
same way she'd known about Cluck bringing Lace to the hospital.

Clémentine rummaged in an old trunk until she found a wide-
brimmed hat, its ribbon the color of lipstick. She set it on Lace's head.
"Now no one will see your face."

Lace caught her reflection in a window. The hat must have made Clémentine and her cousins look like actresses sunning themselves, but it made Lace look like she'd gotten into the attic and was playing dress-up.

Clémentine adjusted the brim. "I'd go if the flower crowns made themselves, but they never do. Don't forget a nectarine."

"Just one?" Lace asked.

"For Nicole. She'll only eat one and nobody else likes them."

So Lace went and bought coral peaches, that single nectarine, a Moon-and-Stars watermelon from the woman who knew she didn't like rain.

Lace watched for the brown-black of her mother's or aunts' hair.

The first face she recognized wasn't a Paloma, but a Corbeau. Dax stood on the edge of the market, jaw held tight, ready to throw his fists.

Her hat blocked her view of who he was facing. She turned her head, lifting the brim.

Matías. Dax stood across from her cousin.

Matías held one foot a little in front of the other, set for a fight. He'd never beat on anyone, three against one, like Justin and his brothers. But if another man set down an insult, and if the other man was his size, he'd take the fight. Once he didn't like the way some *gabacho* was looking at Martha at a gas station, saying things about how she should wear a tighter dress so everyone could see her. Matías left the man a bloody nose, and came away with a black eye. His aunts called him their little Quixote, all *caballero*, no brains.

Dax was bigger than Matías, broader by a little and taller by a lot. Matías always fought fair, never kicking shins or holding shirt collars. But Dax had been a few minutes from bringing a bloody tail to her family's motel. There was nothing Lace could count on him not doing. Matías would get out no better than that shredded, stained *cola de sirena*.

Dax said something Lace couldn't hear.

"We got as much right to be here as you, *puto*," Matías said.

Dax moved toward him, making him back up. "You stayed because we stayed. You can't even think for yourselves." He shoved Matías.

Matías shoved him back, so hard Dax almost fell into a farmer's stand. "You want to say that again?"

Lace dropped the bag of fruit and ran. She slipped between them and pushed on her cousin's chest. "Stop it," she yelled. *El caballero* would get himself killed.

Before Matías could check under the hat, Dax grabbed her. He dug his hands into her upper arms, fingers pressing her sleeves into her skin, and pulled her out of the way. He moved her, quick and clean as lifting one of his cousins during a show. Then he jammed a fist into Matías' jaw.

Matías returned it, hitting the side of Dax's face. His punch fell easily as a stone skipped on the lake.

"Stop it," Lace screamed, loud enough that even Dax and Matías felt faces turn like the heads of sunflowers. "Just stop it."

Now half the market watched them.

Dax dropped his raised fist. He and Matías both lowered their stares. Matías bent his neck to see under the hat brim, looking for the interrupter's face.

The start of a smile tensed the corner of his mouth, like her being there was so strange he had to try not to laugh about it.

Leave it to Matías to find all this funny. She couldn't have laughed if Justin had shown up and done his mermaid impression, batting his eyes like he was preening on a rock. She could still feel where Dax had grabbed her and pressed his thumbs into her, that sense that she might leak blood like sugar-water off bruised fruit.

She waited for the rage in her cousin's face. It didn't come. Confusion made his eyes and mouth look lopsided, a hitch unevenly weighted.

"You do this, one or both of you ends up in jail," Lace said. "My guess is you both have people at home who don't want to see that happen. So look at each other and ask yourself, is he worth it?"

They exchanged glares, scorn-sharpened. But they each took a step back, and Lace dropped her hands. They knew she was right. Matías thought of his aunts; Dax, his mother.

"Good," she said. "Then go home."

She stood her ground, made them leave first. Then picked up her bag of fruit and kept walking. The town went back to its chatter. Their stares dwindled to glances.

Matías was waiting for her around the side of the next fruit stand. He held his arms crossed, one shoe kicking the dirt. "So you're staying in Terra Bella, huh? What, you thought you'd come all the way back here to buy some fruit?"

She checked to make sure Dax wasn't around.

"You got a death wish?" Matías asked.

"Do you?" she asked.

Matías rubbed her upper arms. "Are you okay?"

"I'm fine."

"He touched you."

"It was my sleeves," she said. "I'm fine."

"He still touched you."

Not even Matías could keep *las supersticiones* straight. All he knew was that hitting and kicking were safe.

"I'm pretty sure it has to be skin on skin," Lace said.

"Where've you been?" Matías asked. "Where are you staying?"

Her body flushed with the feeling of Cluck tying wings to her back.

"In town," she said. "I thought if I waited *Abuela* out she might change her mind."

"Can I tell *Tía* Lora?" Matías asked. "She's worried about you."

Lace wished he could. But she didn't want her aunt looking for her and finding her at the Corbeaus'. She hated thinking of her great-aunt catching her in those wings, cringing when she realized Lace was living among the people who had murdered her husband.

"No." She picked a peach from the paper bag and held it out; Matías took it. "Don't tell anyone. If *Abuela* finds out I'm waiting, she'll dig in her heels."

He turned the peach in his hand. "Hey, Lace?"

"Yeah?"

"It wasn't fair," he said.

It was all he said.

"Thank you," she said back.

He knocked her hat brim. "What the hell are you wearing?"

She pinched his elbow.

To him, she was another Licha, cast out from the family. He probably thought she'd get by okay; Licha did nails now and made good money. But she'd never come back to the show, and she never saw the family except for Christmas and *Pentecostés*.

But she was no Licha. Licha had peeled off the emerald green of her tail and left it behind, never aching for it again. Lace wanted to lift up the back of her dress and show Matías her *escamas* were all still there. They were her sign from *Apanchanej* that she was still *una sirena*, even if not a Paloma.

She felt a stare still on her. Her eyes crawled to its source. A little girl stood by her mother's legs. She was short enough to see under the hat brim.

Lace touched her cheek, wondering if she'd forgotten to brush on a last layer of powder.

The girl rocked on the balls of her feet. The sun flashed off her shoes. Pink jelly sandals. Lace had last seen those shoes on the wet ground near the lake.

She wasn't staring at Lace's cheek. This was a girl who'd reached a small hand out for a grapefruit-pink fin. She'd seen Lace as a mermaid. Now she'd seen her out of her tail, no longer *la sirena rosa*, no longer a Paloma.

Lace put her finger to her lips, asking the girl to keep the secret.

The girl's smile spread through her whole face. First teeth, then eyes. To her, Lace had shed her fins and grown legs, maybe until midnight, maybe forever. She probably thought Matías was a prince she'd come on land for. If she noticed that Lace had been the only mermaid without river pearls or shells in her hair, maybe she took it to mean that the pink mermaid was not so tied to the water that she could not walk.

"Lace?" Matías said.

"Yeah?"

"Go stay with Martha's friends," he said. *"Abuela's* never gonna change her mind."

Cual el cuervo, tal el huevo.

The egg is the same as the bird.

Lace stopped at the end of the hall and reached into the fruit bag. She'd bring Nicole Corbeau her one nectarine. Not because she liked her, but because Clémentine had asked her to. Nicole Corbeau may have taught Lace to fix her cheek, but she'd also turned her back on her youngest son, the son who didn't start fights in fruit markets.

She knocked on the bedroom door. "Nicole?" She listened for the floorboards' groan.

She knocked harder. The latch gave under Lace's hand, and clicked undone. The door eased open, hinges squealing.

"Nicole?" Lace said.

The door opened a little more and showed an empty room. Bed neatly made. Doilies centered under lamps. Everything in place but a photo album splayed on the desk.

Lace set the nectarine next to it.

The album's cover gave off the must of old leather. The two open pages showed the same two people in eight different photos. Nicole Corbeau, her face almost the same, her hair shorter. And a little boy strangers must have called handsome. In one, they both gave the camera their smiles. In another, the boy chased a squirrel across a park, and the woman clapped her hands to her mouth, mid-laugh. Another showed her in a car's passenger seat, him in the driver's, small hands pretending to steer.

Lace flipped through the album, backward and forward, and found the same two people a hundred times. The woman clasped the boy's hands as he got the feel of walking. They held the ugliest poodle Lace had ever seen. They lifted their flour-covered hands toward the camera. Some were just of the boy. Halfway up a tree. Showing off a model airplane.

In the background of a few, there was a second boy. Smaller and darker, hair a little longer and messier, curls brushing his collar. In one, he sat on a patch of far-off grass, hands cupping a feather. In another, he was just a blur of motion, like a comet's trail. Never in focus. Never a suggestion that Nicole Corbeau knew there was another boy in the frame. This left-handed boy, nothing more than a smudge.

"Do you like the book?" Nicole Corbeau's voice hit the back of Lace's neck.

Lace snapped her head toward the door. "I'm sorry. I just wanted to look."

"Look all you like." Nicole Corbeau sat on the bed. "If I didn't want them seen, I wouldn't leave them lying around."

"Do you have other ones?" she asked. "Other pictures?"

"Of who? *Le petit démon?*" Nicole Corbeau laughed, sharp and beautiful as cut crystal.

Lace didn't need to speak French to understand. *Le petit démon.* She pulled away from the desk and left the room. "Enjoy your nectarine."

"For God's sake, laugh," Nicole Corbeau called into the hall. "Don't they have jokes in this town?"

Lace emptied the peaches into the kitchen's fruit bowl. She left the watermelon on the counter and crumpled the paper bag.

Whoever Cluck and Dax's father was, Cluck must not have looked enough like him to satisfy Nicole Corbeau. Cluck had that blue-black hair, his olivewood skin, the shape of his eyes. He'd gotten them from his grandfather. They'd stayed hidden in Nicole's generation, but showed up in Cluck like a photograph developing in solution. Dax, with the lighter brown of his hair and his eyes like haze, must have convinced Nicole that tamping down the Romani blood took only strength of will. He had done it. Cluck hadn't, and it, along with his left-handedness and the red in his feathers, made his own mother call him *le petit démon*.

The back door flew open and slammed into the wall.

Dax came in and grabbed Lace's forearms. "You should've stayed out of it."

She cried out at the feeling of his skin on hers. No sleeves in between. She twisted her arms, trying to pull away. "Let me go."

He backed her against the counter. "It was none of your business."

"Was that guy worth a night in jail?" She jerked her head up, finding his eyes. "What were you gonna do? Push him into a stack of cantaloupe crates in front of half the town? How do you think your mother would've liked that?"

This logic had worked on Justin. He'd wanted to keep his mother happy, so he'd listened. Same with Dax. He must've known he was the only one in his mother's scrapbooks.

Dax's hands made her forearms cramp. If he gripped her any harder, the feather Cluck left on her would grow blades for barbs and slice his palms.

She looked for a little of Cluck in his face. His brow bone. The line of his nose. The shape of his jawline.

"I appreciate the thought," Dax said. "I really do. But stay out of this."

She came up empty. Dax and Cluck may have been made of the same things, but they were no more alike than sand and glass.

"You're loyal." Dax threw the crumpled bag on the table. "That counts with us. But stay out of things you don't know anything about."

He yanked her over to the kitchen sink and turned on the tap. He held her hands under and squirted dish soap into her palms.

"What, you think my hands aren't clean?" she asked. "You think I'm gonna make everything dirty?"

"This isn't for us." He rubbed his hands over hers. "It's for you."

"I know how to wash my own hands."

He scrubbed her harder. "Do you know what happens to people who touch them?"

"Who?"

"The guy you shoved."

The feel of his hands and the soap's fake lemon reached her stomach. She swallowed to keep everything still.

Her words stalled in her throat. They turned to a weak hum. Her hands went limp in his.

The Paloma instinct still ruled her. Even to stop a fight, she'd touched Matías instead of Dax. And this family was as afraid of touching a Paloma as hers was of touching a Corbeau.

"If you touch them and you don't know what you're doing, they make you sick," Dax said.

Know what you're doing. Hitting. Kicking. Things that drew blood.

Dax splashed a last rinse over her hands. He loosened his grip and reached for a dish towel.

She pulled her hands free and ran out the back door.

"You should be thanking me," Dax yelled after her.

She kept going until she got to the river. She searched the water. The dull pink hadn't surfaced. Her tail hadn't washed up again. She plunged her hands in, looking out for the fabric and beads, letting the river strip away the dish soap and the feel of Dax's hands.

The sun fell below the tops of the trees. Cluck found her as the light turned the branches gold.

"What were you thinking?" he asked.

She kept her eyes on the water. "News travels fast."

"I hired you," he said. "Anything you do, I hear about it. What if Dax had figured out who you were? What if—who was he, your brother, your cousin? What if he'd figured out *where* you were?"

"But they didn't," she said.

He got in front of her. His eyes adjusted, almost red in this light. When the sun hit his hair, long and messy enough to hide his feathers, it looked copper.

"You think you're outside of this," he said. "You think because your family threw you out you're not part of this. Guess what, it doesn't work that way."

She looked past him at the water. Sundown cast a sheet of rose gold over the surface.

"I get it," Cluck said. "Believe me, I do. I wouldn't want Dax messing up anyone I cared about either."

Lace looked at him. "Are you kidding? Matías would've kicked his ass."

His shoulders relaxed, and he almost smiled. "Then I'm sorry I didn't get to see it."

She unbuttoned his shirt, slipped it off him. Pulled his undershirt off by the bottom hem.

"What are you doing?" he asked.

She took his hands and led him into the river, making him walk with her until the water lapped at his thighs and her hips.

It swirled around them. The rose gold curled into scrolls. The sun's hands warmed his bare back. She set her palms on his skin and found it fever-hot.

The scar on her forearm meant she could never be loyal to her family. Her name meant she could never be loyal to the Corbeaus. The only one left to be loyal to was him.

"This is the border between my family's part of the woods, and yours," she said. "Right here, we're not standing anywhere that belongs to anybody."

"Yes, we are," he said. "Because it's water."

"I was careful," she said.

He held a wet palm to her cheek. "I don't want you getting hurt."

"Everybody gets hurt," she said. "You know that."

Jamais couard n'aura belle amie.

Faint heart never won true love.

He gave Lace a head start, so she'd get back to the house before he did. He'd wait a few minutes and then follow. The last thing they needed was Dax seeing them both together, soaked in river water.

His wet clothes stuck to him. He turned his back to the river. Every glint off the water felt sharp as a glass shard. Every rustle of the current through the tree roots stung. In a few days his family would pack up, leave Almendro for the next town, and put a long stretch of highway between them and this river.

Lace's shadow disappeared into the farthest trees, and all the sharp edges settled into his chest.

It wasn't this river he'd miss. It was the girl who kept pulling him into it.

He went after her. He wanted them both to stand in the winter rain of the Carmel River, the shallows like topaz. He wanted to show her blue hour Mexican jays and vermillion flycatchers, bright as flames, lured hundreds of miles outside their range by the silt of the Pajaro. He wanted them both to find their footing in the glacier-carved bed of Fallen Leaf, the water new from the rain turning over the whole lake every eight years.

"Lace." He caught up and put a hand on her arm.

She turned into his touch, but said, "I thought the whole point was showing up at different times."

He dropped his hand from her arm. "Have you thought about what you're gonna do when we leave town?"

The shadow of a few leaves crossed her face. "Not really."

He tried not to nod, knowing his nod would look slow and heavy. With her two-word answer, the disappointment crept up on him. He hadn't realized until he'd asked the question that he'd wanted her to say yes, she'd worried about it like he did when he saw the light on the water. Or no, that it hadn't occurred to her. Something surer than "not really." "Not really" was her version of a shrug.

Maybe after this week, he wouldn't be anything more to her than the guy who showed her how to climb a tree. She'd remember him putting white feathers on her back, but she'd forget, one color at a time, the way the sun hit them.

It was still worth asking. She'd already covered him like beads of river water.

"Would you consider coming with me?" he said.

The sky flashed gold in her eyes. "What?"

"I mean coming with us," he said. "We're heading out on Monday. Madera County, then Mariposa. I know it means you wouldn't be near your family, but how much are you really seeing them now?"

"I don't want you to feel sorry for me," she said.

"I don't. I'm saying you have a job with us if you want it."

"You don't have to look out for me."

"Do you have somewhere else you want to go?" he asked. "Do

you have somewhere else you want to be more than you want to be with me?"

Her lips parted, her eyes going over the ground like she was searching for the glimmer of something lost. But she didn't say anything.

"Sorry," he said. "You don't have to answer right now. You can think about it."

She lifted her eyes from the ground. "No."

"No, you don't want to think about it?" he asked.

"No, there's nowhere I want to be more than where you are."

He felt the sky shifting deeper blue, falling toward the dark of the water.

"What?" he asked.

"I haven't thought about what would happen when you left town because I didn't want to," she said. "I didn't want to think about being somewhere you're not."

"Is that a yes?" he asked.

She smiled, and the woods turned from shadow to all blue, pure and dark. "What do you think?"

He slid a hand onto the back of her neck and pulled her into him.

The harder he kissed her, the more he picked up the taste of river salt, pink as her tail, glinting on her mouth like glass beads. He could smell the sun-warmed water and wild sky lupines of Honey Lake. He could feel them both getting their clothes soaked in the Estrella River, its water stirred by a hundred little earthquakes they'd never feel unless he held her so close and so still his breath sounded the same as hers.

Lace pulled away and brushed his hair out of his face. "How are you gonna explain this to your brother?"

He spread his hands over the small of her back, feeling for the heat of her birthmarks through her dress. "Let me worry about that."

Ce que chante la corneille,
chante le corneillon.

As the crow sings, so sings the fledging.

C luck scrubbed the same places over and over. It left his chest reddened, his arms raw. But he still felt the brush of the current, his skin made hot by sun and then cooled by water.

If he didn't rub it all off, someone would know. This must have been like the guilt that men who cheated felt. How they washed other women's perfumes from their shoulders. But instead of a mistress, Cluck had Lace and her river. Instead of a wife, he had feathers that told him not to touch a girl with scales. A family that would smell the silt and water vines if he didn't scour away the scent.

He turned off the water, and dressed, damp feathers scratching the back of his neck.

He owed Clémentine. She'd agreed to be the one to say she wanted Lace to stay on. She hadn't hidden the smile at the corner of her mouth when Cluck asked her, but she must have known why she had to do it instead of him. Clémentine was one of *les vedettes du spec-*

tacle, as much a lead in the show as Dax was. She had the standing to ask for things. Cluck didn't.

His grandfather's coughing carried down the hall. It took on the hard, deep sound of shaking his lungs. It had gone farther into his chest.

Cluck opened the door without knocking.

The orange prescription bottle sat on his grandfather's dresser, the pills as high as the day it was filled.

Cluck's lungs felt as full of water as when Lace held him under. He should've known his grandfather wouldn't swallow a single one unless Cluck made such an annoyance of himself about it that *Pépère* considered it less trouble just to take the damn pills.

But Cluck hadn't done that. He'd forgotten. He'd been too busy kissing Lace, taking her up into the trees, letting her pull him into the river.

Cluck shook his head. *"Pépère."*

His grandfather finished coughing into a handkerchief, his back turned. "I told you I didn't like that *gadji*."

The words flared through Cluck's face, the same shame as when he was small and his mother caught him petting wild birds. She would yell at him, say he would bring the bird's sickness home to his brother, and was that what he wanted?

Pépère's voice had never made his forehead feel hot. His grandfather did not scold or yell. He gave advice, his words ballasted with a calm that told Cluck if he did not listen, he would find out himself.

Use your left hand when they are not looking, but always the right when they can see.

Since your feathers are too many to pluck, wear your hair long to cover them, or the gadje will gossip more than they already do.

Stay away from water, or the nivasia will kill you.

Cluck shut the door behind him. "You're not taking your pills."

"Don't talk to me about pills." His grandfather folded the hand-kerchief. "You don't know what you're doing."

The faint outline of his grandfather's face showed on the window glass. Cluck couldn't make out his expression, only the white flash of the handkerchief.

"You didn't know what you were doing when you hired her," *Pépère* said. "And now we are bringing her with us, and you still don't know what you're doing."

Cluck hunched his shoulders, wishing he'd had the chance to tell his grandfather before word got around the family. Clémentine worked fast.

"You'd like her if you got to know her," Cluck said.

Pépère gave a curt laugh, made rough by his torn-up throat. "Why would I want to know a *nivasi?*"

The floorboards wavered, turning to water.

Nivasi.

His grandfather knew. He knew Cluck had brought a Paloma into their house.

"You think I don't see what she is?" *Pépère* asked.

The floorboards swelled liked waves, ready to swallow Cluck.

"How long have you known?" he asked.

"Longer than you have."

The rattled feeling inside Cluck sharpened into anger. "Then you should have told me."

"And what would that have done?" his grandfather asked. "You found out. It made no difference."

"If you had a problem with her being here, why didn't you say something sooner?"

"I had no problem with her being here. I have many problems with her being with you."

Cluck put a hand on the dresser, steadying himself.

"I taught you better than this," his grandfather said.

"Whatever happened, she didn't do it," Cluck said. "They don't even want her. They threw her out."

"She's the same blood." *Pépère* almost yelled now. "You know nothing about that family."

"Then tell me." Cluck slammed his hand down on the dresser. The pills rattled in the bottle, a reminder like a sharp whisper that they had not been touched. "You tell me the plant did worse things than I know, but you won't tell me what. You tell me I shouldn't be with her but you won't give me any reason better than her last name. What do I do with that?"

"If you find a *nivasi* you leave her where you find her." His grandfather turned. "End it with her."

"If you didn't want me with her, why did you let her stay?"

"Because I wanted her to get you out of here."

"What are you talking about?" Cluck asked.

"It wouldn't have been long until someone figured out who she was," *Pépère* said. "And you're the one who brought her here. You're the one who knew what she was. This family would throw you out for that the same as hers threw her out."

The book-smell Cluck's grandfather brought with him into every room he stayed in faded. The scent of Lace's river, all wet reeds and sun on her body, faded. Nothing stayed but the dry earth smell of his own feathers.

"You wanted them to find out?" Cluck asked.

"I wanted them to find out you'd hired a Paloma," *Pépère* said. "Not that you were going into rivers with her. If they knew that, if they knew what you were really doing, they'd kill you. I'm not going to let that happen. But if they'd thought she was only some girl you were looking after, they'd just throw you away like her family did to her."

"And that's what you wanted?" Cluck asked. "You wanted me to end up like her?"

"I didn't want you to end up like me." His grandfather threw his hand toward the window, the white square of his *mouchoir* almost brushing the glass. "Stuck here, following everyone else's rules."

"You didn't have to do this," Cluck said. They'd talked about this so many times. About Cluck going to community college, transferring to a four-year, then graduate school if he could get a scholarship like *Pépère*. That had been their plan since the day *Pépère* explained bird flight to Cluck, and Cluck had listened as closely as his youngest cousins did to fairy tales. "I didn't plan on staying with the show forever. You knew that. I was always going to leave."

"You mean the way I've left?" his grandfather asked.

His grandfather's tired smile stung him.

"That's not fair," Cluck said, hating how the words sounded as soon as he said them. He'd meant it wasn't fair to *Pépère*.

"You're eighteen," his grandfather said. "You finished the high school curriculum a year ago. When were you planning on leaving?"

"I'm saving for it," Cluck said. "I need money before I can leave."

"There's never enough money." *Pépère* cleared his throat into the handkerchief and then folded it as neatly as if it were clean. "You'll be waiting forever."

That smile on his grandfather's face, sure and sad and bitter, killed any protest in him.

Cluck had never set a date to leave, never made plans to enroll in the fall.

His grandfather had been right about Lace too. Cluck had wanted to take Lace with him to the next county, keep her like a cat. He'd never thought of leaving with her, finding a place where neither of their names was the same as an oath broken. He'd just wanted to bring her with him to where this family was going next.

Lace's was not Cluck's freedom. He was her captivity. People did not leave this family, not for good. Margaux would be back eventually, a boyfriend or new husband with her. Whether Corbeau by blood or marriage or simply by working for the show, they did not leave. They stayed, and they followed the law set by pure black feathers.

"You know the way this family is," *Pépère* said. "They pull you. They keep you."

Any anger Cluck had sank beneath this understanding. *Pépère* wanted to take the choice from Cluck. He did not want Cluck to have to turn his back on this family, so instead he wanted them to turn their backs on him.

The fact that *Pépère* once had a house that did not move and a job that followed a steady clock, that he once didn't have to listen to this family about whether he should see other women after *Mémère* died or whether he should put eggshells around the base of the lemon tree outside his kitchen window, these were all miracles, small but heavy. Miracles revoked when the plant took them from *Pépère*, and he had nowhere else to go.

"I was afraid you were never going to get out unless they made you," *Pépère* said.

"If you wanted me to get out why do you care if I'm with her?" Cluck said, breathing on this small ember that made him wonder if Lace asked him, would he leave with her.

But *Pépère* just said, "You weren't supposed to be with her that way. You were so protective of her I thought she was another Eugenie to you. A little cousin or sister."

"And you just assumed I'd never feel anything for her?" Cluck asked. "You just banked on it?"

"You've never shown interest in any girls." *Pépère* cleared his throat with a hard cough. "You've never shown interest in anyone."

"Why do you think that is?" Cluck asked. "Everyone around here has made it pretty clear I'm supposed to stay away from any girls I'm not related to."

"Then stay away from her."

"Tell me why."

Pépère coughed into the handkerchief again, trying three times before he got out, "She will ruin you."

Cluck grabbed the prescription bottle off the dresser and forced it into his grandfather's hand. "You don't know that."

"Yes, I do." His grandfather threw the bottle down. "Because one of them ruined me."

It cracked open. Half the pills scattered across the floor.

Cluck bent and picked out one left in the split bottle.

His fingers froze in the orange plastic, his grandfather's words echoing, registering.

One of them.

But it was all of them. They'd all spread the lies about him.

Another coughing fit kept his grandfather from speaking.

He waited it out, and cleared his throat. "It was after your grandmother died."

"What are you talking about?" Cluck asked.

"I was with one of them," *Pépère* said, his words sharp as when Cluck couldn't answer one of his questions about bird flight or earth metals. "I know about them better than you do."

Cluck crouched over the prescription bottle. "A Paloma?" he asked, the words as weak as when he had to guess an answer to one of those questions *Pépère* thought he should've known. "You were with a Paloma?"

"And after, she claimed I forced her," his grandfather said. "This is how that family is. They can get their own to say anything."

He said it without hesitation, clean and even. These were facts etched into his life, as much as being let go from the plant.

He started coughing again, each inhale splintering the wood of the floorboards. The sound cracked Cluck open, knowing that he could have stopped this.

Cluck stood, a pill in his palm.

Pépère held a pointing hand between them, a warning, a sign that he would take nothing from that bottle. "This girl will do the same to you. That family will get her to do the same to you."

"Who was the woman?" Cluck asked.

His grandfather hacked into the cotton square. "It doesn't matter."

"If it doesn't matter, then tell me."

His coughing got quieter, but still shook his frame. "End it."

The words got into Cluck's body. Their weight came down on him, but he couldn't get his hands on the meaning, wet and slipping from his grasp.

Pépère looked at the door. "You."

Lace froze at the threshold, eyes flitting between Cluck and his grandfather.

"I let you stay," *Pépère* said. "I knew and I said nothing. And you went after him."

"*Pépère*," Cluck said.

His grandfather ignored him. "You will ruin his life," he said to Lace.

Cluck saw Lace try to speak. Her mouth moved. But the sound sank under *Pépère*'s coughing.

Cluck reached out for his grandfather's hand, to set the pill in his palm.

But his grandfather's hand slipped down and out of reach, his body falling with it.

Cluck dropped to his knees, calling him back. *Pépère. Alain.* Any name he might answer to.

The handkerchief fluttered to the floor, the blood spray dense as the spotting on an umber-brown mushroom. The chemicals sharpening the air had needled *Pépère*'s smoke-worn lungs into forgetting they were for breathing.

Lace called. The sirens came for Alain Corbeau.

As they took him, Cluck opened his fingers and set his rosary in his palm. The string of dark, carved beads and the medal of *Sara-la-Kali* would be his grandfather's guard against things left in the air.

Cluck got in the Morris Cowley and followed them.

But *Pépère* was faster than Cluck. He had always been faster. He left the whole world behind before Cluck even caught up to the ambulance.

Cluck got to the hospital in time for the doctor, shaking his head, to stop him in the hallway and tell him there was nothing they could do. That his grandfather's lungs had forgotten how to breathe and his heart could not take it. That he was sorry. That Alain Corbeau was already gone.

A few minutes later the rest of his family was there, Clémentine sobbing so hard the echo vibrated through the waiting room.

A nurse set Alain Corbeau's rosary into Cluck's palms, the beads still warm from his grandfather's fingers.

No todo lo que brilla es oro.

Not all that shines is gold.

H e looked misplaced, an obsidian shard in a bowl of flour. In sunlight, his skin was the brown of unfinished wood, but here, the fluorescents stripped its warmth. His hair stood out against the hospital linoleum and walls. His dark trousers, inherited from the man he'd just lost, did not belong among the white coats and pastel scrubs.

The nurse who always wore purple came down the hall, eyes on the floor. She patted Cluck's shoulder on her way by. Lace could tell by her face she knew he wouldn't feel it. He didn't react. The touch didn't register.

Cluck poured his grandfather's rosary from one hand to the other, then back. He stared down at the carved wooden beads. His thumb circled the saint's medal.

The last words Lace had said to Alain Corbeau clung to her mouth. They left her tongue hot and dry. *I love him.* She knew she'd said it. She'd felt her mouth forming the shape of the words. Her throat hummed with the sound. But Alain Corbeau hadn't heard it. Neither had Cluck.

She stood in front of him.

He saw her. The wavering of his eyes spread through her.

"I'm so sorry," she said. She tried to hold him.

He set his hands on her upper arms. "Don't," he whispered. "I can't. I want to, but I can't."

Lace brushed a piece of hair out of his eyes. She would not hold him to words those rosary beads bled out of him.

"Don't say anything," she whispered, and tried to put her arms around him again. "Not now."

He took a step back. The metal-and-earth scent of violet-black salt pulled away with him.

His face hardened. Losing Alain Corbeau had set him like clay.

"I can't be with you, Lace," he said.

His words fell against her lips, parched them like wind and dust. It stripped the words off her tongue.

I love him, her defense against everything Alain Corbeau thought she'd do to Cluck, was as weak as it was true.

He walked away. Back to the family who thought of him as a blur in a photograph. Back to the brother who threw him against walls to see if he'd break.

A few steps, and the distance opened like the height from a bough. It shook through her like a branch snapping.

She went after him.

A hand on her arm stopped her.

"Don't," Clémentine said, her eyes pink-rimmed. "Not now. He won't listen. The only one he'd listen to now is gone."

Clémentine left, biting the side of her thumb against sobbing.

Lace opened her hand. A black semiplume, the barbs striped

deep red, crossed her palm. She lifted it to her face, and her breath trembled the afterfeather. A perfect copy of the plume still burned into her arm, first a curse, now the only thing she had to prove that he had ever touched her.

No puede ser más negro el cuervo
que sus alas.

The crow cannot be blacker than its wings.

She went back to the Corbeaus' trailers, the place she had never belonged and now belonged less. Cluck had been the one holding her passport. He had taught her the language and the landscape, shown her this country's trees, the secret thrill of almost falling.

She took her suitcase, the clothes inside flecked with the black and red of Cluck's lost feathers. She took her tail, the fabric stiff from drying. She folded up the wings Cluck made her.

The money her father had given her was still hidden in the lining of her suitcase. She slipped it out and used it to check into the cheapest motel in Almendro that was not the River Fork.

Her suitcase bounced on the bed, the lock clicking unhinged. She shoved it off the comforter. It thudded on the floor and flopped open.

A few black feathers floated out, like air bubbles underwater. They drifted toward the ceiling. Then one fell and brushed her fingers, the plume soft as the underside of Cluck's hair.

First a dozen. Then a few dozen. Then hundreds more than she'd kept. More than could have fallen from Cluck's head in his life.

Those black and jewel red plumes filled the air like dandelion fluff. The dark cloud rose up and then dispersed, raining red-streaked black over everything. She opened her hands to catch them.

Coverts spun down onto the bed. Secondaries wafted over the dresser. Some feathers were small, all down. Others were primaries, long as quill plumes, bigger than any that had grown in with Cluck's hair. But they were all his, all marbled with his same red. Whether they'd fallen from him or not, they were his.

She went back to that old Craftsman house, ready to sneak into the blue and white trailer. But the few Corbeaus who saw her just nodded as she passed. Cluck must not have told them he didn't want her there anymore. Not that they'd ever cared what he wanted.

She stole things no one but Cluck would miss. Scraps of wire. A few spools of the darkest thread she could find. Scrapped ribbon, red as a blood orange, leftover from trimming a dress.

The blank wing frame leaning on Cluck's old mirror, bare as a February tree.

She'd never blamed Cluck for wearing his hair long enough to hide his feathers. She wouldn't have wanted questions from strangers either. But if she left him alone with his family, without his grandfather, without her, they'd break him until he hated the red in his feathers as much as they did. He'd start thinking of it as a sickness that held onto him.

She wasn't letting that happen. Even if he didn't want her anymore, she wasn't letting anyone, not even the Corbeaus, make him think the red that streaked every one of his feathers was a thing to hate.

Les petits ruisseaux font les grandes rivières.

Tall oaks from little acorns grow.

They kept saying his grandfather's name. They would not listen to Cluck when he told them *Pépère* would not have wanted them saying his name.

His grandfather did not say *Mémère*'s name for weeks after her death, so her soul could break free from her bones. But now they all said his, throwing it around without thinking. If everyone kept saying *Pépère*'s name, his *mulo* would get tethered to his body, stuck as a balloon tied to a weight.

But they wanted to be French, all French. Cluck told them, "Don't say his name out loud," and they looked at him as though he'd spoken of broken mirrors. Like he was an old woman who wouldn't let a black cat into the house.

They forgot they had Manouche blood of their own. But they had thrown it away with the rest of *Romanipen*.

His mother and her older sisters made the arrangements. A priest, a friend of Cluck's aunt, would drive in from Linden for the service.

None of them knew that Cluck could have saved him, if he'd just thought for one minute about those pills instead of about a girl who loved water as much as he loved the sky.

The owners of the chemical plant offered to buy a plot in a cemetery on Almendro's east border. They presented it as charity, not an admission. They said it was to express their condolences, to thank the family for the work Alain Corbeau had done for the plant decades ago.

It was their way of keeping the Corbeaus from wondering what killed him. The plant didn't want them thinking about it too hard, considering if the fallout in the air had turned the wet surfaces of his lungs to blood.

"They're being very generous," his eldest aunt said, signing the papers. "We should be grateful."

"They just want the body in the ground before a medical examiner can look at it," Cluck said.

His eldest aunt's husband slapped him and told him to show some respect.

Cluck held his palm to his right cheek. He breathed into the pain, knowing he deserved it. He'd failed, left those pills undisturbed in their bottle.

But that didn't mean he had to like how they were taking the *gadje*'s blood money, crumpling up *Romanipen* like an old map. And they wanted respect out of him.

His aunts and his mother accepted the plot. Dax kept saying, "This is the best thing for him and for us," as though he had made the decision.

Cluck only heard in time to see them sign the papers, God knew what they said.

It should not have been this way. The thought of *Pépère* in that shellacked wooden box, surrounded by this family who had made themselves *gadje*, sharpened the pain on Cluck's cheek. How many times would they say his name during the service, and then over the next month?

Years ago, they would have set fire to his *vardo*, his wagon, all the dead man's possessions lain inside. They would have decorated it with flowers and the dead man's things, and then lit it. But Cluck couldn't do that. He couldn't torch the house or the blue and white trailer, set half the woods on fire along with it.

Cluck went back to the blue and white trailer, shut the door, took off his grandfather's trousers and collared shirt. He could not burn everything for *Pépère*. But he could do this.

He found the pair of corduroys and the long-sleeved shirt his grandfather had bought him. He cut off the tags, pulled them on, bracing against the red of the shirt like it was cold water. They felt so unworn. But except for his underclothes and shoes, the things his grandfather had bought him were the only clothes he had that were his, and not once *Pépère*'s. A few shirts, a couple of pairs of pants, a jacket Cluck had kept but never put on.

The rest belonged to his grandfather. The suits and vests, the detachable collars on the ironed shirts, the dress pants. The things *Pépère* had asked Cluck to burn for him when he died.

He gathered them all, took them to the abandoned campground a quarter mile beyond the property, and threw them in a fire pit. The Corbeaus had left this tradition behind when they left *le Midi*. If Cluck did not do this for *Pépère*, no one else would.

He added fallen branches for kindling, then a lit match, and Alain Corbeau's clothes caught.

Embers clung to the edges, dense as a band of stars. The fabric burned and thinned. It glowed translucent, and then crumbled to ash. The thin wood of the porcelain vines released the scent of their blue berries, and the lemon of the rampant wild roses turned to rind oil and pith.

He threw in white, pink-centered bitterroot. The red buds of pallid milkweed. Larkspur, violet-spindled. Paintbrush, red and sticky with resin; he tossed it in, and the fire flared white.

The wildflowers dissolved into cinders, and turned the air to perfume. His grandfather's rosary weighted his pocket. He picked it out, and held it over the fire.

The moon and the firelight shone off the saint's medal, the little copper image of *Sara-la-Kali*. The flames turned it hot so fast, the metal burned Cluck's palm. He almost dropped it, but his fingers clutched at the wooden beads, and pulled it back.

He held the rosary to his chest. The metal's heat spread through him as though he wore no shirt. He had lost the armor his grandfather's clothes gave him. They had made him someone else. If he burned his hand or cut his arm, if his brother shoved him into the side of a trailer, the pain was not all his. He shared it with the years *Pépère* wore those clothes, stringing it out over decades until he barely felt it, the faint static of an untuned radio.

Now, if he let a girl touch him, it would be his body to feel it. He would not be able to thin out the feeling of her fingers. If she took his left hand and slid it under her blouse, it would be his own left hand, blighted, with ruined fingers. He would not be able to pretend his left hand was someone else's, perfect and unbroken, or that it did not shudder to touch her more than his right.

His grandfather had not willed his right-handedness to him. It was not Cluck's to inherit.

The rosary metal gave his body all its heat, and grew cool. The sting of that burn was only his. These clothes had no history to take the weight. Only his grandfather's wish that he fear no color, not even the red of his own feathers. That he remember how red-winged blackbirds did not fear crows or ravens twice their size.

Cluck had not understood before why *Pépère* wanted him to wear his own clothes. But he understood now.

Pépère wanted Cluck to know the feeling of putting on something blank and new, clothes that did not speak of another man's life. *Pépère* wanted him to grow a scent of his own, not offer his shoulders and hair to his grandfather's smoke and wild chervil.

He wanted him to grow his own skin.

Cluck kissed the medal of *Sara-la-Kali*, and tucked the rosary into the pocket of his corduroys. He should have burned it with his grandfather's clothes, but couldn't. If he burned it, he would forget the feeling of the copper's heat spreading through him. He would forget why he should wear his own clothes, and not another man's. He would forget why he had burned *Pépère*'s suits, and he would want them back.

De malas costumbres nacen buenas leyes.

From bad customs are born good laws.

ace kept her distance. She dressed in black anyway, the
same dress she wore to her own grandfather's funeral. She'd
grown, so it was shorter now, ending three inches above her knees.
It fit tight across her hips. But it was the only thing black she had
with her in the motel room where feathers had rained down on
everything.

She stood so the Corbeaus' backs were to her. To anyone but
them, she'd be a mourner who'd stepped away for a prayer or a cigarette.

Dew left the cemetery wet and green, lichen blooming over the
stones. The drops caught the sun, scattering the light.

The morning was still cold enough to make her shiver. Cap sleeves
exposed where wiring the feathers onto the wings had left her forearms scratched.

She almost didn't recognize Cluck. He stood next to the open
plot, hands at his sides. His jaw was still set, his face hard as the wood

of his grandfather's rosary beads. She'd gotten used to him in button-downs. Now he wore a dark red shirt, crew neck, not collared, and he stood out from all his family's black suits.

The women, in black skirts down to their calves, looked over at him, but he did not turn his head, did not notice the glares. They must have taken it as disrespect, insolence. Worse, that he would dare to throw in their faces the color that stained his feathers.

If they knew him at all, they'd know better. His grandfather's suits were the only ones he had, and maybe they reminded him too much of losing him. Maybe he couldn't look at one of those suits long enough to put it on. Or he had, and that age-darkened mirror had cut into him, showing him how much he looked like a decades-old photograph of Alain Corbeau.

She stayed at the tree line, where the cemetery broke into the woods. She didn't want Eugenie noticing her and asking why she was there.

She was there to pull Cluck to his feet and keep him there if he couldn't stand. To make sure none of the pieces of him got lost if he broke. In case his mother, neat as a greenhouse tulip, failed to notice that he was not dust or cracked glass, and reached for a broom.

Lace would gather up those bits of him before they got swept up and thrown out. How he climbed trees as quick as a feral cat. The black salt smell of his hair and sweat. The way his wrecked hand moved over her body. How the sun and water dripped off his back, how warm it stayed even in the river.

A shadow cut through the pale sunlight. "Lace?" said her great-aunt's voice.

Lace turned.

This *Tía* Lora was not the same as the *Tía* Lora Lace had left behind. She looked taken by a spirit, like a specter had spread through her limbs. It was a calm possession, not the thrashing rage of a vengeful ghost, but the deep-river stillness of *Apanchanej*, the water goddess who'd given the Paloma women their *escamas*.

Instead of her usual sweater and high-waisted skirt, *Tía* Lora wore a black dress, the cut plain and straight. It showed enough of her figure that she looked her age instead of *Abuela's*. Her usual skirts started at the bottom of her rib cage and ended in the middle of her calves, making her seem the eldest among her sisters-in-law even when she was the youngest.

Her everyday braid showed mostly the silver. Now her hair was loose to her waist, the black streaks free. She wore no lipstick or mascara, but a layer of powder evened her color. Blush warmed her cheeks.

Though she had no children, Lora Paloma had always looked, to Lace, like a grandmother. But not now, not in this dress and this light. Now she was a woman retired men might wink at. They would take her out for early dinners and almost-late dancing. Twice a year— Valentine's Day and her birthday—they would bring her twelve red roses, perfect and identical as folded napkins.

The sun made her glow like she was made of scales. Her skin shimmered with something a little like that pale iridescence.

Lace remembered Cluck telling her that iridescence was a dangerous thing. When birds or dragonflies grew into the glint of their own wings, they were weak, more open to damage than creatures that were plain colors. Lace wondered if *Tía* Lora had spent the last few days alone in her motel room, fragile and still, so she could emerge beautiful and made of light.

"*Mijita?*" her great-aunt asked. "What are you doing here?"

"Me?" Lace's laugh was soft as the color on *Tía* Lora's cheeks. "What are you doing here?"

Behind the veil of blush, her great-aunt's color drained. She turned and walked into the woods.

"*Tía* Lora." Lace went after her, her heart tight and raw.

Now her great-aunt knew where she'd been hiding. She'd picked up the oak and earth smell of the Corbeau boy's feathers.

Lace caught up and stopped her. "Why are you here?"

Her great-aunt looked past her. Her eyes fell on the funeral. The wooden casket. The boy who stood by the gravesite. Even in corduroys and a plain shirt, instead of those passed-down suits, he looked like a young copy of the old man they were laying in the ground. A print left behind.

"*Tía* Lora," Lace said. "Tell me."

À bois noueux, hache affilée.

Meet roughness with roughness.

The priest from Linden spoke, but Cluck didn't hear the words. He watched a crow pecking at the grass, feathers shining like slices of water. It kept his eyes from the varnished coffin, a burst of carnations and filler fern splayed over the top.

His aunts must have told the florist nothing but that they needed a funeral spray. *Pépère* never would have wanted the fuss of baby's breath and these ruffled, bloodless flowers. If there had to be flowers, his family should have covered the wood with the kind of wild periwinkles *Mémère* let take over their back garden.

His family's scorn whipped against him like wind-thrown branches. He didn't care. They could think what they wanted. He'd burned as many of his grandfather's things as he had the right and the stomach to. His family would have sold *Pépère*'s clothes, or let them wrinkle and yellow at the bottom of a wooden trunk.

Eugenie stood at his side, her small, set face daring her mother and father and older brother to say anything.

The crow beat its wings and lifted off. Cluck looked over his shoulder and watched it fly.

A shape at the tree line moved like a shadow. For that second, he thought he saw her, Lace Paloma in a black dress so short his mother would not have let her cross a church nave. Then she vanished.

This shadow of her was haunting him, reminding him that his grandfather would not have died if Cluck had not been so caught up in her. All he could do now was what he'd done, given her up, just like his grandfather wanted. Cluck wouldn't be with the same kind of woman who had told lies about *Pépère*, and he wouldn't trap Lace in this family.

He turned back toward the service, wanting to shake off that glimpse of her shape. He squeezed his eyes shut so tight that when he opened them, flecks of blue light swam in the air.

Clémentine's eyes flashed toward Eugenie. Her *Is he alright?* face. It was the same for her cousins, for children, for a stray cat they fed that always held its head tilted to the side.

Eugenie squeezed his hand. "*Ça va?*"

He forced a nod, his tongue pressed against the back of his teeth.

After the service, most of the family did not speak to him. Those who did—an uncle, a few cousins—all told him how much he looked like his grandfather. A great-aunt made him bend down so she could kiss his forehead, and told him, "You are a picture of him." A second cousin said, "I bet you'll be just like him when you're that old."

What did they want him to take from these words? That if he missed *Pépère*, he could just check a mirror? That the more he aged, the closer he'd get to him? Like getting older would seal up the empty place.

Cluck knelt next to the grave, damp earth cooling the knees of his pants. He reached down a hand—the right, he made sure of it— and gathered a fistful of earth. It smelled of new roots and week-old rain. He would keep it with him until he could throw it in a well, the way his grandfather's family had done for their dead since long before *la République française* existed. Another small thing to help *Pépère* flee this world. Cluck prayed, and told *Pépère* he would do this for him.

He finished praying, and walked away from the gravesite.

The sight of a man who was not one of them stopped him. He wore a navy suit, like he had in the hospital, one too nice for anyone who lived here. A suit not made for mourning.

A risk manager, Eugenie had called him. A man here to disperse the few protestors left as though they were rabbits. To take this town's silence not as fear for their jobs, but as assent. He would ignore the families who depended on the plant workers. He would ignore the town's unease that if too many of them protested, if they got too loud about safety standards, the plant would just pull out of Almendro. He'd ignore their dread about how it would gut the town, a worry so sharp it made the air hum.

The risk manager didn't see any of that. His job existed because *Pépère*'s did not.

The man shook Dax's hand with both hands, gripping with the right, patting with the left. A business handshake.

Cluck stood in the man's path, blocking the way to his mother and aunts and uncles.

"What are you doing here?" Cluck said in a low voice.

"You're Alain Corbeau's grandson," the risk manager said.

Cluck held the handful of dirt tighter. A few grains slipped between his fingers. "Don't say his name."

The man put on his best condolence face. He must have rehearsed it. The mouth was too tight, the eyes too pinched. "Alain was a great man."

Cluck packed the earth against his palm, perspiration turning the outer layer to mud. First his full name, and now just the first. Worse than speaking his grandfather's name, this man spoke as though he knew him. He wasn't even old enough to have seen him checking gauges and managing cleaning procedures.

"Please," Cluck said. "Don't say his name."

But the man didn't understand, and went on with his speech about how vital Alain Corbeau was to the plant "back then," how Alain's dedication to his work inspired those around him, that Alain Corbeau would be remembered fondly as part of the Almendro community.

He used *Pépère*'s name so many times the words sounded like a printed obituary. He repeated it, full or first, over and over, until Cluck could hear his grandfather's soul screaming back toward this world, a meteor of pure nickel and iron.

Cluck had already betrayed *Pépère* by loving a Paloma so hard he forgot to look after his own grandfather. He could not let this go.

"Anyone who worked with Alain Corbeau speaks highly of him," the man said. "I want you to know that."

Cluck's left hand flew. It hit the man in the jaw, closed-fist, his right palm still holding the handful of *Pépère*'s grave.

The man stumbled, holding his hand to his face. The practiced sadness slipped out of place like the lid off a jar.

The pain of a jammed finger throbbed through Cluck's hand. It hadn't faded by the time the police came for him.

His family's murmurs and his mother's shouting all faded under the crisp flapping of the crow's wings.

The soreness in Cluck's left hand gave way to the weight in his right. With as many times as the risk manager had said *Pépère*'s name, Cluck needed, even more, to leave this handful of earth in a well.

"Please," Cluck said as they tried to force his wrists behind his back. "There's something I have to do first." He had to do this one thing right for *Pépère*.

He would not open his right hand. If he did not reach the well, no one would do it in his place. His family would call these things old superstitions. They would leave *Pépère* held to the earth like a moon.

Cluck fought their hold. "No." But they clicked the locks into place. He felt small hands under his, taking the earth.

Eugenie stepped into his sight, the soil filling her palms. She held it in both hands, cupping it in front of her like she'd caught a finch. She was so little, so quick, that she'd slipped behind him and away again before the police could think to stop her.

"Please," Cluck told her. "There's a well out by County Road 27."

"By the almond orchard," she interrupted him. "I know. I'll bring it."

Her hands had been raining petals onto their audiences for years. They knew when to stay so closed it looked like she held nothing, and when to open.

"*Nais tuke*," he said as they pulled him away. *Thank you.*

She smiled. "Always."

Cluck breathed out until he'd emptied his lungs. He stopped fighting, and let them take him.

El amor es ciego.

Love is blind.

*T*ía Lora told her not to go back. This was what she asked in
return for the things she told her.

"There is nothing for you there, *mija*," she said, making Lace drink
borraja tea to calm her, the honey taste of the flowers helping the bite
of the leaves go down.

But Lace went anyway, her hands prickling with the truth of what
happened the night the lake swallowed the trees, a truth only she and
Lora Paloma knew.

And how Justin, Oscar, and Rey could have called Cluck a *chucho*, a
word that meant not just wild or stray but mutt. Why Cluck's *gitano*
blood showed so much more in him than in his mother and brother.
This truth half the Corbeaus knew. They just hadn't bothered to tell
Cluck.

Lace didn't find him in the trailers. She searched the mourners
in the Corbeaus' kitchen and dining room. But she did not see
Cluck.

She didn't see Dax either. So she threw open his bedroom door without knocking.

Dax looked up from a writing desk, hand paused over a ledger like his mother's.

"Where is he?" Lace asked.

"Who?" Dax asked.

"Cluck," she said, yelling more than she meant to.

"Where do you think? He's in a holding cell."

She held her hands to her sternum, her great-aunt's truths stinging her through her dress. "What?"

"He hit one of the men from the plant. Some lawyer or actuary, I don't know. Eugenie didn't tell you?"

"No," Lace said. She hadn't seen Eugenie.

"Don't worry, we'll get by without him. Call tonight is the usual time." He went back to writing.

Lace set her back against the wall. "Dammit, Cluck," she said under her breath. He'd never hit anyone in his life, and he had to start with a lawyer.

"Stop calling him that," Dax said. "He's not a chicken."

Her shoulder blades pressed into the wallpaper. "And you're just leaving him there."

"Suis-je le gardien de mon frère?" Dax asked.

"What does that mean?" she asked.

"Genesis four-nine." He took a Bible off the bookshelf and handed it to her. "If you're going to keep working for us, you'll need to learn a little French."

The Bible was in English. She wondered if it belonged to him, or Nicole, or whoever rented them this house.

She turned to the right chapter and verse. She only knew one word, *frère*, but it was enough to tell her the right part of the verse. *Am I my brother's keeper?* The line in scripture that had let men pass the buck for thousands of years.

She shut the Bible and threw it on the desk. "Did you know? This whole time, did you know?"

"Know what?" He put the Bible back on the shelf.

She set her hands on the edge of the desk. "Where were you in all this?"

He kept working.

She grabbed the pen from his fingers.

His hand shot out toward hers, gripping it. "Let it go."

She tried pulling her hand back. Trying to twist free made his hold worse.

His thumb pressed back on her index and third fingers. "Let go."

She doubled over the desk. Her fingers would not give up the pen. A spot of ink bled onto Dax's palm.

"Stop," she choked out.

She tried to let the pen go, but now he was smashing her hand into it. The pressure built in her joints. If he kept bending her fingers back, the bones would give and crack.

"Let it go," he said, low as a whisper. The alcohol of his cologne stung the back of her throat.

Her hand trembled, her mouth trying to make the word *Please*. If he kept holding her this hard, twisting her knuckles, he would break both her fingers in one snap, like Cluck's hand, ruined by a single thing he would never tell her. Jousting or bullfighting. Lies more ridiculous than his fake names.

All those stories about car doors and falling out of trees.

Genesis, fourth chapter.

Am I my brother's keeper?

Cain's answer when God asked where Abel was.

Dax had wrecked the hand Cluck thought he should never use.

The numbers floated through her brain like math on her father's worksheets. Cluck was eighteen. It had happened nine years ago, when he was nine years old. Dax couldn't have been older than fourteen. How had his fingers held that kind of brutal will?

This was the sin of mothers and fathers, thinking their children were too young, too much children, to be cruel. Oscar and Rey weren't any older when they joined their uncles shooting crows.

Lace's stomach clenched and then gave. The *borraja* tea came up. The acid burned her throat, and she coughed it out. It sprayed Dax's suit. He jumped back and let her hand go.

She dropped the pen and ran out of the room, hunching her shoulder to wipe her mouth on her sleeve.

Nicole Corbeau stepped into the hall. She held out a hand to stop Lace. *"Tu couve quelque chose?"*

The water in Lace's eyes beaded and fell. She rubbed it away with the heel of her hand. "How could you lie to him like this?"

The blue of Nicole Corbeau's eyes lightened, like water draining from a bathtub. She knew what Lace meant. Who *him* was. What *this* was.

"How could you let him believe all this?" Lace asked. Her voice would have broken into screaming if she'd had the air. She heard the full, heavy call of *arundo* reeds creep into the words, their breath holding up her weak voice. She didn't care. Let Nicole Corbeau hear it. Let her know Lace was a *sirena* who would not keep Corbeau lies locked under her tongue.

Nicole Corbeau pressed on Lace's back to get her into a side room.

She shut the door. "I didn't decide it. My sisters did."

"But you went along with it," Lace said.

"Dax's father left. He wouldn't marry me. You don't know what that means in this family." She folded her thin arms over the black linen of her dress. "They decided this was my penance for having the son I wanted. Being forced to raise another who wasn't mine."

Two *bastardos* who would think they shared a vanished father.

"Dax doesn't know?" Lace asked.

Nicole's laugh was small but sharp. "He thinks he remembers when I was pregnant. He was five. You can convince a child that age of anything."

"And your father?" Lace asked. "How'd you convince him? He agreed to this?"

"This whole town called him a rapist. He thought if he raised *le cygnon* himself the name would brand him too. That the scandal would follow *le cygnon* his whole life."

Le cygnon.

"You can't even say his name, can you?" Lace asked.

Nicole Corbeau could not have known then that Cluck would turn out left-handed. That, as he grew, the black cygnet down would give way to red-streaked feathers. That he would look so much like Alain Corbeau, *el gitano*. She hated him for all these things, but most of all she hated him because she could not love him as she loved her own perfect *bastardo*, the son she wanted even if his father did not stay.

"Who told you?" Nicole asked.

"Does it matter?"

"Does he know?"

"No," Lace said. "He doesn't."

"Are you going to tell him?"

"Would you care if I did? If I tell him, he'll hate you. He'll leave. And then you'll never have to see him again."

A wince tightened Nicole's face and stiffened her shoulders. For a second Lace felt sorry for the woman Nicole Corbeau had been back then. A young mother shamed for having a child but no husband. A woman not much older than Lace, who had no more power to fight the law of her family than *las sirenas* had to defy *Abuela*.

Like *Tía* Lora, Nicole Corbeau paid for having a son when she was not married. But while *Tía* Lora's punishment was losing a son, Nicole Corbeau's was being given one she did not want.

Lace sobbed into the air, her hands too wet to take it. She cried not just for Cluck and for *Tía* Lora, but for the young woman who had hardened into the Nicole Corbeau who now stood in this room. The salt of her tears seeped into her burn, dragging through like a safety razor slipping. "Did you ever want him?"

"I already had the son I wanted," Nicole Corbeau said.

There was no sharpness in her face, no cruelty. She said it as plainly as whether the eggs this week were good or not.

"You could've gotten rid of him months ago," Lace said. "He's eighteen. You could've kicked him out on his last birthday. There wouldn't even have been paperwork."

"It's not up to me to decide where he goes," Nicole said. "It never has been. This family keeps him here to teach him, to help him be something better than he was born. He is our blood. It's up to us to look after him."

"Is that what you all think you're doing?" Lace threw the door open.

"Where are you going?" Nicole Corbeau asked.

"If you won't get him out, I will," Lace said.

"Take him. *Avec ma bénédiction.*"

The words hooked into Lace, pulling her so she almost turned around. They almost got her to talk back, to say *That's what you want, isn't it? So he won't be your problem anymore? So you all won't have to contain how evil he is?*

But she did not stop. She did not stop when she reached the back door, or the dirt road, or the paved street. She did not stop until she reached the chemical plant's fence line.

The few remaining protestors sent their chants through the chain link. She wove through, keeping her eyes off the mixing tanks, so the sight of them would not stab into her cheek.

She slipped her fingers into the fence. "Hey." She rattled the chain link and yelled over the protestors' chanting. "I want to see your lawyer. Your actuary. Whatever you call him. Whoever showed up at the cemetery this morning, I want to see him."

A security guard approached the fence, his steps slow, one eye half-shut. He was a younger one, still getting the bearing of the job. He had the kind of extra weight that made him look soft, but that heft gave his arms power. Lace knew because of Justin. His body had that same look, and Lace had seen the blood and bruises he left.

"He came here to handle people, didn't he?" Lace yelled, shaking the fence. "Tell him to get out here and handle me."

If she had still been with her family's show, *Abuela* would have fired her, swept all her things into an empty suitcase like she had Licha's. *Las niñas buenas* did not stand outside fences, squawking and making shows of themselves.

But what had all this behaving gotten *Tía* Lora? A lover she had not been allowed to see. A lie that ruined the one man who'd been kind to her. And a son she'd barely gotten to hold. A boy who grew up thinking his father was a man he had never known, and his mother a woman who considered him nothing more than a weak copy of his older brother.

The security guard watched her, the dilemma pulling at that half-closed eye. She could see it twisting the muscles at the corners of his mouth. Should he escort her off the property? Throw out the girl the chemical plant cooked? Right now she was nothing. A number, an injury, an item so low on the lawyers' list she drifted off the bottom of the page. But if some in-town reporter caught the story and got it into the next day's paper, the bad publicity might stick.

The red heart on Lace's cheek already showed. She turned her head so it was all he could see.

She lowered her voice. "Get him out here, or I start talking."

He knew what she meant. She'd hidden from the papers and local station camera crews, first with her family, then with the Corbeaus, *los gitanos* the reporters wouldn't get near. But she didn't have to. Some county paper could print her picture, the garnet on her cheek showing up even in black-and-white.

The guard nodded to another guard. She waited five minutes, and a man in a newly pressed suit came out to the fence line. He held an ice pack to the side of his face.

She could smell his aftershave through the fence, the sharp resin of synthetic pine. His hair, neat and styled, made her think of leather briefcases, dry cleaners, first class red-eyes.

She pointed at his cheek. "Luc Corbeau gave you that, right?"

A sneer wrinkled his upper lip. He smoothed it, and said nothing.

"Are you pressing charges?" she asked.

"That's none of your business."

He started walking away, giving the security guard a look of *don't let this bother me again.*

"Actually it is." Lace held the fence and stood on her toes. "Because I want to know if I'm going to the county paper tomorrow morning."

He stopped, the heel of one polished shoe lifted midstep.

The chanting pressed into her back.

"They're afraid now," she said. "They don't want to lose their jobs. But if the news crews come in, they're gonna find out what everyone's too scared to say."

The plant should have installed an overfill pipe. Cluck knew it. This man must have known it. And he must have known of a dozen other little mistakes. A disregarded pressure gauge. A broken thermometer. Pipes that hadn't been cleaned. Slip blind procedures skipped. A shift worker so bleary from overtime he could barely read the numbers.

These things would come out. The question was how fast, and if Lace would help.

The man turned around. "Nobody knows who you are."

"You're right," she said. "And this isn't a story. It's two lines in anything but the local paper. But it could be bigger. It will get bigger. All that noise is coming. You know that. So my question is, do you want me to be part of it?" She turned her face again to show her cheek.

"I don't have time for this." The man turned his back, shaking her off through that chain-link fence.

All Lace had left was a thing that was not hers to tell. What Lora Paloma had figured out with Alain Corbeau's help. Not because *Tía* Lora wanted justice for her dead husband, but because she did not want the sinking of a grove of trees to destroy the family she now called hers.

Alain Corbeau was the one man who could have told *Tía* Lora if she was right, and who might have wanted to see the fighting end as much as she did. He was the one Corbeau who, years ago, did not travel with his family's show.

The mineral extraction work being done under the lake. Alain Corbeau had found the records that proved the lake swallowing the trees was an act neither of God nor of either family, but the fallout from the crumbling of a salt dome beneath the lake.

The plant's owners had sunken a well into that salt dome. Shoddy work, and orders for more salt faster, made the wall of the well cave. Rock slipped down into the empty space, trapped air bubbled toward the surface, and the lake opened up. A sinkhole took out all those trees before the water settled. The river's sudden roughness, the thing Lace's family blamed on the Corbeaus' *magia negra*, had been from the force and debris off the collapsed lake bed.

All of this an act of no one but the chemical plant's owners, who'd covered it all up so well that the whole town thought it was a natural disaster, a tragedy no different than a lightning-strike fire.

But before Alain Corbeau could steal or copy the records that would prove what he and Lora knew, the plant managers had found out and fired him. Then he had nothing to show he was more than a madman with his theories.

Tía Lora didn't have those records. Neither did Lace.

All she had was lying.

"Maybe you wanna talk about the sinkhole," Lace said through the fence.

The shift in the man's walk gave him away. He stopped in the middle of his stride, and turned around. His eyes got tight.

"You don't know anything," he said.

"And you don't know how much of a pain in your ass I can be," she said. "You really want to find out?"

The man's face relaxed, but there was no more of that smirk, that ridicule. The man may not have believed her threat had any more weight than a string of paper dolls. But he knew the way to make it not matter. It was a small thing to let Luc Corbeau go.

He could make her go away, and he knew it.

Lace pushed herself off the fence. "Get him out."

De lo perdido, lo que aparezca.

From what is lost, what comes back.

Her toothbrush cleared out the bitter taste of starflower leaves. But her stomach didn't settle.

She thought of the Corbeaus in that rented Craftsman house. They carried with them so many years of lying Lace waited for the clapboards to split.

She put on the white wings Cluck had made her, tied the ribbons under her breasts, and waited in the blue and white trailer.

When Cluck opened the door, he didn't look surprised to see her. He didn't look happy either.

"What the hell did you do?" he asked.

She got up from the built-in bed.

He threw the trailer door shut. "You went to the plant?"

She set her hands on his upper arms, checking that he was all there. The red shirt and brown corduroys she'd never seen him in before that morning. His hair that looked neat at the funeral but uncombed now. The three fingers Dax had broken.

"These aren't the kind of people you want to deal with." He put his hands on the side of her face, the heat of his palm stinging her burn.

She didn't stop him.

He gripped the back of her neck. "You know that, right?" He didn't raise his voice. Today had hollowed him out too much. He didn't have the sound left to yell.

"I don't care." She dug her hands into his back. "I wanted you out."

He kissed her, hard. She kissed him back, almost biting his lip.

His hands found the feathers on her back. "What are you doing in these?"

She made him stand in front of the mirror, eyes closed, like he'd done to her. She tied to his body the things she'd made. Those hundreds of black and red feathers threaded to the empty wing frame, filling in the wire shapes until they were thick as crow's plumage.

She fastened the red ties to his shoulders and across his chest.

The feeling of the ribbon against his shirt made him open his eyes.

She watched his face in the mirror, his eyes half-closing again, his mouth a little open. He took in the spread of black feathers. Red streaks wove through, like the petals of French marigolds on dark water.

She stood behind him, her fingers tracing the wingspan. "I borrowed the frame," she said. "I hope you don't mind."

He met her eyes in the mirror.

"I just tried to copy what you did on mine." She moved between him and the mirror. "It's nowhere near as good as your work, and they'll probably fall apart in about two days. But I had the feathers."

He held her against the mirror, the hollow shafts of the white peacock feathers pressing into her back. His breath fell hot on her mouth. "Why?"

The night she stole the thread and ribbon and the wire frame, it was to get him back. But now she'd tied them to him so *Tía* Lora would know him, so she would not have to ask if this was the boy.

Lace hadn't told *Tía* Lora she would do this, but her great-aunt would know. The boy in the black wings, brushed red, was the one Lora Paloma needed to tell the things she'd told Lace. Lace was afraid if her great-aunt had to ask, if she heard herself say the question—*Is this him? Is this the boy?*—she'd shrivel back into herself and never speak.

Lace held her hand to Cluck's chest, so neither of them would close the space between their lips again. "There's someone you need to see."

She led him across the woods, both of them still wearing their wings, a shared sign to anyone who wanted to look that they would not let this go on. All these lies would not bleed into two more decades.

The motel hallway was empty. *Tía* Lora waited behind an unlocked door, fidgeting with a handful of thread and glass beads.

A flicker of recognition passed between her and Cluck.

Lace shut the door. Cluck and *Tía* Lora stood in the middle of the room, him looking a little down, her a little up.

Tía Lora lifted a hand to his cheek, as though she could know him by the grain of his skin.

His wings made him so much bigger than Lace's great-aunt. He loomed over her like an archangel. He must have felt it too. He untied the wings from his body, took them off, and laid them on the bed.

Lace knew she should leave them alone. But if she did not stay, did not needle her great-aunt into repeating the things she'd told her this morning, the truth would sink under the river silt, and never be found.

So Lace stood at the threshold, guarding the door, where *Tía* Lora could see her.

Tía Lora hesitated, and Lace gave her a nod, a look of *go on, tell him.* Lora Paloma had been silent so long. A few more minutes would be too much. She would wither like a crepe paper poppy.

Tía Lora set the glass beads on a nightstand and made Cluck sit on the edge of the bed. She sat next to him.

Cluck set his forearms on his knees, looking at the patterned carpet. Lace could not hear most of their words, especially her great-aunt's soft, low voice. But she knew what *Tía* Lora was saying. She had said it all to Lace this morning. And now she told it to Cluck like he was small, and it was *un cuento de hadas*, some fairy story, dark and sharp.

Tía Lora had been with a man named Alain, a small romance rooted as much in shared loneliness as love, grown from their shared search for the truth about the salt under the lake and the sinkhole that took the trees. They still did not know what to do with what they knew but could not prove when Lora found out she was pregnant.

That morning, *Tía* Lora had told Lace how her sisters-in-law had whispered. *Imagine, at her age? A forty-five-year-old widow? You'd think God would have closed her womb, sí? Dime, which* cabrón *you think did it? Maybe that mechanic in Calaveras? You saw how he looked at her. ¿Te lo crees? A man losing his head over Lora.*

But *Tía* Lora didn't tell Cluck these things. Instead she told him how during those months she did not speak, would not say who her child's father was no matter how many Palomas asked her, until her time came, the day her son was born. No one asked who the father was again. They knew. In the place of hair her son was born with the dark, soft down of a black cygnet.

"Those feathers," *Tía* Lora said. "It could have been any Corbeau." She held her right hand balled in her left, and then switched, back and forth. "I don't know how they knew it was Alain."

Lace could guess. If anyone had seen them together, even once,

Abuela would have heard about it, the same as she'd heard about Cluck holding Lace in his arms the night of the accident, her dress in pieces.

But Lace didn't speak, afraid if she startled them *Tía* Lora would stop talking and Cluck would leave, spooked like that Camargue colt. So she stayed quiet.

Tía Lora kept kneading her fingers, holding one hand closed inside the other. She told Cluck that before she had even gotten to hold her son, the Palomas brought him to the *gitanos* who grew feathers in their hair. They left him with them, the black down bearing witness that *This, this is clearly yours.*

Neither Paloma nor Corbeau knew that once his down fell away and his semiplumes came in with his hair, they would be streaked red.

"They said it was because I was bad," Cluck said, more to his own hands than to *Tía* Lora. He did not lift his eyes from the carpet. There was so much in *Tía* Lora's *cuento de hadas,* so many things he had to hold in those hands, and this was the one small thing he could take in right now, the reason for the wicked color in his feathers. He held it, turned it over like a river stone, invisible except to him. "Like how I'm left-handed."

Tía Lora did not have to ask to know he had taken it as truth, undeniable as the red itself. She put a hand on his arm, to tell him she did not believe it. He flinched, but then Lace saw his muscles settle into the feeling of her hand as she told him the Palomas had given her a choice. Leave with her new son, her little *cuervo,* leave the only family she had left, or give him to *los gitanos.*

They did not need to tell her that she could not go with the Corbeaus, with Alain and their new son. She was a Paloma, by marriage and by name, and the Corbeaus would no sooner take her as they would adopt a fish from the river.

"But why didn't you leave with my grandfather?" Cluck asked. "He would've. I know he would've."

Tía Lora told Cluck that Alain had never loved her the way she had loved him, that she did not want to force him to be with her because he had made her pregnant. She did not want him growing to hate their child for it.

"He wasn't like that," Cluck said.

But it was more than this, *Tía* Lora told him. She had seen the feud building between the Palomas and the Corbeaus. She'd seen the fights, the threats, the sabotage, and how the accident had deepened all of it. She knew a child born between a Corbeau and a Paloma, even a Paloma by marriage, would not bring the families together.

It would just destroy the child. Both families would reject him, leaving him with no one but a mother, a father who stayed out of obligation, and all those voices telling him he was worth nothing. Or each family would pull on him so hard, wanting him to choose their side, that he would break apart.

So *Tía* Lora had kept her pregnancy from Alain, avoiding him when her clothes could no longer hide her shape. But when her son was born with down for hair, and the Palomas set the choice before *Tía* Lora, she thought the better life for her son would be one surrounded by others who grew feathers. A family who could care for him better than she could alone.

But the Palomas saw her wavering, heard her wailing in her sleep like a cow with its calf torn away, so to save her from her weakness, they made sure that every Corbeau would hate her, including Alain. Especially Alain.

The Palomas told everyone close enough to hear that she cried out in her sleep because this pain, this bleeding in her womb, was all because a Corbeau had forced her. He was *un violador*, and he would pay.

The police took Lora Paloma's wailing and bleeding as proof of the story her family told. All the crying and the things dripping into her through the IV kept her from hearing their words, and speaking her own.

She would have said she loved Alain Corbeau, even if the only woman he would ever love was a wife he'd lost years earlier. And when the cloud the IV had left around *Tía* Lora cleared like haze burning off a morning, when she heard what the Palomas had done, she went to the police herself.

She did not tell Cluck that her womb had still been swollen and sore as she waited in the station. She did not tell him about the feeling of blood collecting inside her like rain. These were things for Lace to know, not her son, not a boy becoming a man.

But she did tell him how she made sure the police knew there was no *violador*, that she had wanted Alain Corbeau more than she had ever wanted the dead man who was once her husband. If her family would not let her have her son, they would let her have this, lifting the weight of the truth off her tongue.

She kept Alain Corbeau from jail. But even if she'd knocked on every door in Almendro and told them the truth, it wouldn't have kept him inside the chemical plant's fence line. They caught him looking at records he should not have seen, files about the lake and the salt mining, and they let him go.

Along with his job, he lost any chance of proving what happened the night the trees sank, so the hate between the Palomas and the Corbeaus burned bright, and Lora and Alain had no breath to blow it out or water to drown it. The town shunned Alain Corbeau, *el gitano y el violador*. And he never spoke to Lora again. She never had the chance to tell him that she hadn't been the one to tell those lies, to call him *un violador*.

Cluck stood up. "I don't want to hear any more."

"It doesn't matter what they think of him," *Tía* Lora said. "You knew him."

He turned away. "I don't care." Cracks came into his voice. "I don't want to hear this."

"Lucien Corbeau, sit down," Lora Paloma said.

Lace held the door frame. She had never heard *Tía* Lora raise her voice. Even once when Lace tried to run into the street after a cat, her great-aunt had only gripped her arm and whispered, "No, *mija*. This is how you die."

Lucien. The name stilled him in a way that made Lace sure it was his. He hadn't even told her when she asked. He'd just given her Luc, the first syllable. He'd let her take off his shirt before he'd been willing to let her have those last three letters.

"How do you know that name?" he asked.

"I gave you that name," *Tía* Lora said.

Cluck sat down and dragged his fingers through his hair, holding his head in his hands. *Tía* Lora put her palm on his back, and Lace could guess what she whispered. These were the words she needed to say to him. *Él era tu padre y yo soy tu madre.*

He was your father, and I am your mother.

Cluck would not know the words, but he'd understand the meaning, the sum of all these things she'd said.

He moved his hands to his eyes. When Lace stilled her breathing, she could hear him sobbing into them, the gasps in for air, the wet breaking at the back of his throat. His tears spread over the heels of his palms. His wrists shone wet.

Tía Lora and her truths had broken him. These things he did not know broke him. These were things he should have learned over years. That way they might have worn into him slowly, water cutting a place in rock. This way, all at once, they cracked him like shale.

"I killed him," Cluck said. "I was supposed to take care of him and I didn't."

Lace's fingernails worried the paint on the door frame. This was what he thought? That his grandfather's death was on him?

Tía Lora rubbed her palm up and down his back. The forwardness of it, like she'd been doing it since he was small, made Lace part her lips midbreath. *Tía* Lora had never been a woman anyone would call bold. But now that she could touch this lost son, she treated him like there was no question he belonged to her.

"You know that's not true," *Tía* Lora told Cluck.

Cluck let out a rough laugh, quiet and small. "I do?"

"You should." *Tía* Lora put a hand under his chin to make him look at her. "Because I do."

The pain didn't leave Cluck's face. But Lace saw one small break in it, a second of easing up, like a candle flame darkening before the wick caught again.

He almost believed *Tía* Lora. The only person who could tell him he didn't kill the man he did not know was his father was the woman he did not know was his mother.

He pressed his lips together, hiding the faint tint of violet Lace always looked for on the inside of his lower lip.

This possibility, that Alain Corbeau being gone was not his fault, was putting another handful of cracks in him.

But *Tía* Lora did not let him splinter. She got him to his feet, took the black wings off the bed and tied them to his body. She fastened the ribbons, her hands as gentle and sure as if he'd always been hers. Like she would have buttoned his coat when he was six, straightened his collar when he was ten, fixed his tie when he was fifteen.

He straightened his shoulders, holding up those dark wings.

"*Eres perfecto y eres hermoso,*" Lora Paloma said, her voice still low. *You are perfect, and you are beautiful.*

Cluck shut his eyes, salt drying on his cheeks. He nodded without understanding. If he had understood, he might not have nodded. He did not believe he was perfect or beautiful. But if no one told him what *Tía* Lora's words meant, he would nod, and she would think he believed.

Lace kept a last handful of secrets for both of them. She did not tell Cluck that Lora Paloma had wanted a child worse than she wanted her own breath. That the only reason she hadn't had one before Cluck was that her husband had beaten every life out of her but her own. This man the Palomas had called a martyr the night the lake took him.

Tía Lora had told Lace that part, and then asked her to forget it.

Lace hadn't told *Tía* Lora that Cluck had grown up never knowing when his brother might leave a bruise on his temple or throw him against a piece of rented furniture. She didn't tell her that, to Cluck, trees were as much a place to hide as a way to find the sky.

This was the bond they shared that they'd never know. They had both been beaten by men who decided that the only things worth less than their souls were their bodies.

Cluck said something to *Tía* Lora. She nodded, and he left.

"Go with him," *Tía* Lora said. "Tell him to wait. Tell him not now."

So Lace caught up in the motel hallway. Even down, his left wing brushed the wall. The black primaries grazed the yellowing paper.

"You okay?" Lace asked.

"No," he said. "No. Not really."

"Where are you going?"

He shoved through a side door. He held it open behind him, but didn't look back at her. "I've got some questions for my family. Or, not my family."

She followed him across the parking lot. He did not go toward the road. He went to the edge of the property that backed against the trees.

"Speaking of family, I guess you and I are, what?" He worked out the math. "Second cousins?"

"First cousins once removed." She'd done the math on the back of a napkin that morning. "But we're not blood related."

She was no more related to him than she was to any other Corbeau. But if her family had let *Tía* Lora keep him, he would have been a Paloma, the only one who neither had Paloma blood nor had married into the family. Lace would have grown up sharing school lessons with him, talking him into swimming, making fun of him if she ever caught him pulling out the feathers under his hair.

But even with the Paloma name, those feathers would have stopped her family from claiming him as theirs, the same as the streaks of red and his left-handedness left him a little outside the Corbeaus.

"Well, there's a silver lining, huh?" he said.

She could feel him grasping at it, looking for a way to make this funny. This was the best he could do. He was reaching for the joke, and his hands found this because it hurt less than anything else. This was how he broke things into pieces small enough to hold.

She got in front of him and stopped him. "You sure you wanna do this now?" she asked. The Corbeaus must have still been in their mourning clothes.

"No, I don't. I want to do this ten years ago. Hell, I'd settle for a week ago." He scratched at his cheek, where his tears had dried into salt. "But now is the best I can get."

Le loup retourne toujours au bois.

The wolf always goes back to the woods.

"Cluck?"

He heard Lace saying his name, but didn't answer.

He understood now. It clicked into place like the last wire on a wing frame. It slashed at him, a knife grown dull from sitting in a drawer. It left a line of little scratches instead of a clean cut.

Pépère had been careful. He'd given Cluck the quiet space to use his left hand and climb trees higher than any in the show. He'd never fought his own daughter on the show's schedule or not taking Cluck to church, because Nicole Corbeau knew the secret that could always get him to back down.

Pépère had felt like more than a grandfather because he was. He showed Cluck more patience than he showed his other grandchildren because Cluck was not one of them.

This was why *Pépère* let Cluck wear his old clothes even when he thought he shouldn't, because they let him be something more to Cluck than what his children had decided.

"Cluck." She held his arm to stop him. "I need to know you can hear me."

"I can hear you," he said, and kept walking.

She went with him.

He didn't like looking at her. Every time he saw the dark stain of the wound on her cheek, he remembered that the plant hadn't just sealed her dress to her body that night. They hadn't just killed *Pépère* with the things they'd sent into the air. They'd caused the accident that killed a Corbeau who'd just learned to walk the highest branches.

They'd turned the Corbeaus and the Palomas from rivals to enemies.

These were the things they'd done that his grandfather would never tell him. And he thought of all of them when he saw Lace.

But she was his witness, the girl who would speak for Lora Paloma when Lora Paloma would not cross the woods to speak for herself. If they wanted to hurt Lace, they would have to kill him.

"Why the hell did my grandfather go along with this?" he asked.

"Because he didn't want you growing up with everyone thinking you were born because he raped your mother," Lace said.

"I wouldn't have thought that."

Now *Pépère* would never know that the lie wasn't Lora Paloma's. She had been the one to pull it back. But it had been too late. The Palomas' lies had already rained over the whole town. Nothing Lora Paloma said could make them forget.

His family had kept him from knowing his father as his father, and the Palomas had kept him from knowing his mother at all.

There wasn't enough of him to hate them all. He'd been able to hate the Palomas because he loved *Pépère*, even if he didn't love the woman he'd thought was his mother and the man he'd thought was his brother. Now he didn't have that love to push against, to give the hate direction. So the hate drifted, unanchored, trying to find a current. It turned over inside him, the edges catching his lungs and heart and stomach. He didn't know how to hate unless he had something to love.

"Lace."

"What?" she asked, and he realized he'd said her name out loud.

"Nothing." He'd been thinking her name but hadn't meant to speak it. "Sorry."

Lace. He could love her. The Palomas had thrown her away too, and she would never be a Corbeau, no matter how many of their faces she painted. He couldn't even make her one, because he wasn't one. That he was both Corbeau and Paloma made him neither.

It didn't matter if he had no Paloma blood. Lora had become a Paloma, taken the name, spent so many years among them they had become her family. The Corbeau and Paloma in him would not mix, like the almond oil and apple cider vinegar Clémentine put on her hair. She could shake the bottle, but the two liquids always pulled apart. He felt himself separating out, becoming two things in one body, one half of him Corbeau and the other Paloma. He was one of the half-leucistic peacocks his grandfather had shown him in books. A pale body patched with blue, a tail fan that was half-white and half-green.

He stopped and looked at Lace. "Go back," he said. "Stay with . . ." He got caught on what to call the woman he had just met for the second time. *Your great-aunt. Lora. My mother.*

Before he could decide, Lace said, "No."

He breathed out. "Please? I don't want you over there. Not for this."

"If you're going, I'm coming with you."

"They're gonna blame you for telling me." The white wings wouldn't do her any favors either. Maybe none of his family spoke Spanish, but they knew what Paloma meant as well as Lace knew what Corbeau meant.

"I'm not going back unless you come with me," she said.

He saw the wager in her eyes, her bet that if she refused to let him do this alone, she could get him to turn back.

"Then I guess you're coming with me." He kept going, and she kept up.

He'd stand between her and his family if he had to, his wings making him a feathered shield.

How many of them already knew? *Pépère*, now in the ground, the truth clutched against his chest with *Mémère's* finest doily. Cluck's mother, and her brother and sisters.

Did Dax? Did Eugenie and his other cousins? Had they wondered why Cluck looked so little like Dax or his mother and so much like old photographs of *Pépère*?

"My mother." The word felt wrong in his mouth. "Her. Nicole. She doesn't even like me."

"No," Lace said. "She doesn't."

That almost made him laugh. He liked that Lace wasn't trying to make any of this soft.

"Then why would she agree to this?" he asked.

"Because your family told her to," Lace said.

"She hates me. She could've said no."

"Really?" Lace asked, the word so sharp Cluck felt it.

"Good point," he said.

Lace knew better than anyone. Once her family came down on her for that feather on her arm, no one short of God himself could help her. In this way, the Corbeaus were no different from the Palomas. Nicole Corbeau's word may have ruled now, but no one got to make Corbeau law without years of following them first.

What Cluck was hadn't made Nicole Corbeau hate him. That he was at all had. It made his rage toward her both smaller and sharper.

Cluck laughed, the noise slight but sudden.

"What?" Lace asked.

"You know I've never seen my birth certificate?" he said.

"Really?"

"Really."

Nicole Corbeau had made sure of it. When he went to the DMV for his driver's license, she had kept it for him, not even letting him hold it long enough to look. She'd told him he'd lose it. He'd taken it the same as he took every other time she rolled her eyes or turned her back. That he was stupid, bad, ugly.

He wanted his birth certificate, the original. He wanted to hold that slip of paper, read it.

He wondered if his grandfather ever thought of leaving with him. But after the plant fired him, *Pépère* had fallen in with the family, given up on getting another engineering job, knowing he'd never get a good reference out of the Almendro plant. The only place for him and Cluck was with the rest of the family. The once-engineer, and *le cygnon* who did not turn white as he got older but only grew darker.

In the dark, Cluck couldn't tell if they'd reached the part of the woods closer to his family than hers. He waited for some shift in the air, like the trailing edge of a cold front, wet warmth turning to ice crystals.

Lace gripped Cluck's arm, stopping him.

"What?" he asked.

A figure stepped out from behind a tree. Cluck recognized the broad shape.

"You back for more, *chucho?*" the figure said. He hadn't gotten close enough for Cluck to make out his face, but the word he remembered. *Chucho.* The two syllables called up the feeling of getting kicked in the stomach, his grandfather's collar coming undone.

Two more figures stepped forward, their silhouettes showing against the trees. Lace's cousins, the ones from the liquor store.

Now his wings told them he was a Corbeau.

"And you brought your girlfriend this time, huh?" one asked.

If they knew she'd been with a Corbeau, they might kill her, treat her like a fallow deer a wolf had gotten its teeth into.

"Run," Cluck said, low enough that the three of them wouldn't hear.

But the break in his voice betrayed him, told her that if she ran, he wouldn't.

"No," she whispered back. "Justin," she said to the biggest one.

But Justin didn't hear her, or didn't care.

They didn't recognize her. Her makeup was too heavy, covering the red heart on her cheek. In the dark, they didn't see past her wings.

Cluck walked up to their line. He wasn't taking anyone, Paloma or Corbeau, standing in front of him anymore.

"Get out of my way," he said.

The oldest one laughed. The other two went at him.

Lace's cousins had not been the ones to call the police about *Pépère*. But their parents or grandparents might have brought the police to the hospital, where the officers accepted Lora Paloma's writhing and sobbing as a statement. Lace's cousins carried the blood of everyone who kept him from his mother.

This time when they hit him, he hit back. Every time one of their fists went into him, his hands returned the blow. Feathers rained from his wings. The salt of his own blood dried out his mouth. This was what his hate could press against. Their hate, and the pain in his own body.

Lace called their names, trying to pull them off Cluck. One tugged on her dress to get her off him, and the fabric tore, exposing her slip. Cluck shoved him and he fell. She kicked another one, and he back-handed her to flick her away. The force knocked Lace's right wing out of place. Cluck hit him in the jaw, a clean copy of how he'd gotten the risk manager.

Lace gripped the biggest one by his shirt collar and yelled into his face, "Justin, look at me!"

Her yelling, almost breaking into screaming, made her cousins freeze. The two younger ones let go of Cluck.

Their stares all met on her face. They stepped back like she could burn them.

"Lace?" the biggest one said, the word choked like Lace had her hand around it.

She looked at Cluck. "Run."

Cluck grabbed her hand to make her go with him. The *fildefériste* blood in him shook awake. The wind shifted, the air sharpened with the scent of iodine. He had never been to the towns in Provence where his great-grandparents strung their wires. He had never walked a tightrope between a town's tallest tree and steeple. He had never waved to the crowd gathered in front of a village church. But these trees were his wires. He could climb higher and faster than anyone in the show.

They'd hide in the cottonwood tree. They could get high enough in the branches that no one could reach them.

He let Lace get ahead of him so he could see her, make sure she didn't turn back. The trees blurred. The moon barely reached the ground. His lungs cramped and stung, but he told her to keep going. The undergrowth crunched and snapped under their steps, the sounds scattering night birds.

But Cluck didn't find the cottonwood trunk standing alone. Another familiar shape broke its line.

Cluck and Lace stopped.

Dax stood near the tree's base, still in his funeral suit. He would have heard the fight with Lace's cousins, the noise in the stretch of woods both the Corbeaus and the Palomas considered theirs.

He took in Lace's ripped dress, her bent wing, her tangled hair. Then he looked at Cluck. "What did you do?"

The pain between Cluck's ribs brightened and spread.

It didn't matter if Dax knew the truth, that this town thought Alain

Corbeau had raped Lora Paloma. Whatever he knew or didn't know, Dax had been waiting for years for Cluck to live up to his left-handedness and the red in his feathers. Cluck was *le petit démon*, the blighted thing that would ravage this family if Dax didn't keep him caged.

Something had lit the green in Dax's eyes. Cluck being with Lace. The white wings that might have been enough to make Dax realize she was a Paloma. The black and red wings on Cluck. Dax wondering if Cluck had been the one to tear Lace's dress.

Cluck got in front of Lace. He'd made her part of this, so he had to stay between her and Dax.

But Dax didn't go after Lace. He grabbed Cluck's collar and shoved him against the cottonwood. The impact went through Cluck's body. He fought to hold his breath in his lungs.

"You never listen, do you?" Dax hit him in the jaw.

The force rattled down through Cluck's neck.

"I told you not to." Dax got him again, left temple this time. "And you did it anyway."

A seam of blood dripped down Cluck's cheek. It stung like a spray of hot water.

He tried to get Lace's eye, to tell her to run even though he couldn't. Dax wanted him. He was the traitor, *le bâtard*. The evil thing that would ruin his family. If he let Dax pin him against this tree, hit him until he had to hold Cluck up by his collar, Lace could get away before Dax remembered she was there.

El que quiera azul celeste, que le cueste.

He who wants the sky must pay.

Lace saw the look, the flick of Cluck's eyes telling her to leave. She ignored it. Blood streaked his face. It stained his collar. If she left him here, Dax would kill him.

So she kept searching the dark ground for anything to stop Dax. She wasn't big enough to pull him off Cluck. If she tried, she'd make it worse, irritating Dax like a wasp. She needed something big enough to knock him out.

The sound of Dax's fist hitting Cluck's skin again made her stumble. Her hands found a branch, heavy and knotted. The bark felt rough as raw quartz. The rain had eaten at the wood. It wouldn't have fallen if the chemical hadn't weakened the bough.

"You always have to do something, don't you?" she heard Dax say.

She picked up the branch and steadied her grip to go at him.

"I don't know what you did," Dax said. "But everything bad in this family starts with you, doesn't it?"

"Yeah," Cluck said.

The hint of a laugh in his voice made her look up.

She stopped, the branch still in her hands.

"It does." Cluck half-smiled, blood trickling from his lip.

Dax stared at him, fist frozen at his side.

The fear left Cluck's face. He opened his eyes, the moon a white fleck in each iris.

Yeah, it does. Those three words, accepting the things his family hated about him. Instead of letting them leave a thousand little cuts in him, he sharpened them himself, held them like knives.

It wasn't true. Everything bad in these trees and that water lived there before Cluck took his first breath.

But Dax could think anything he wanted. The truth didn't belong to him anymore.

Cluck turned his shoulder, getting free of Dax's grip. He drove his fist into the side of Dax's face, and Dax fell. His body hit the under-brush, and he blacked out.

This was just one hit returned out of a thousand Dax must have given Cluck. But it was perfect, and clean, and it belonged to Cluck. All those years of hiding in trees and crouching in corners, every bruise, split lip, broken finger that had held him down like a hundred little stones, now let go of him. She could see his back untensing, not fighting them anymore, until she thought the black and red of his wings would lift him off the ground if they caught the wind just right.

Lace dropped the branch and put her hands on the sides of Cluck's face. "Are you okay?"

His palms slid over hers, warming the backs of her fingers. "Yeah," he said. "I think I am."

A rush of voices drifted through the forest. Both their families were coming for them.

Cluck grabbed her hand and set it on the cottonwood. "Climb," he said. One word, and she got herself up the first few branches. He followed her, their weight disturbing the boughs. Leaves fell, catching in their hair.

She stalled halfway up the tree, where they'd stopped the night he'd shown her how to climb. She set her back against the trunk. Her eyes flashed down, the ground so dark she couldn't make out the undergrowth.

"We have to keep going." He held her waist, easing her away from the trunk. There was strength in his palms, the assurance that whatever his family thought he was, he could own it, make it his. "I won't let you fall."

"I can't," she whispered back. "I'm not like you."

He laughed softly. "I'm not like anybody."

He offered his hand. She took it, and he pulled her up a bough at a time. Her arms and legs trembled, shaking the leaves on each branch she touched. The wings pulled on her shoulders. But she gave him her weight, and he kept her steady.

The two families, Paloma and Corbeau, ran from their sides of the woods and surrounded the tree. Cluck's aunts and uncles. The woman Cluck once thought was his mother, slapping Dax's cheek to wake him up. Eugenie. Lace's cousins.

Cluck got her to sit down on a high bough, close to the trunk. "Don't worry." He sat next to her, keeping his hands on her. "We're too far up. They can't get to us."

The wind made her shudder. If it caught their wings, it could knock them both from the tree like a nest.

What they both knew, what he wouldn't say, was that they'd have to come down. And when their feet touched the undergrowth, everything they'd left on the ground would be waiting, worse for being given room to rage and spread.

The height stabbed into her. It pulsed through the dark. Cluck had brought her so high she thought she could brush her fingers against the moon. Its light reached down through the branches, showing their families' faces.

Lace looked down enough to match the voices to the far-off figures.

"Let her go," her uncles called up to Cluck, not begging. They reprimanded him like he was bothering a stray cat, telling him to leave it alone. Because he was a Corbeau, they thought they could scare him like they would a crow.

"Come down," Cluck's aunts and uncles and the older cousins said, gesturing with their hands as though he'd forgotten the way.

Dax got to his feet and lunged for the base of the tree, ready to go up after Cluck, not caring that he'd never learned to climb as high. He knew now what Lace was, that Cluck had brought a Paloma into their family, and he was ready to make Cluck pay for it.

But Nicole Corbeau dug her fingers into his arm and pulled him back. She whispered something Lace couldn't hear. But Lace could guess. Some assurance that Cluck was not worth it. *He has never belonged with us. Leave him to the Palomas. Let them do what they want with him.*

"I'll kill you, *chucho*," Justin yelled up, his brothers echoing him. "Bring her down or I'll kill you."

Lace gripped Cluck's arm. As long as her cousins were waiting for him, she wasn't letting him go.

"Lace, come down," her mother said. "We'll make sure he doesn't hurt you."

"Are you out of your minds?" Clémentine shrieked. "You'll break your necks."

Abuela called for them to kill him, kill the boy with the *violador* blood in him. Her gaze fixed on Lace's torn wing, the white plumes proof that a Corbeau boy had not only taken Lace, but had tried to make her a feathered thing.

"Please, come down," Martha and Emilia pleaded. "You'll fall."

"Cluck," Eugenie said.

The blunt crack of a shotgun cut through the voices.

A scream tore free from Lace's throat. She ran her hands over Cluck's body, checking for blood, feeling for it because his shirt was too dark and too red to let her see. Wondering which of her uncles had the Winchester and if Cluck was just another crow to them.

The shot's echo wrenched away the few pins holding the inside of her together. They fell away, so softly they did not ring out as they hit the branches, and there was nothing but the ringing of distant glass chimes.

Cluck shook his head and pointed down.

Lace's father stood at the base of a nearby tree, his Winchester pointed at the ground. The muzzle smoked. So did a pile of leaves below the barrel. The dull burnt smell drifted up.

He'd fired it down, at nothing.

Both Palomas and Corbeaus gave his gun a wide berth.

"What's the matter with you?" he shouted to both sides. "All of you."

Her father didn't understand. He had never understood. He cast off his name not because he believed *Abuela*'s superstitions, but because he did not care to argue. Cuervo or not, Sara Paloma would still be his wife, and Lace Paloma his daughter. To him, it was this simple.

He thought the feud was live ash a boot heel could stomp out. He didn't notice it burning down both their houses.

"I don't care what you are, *muchacho*." Her father looked up at Cluck. "Come down. Both of you." He lowered his eyes and held the shotgun at his side, his gaze taking in every face. "If any of you lays a hand on either of them, *que Dios me ayude*."

He tilted his head back up to the tree, his stare broken only by the flickering leaves. "Come on. I won't let them at you. Either of you." His eyes stayed on Lace. "*Te lo prometo*."

She believed him. It didn't matter that he let the Paloma men kill crows with his own gun. He would not let the family he married into slaughter a boy.

This was their best chance, coming down, letting their families take them.

Lace pressed herself against Cluck's chest. He put his arms around her, his hands holding her wings to her back. She wanted to remember how he smelled, the salt and the cottonwood bark. She wanted to memorize the warmth of his body on hers, the only heat that didn't hurt her still-healing skin. When she couldn't sleep, she would think of it, the shimmer of warmth through her breasts when she felt him looking at them.

He held her tight to him, this boy she might have grown up with. He knew what she knew, that safe meant safe, but it also meant never again. A tear on her right cheek met one on his, the only one she found on him.

She let him go, nodding. She'd go back to her family. Maybe her father would even convince *Abuela* to forgive the burn on her arm, and she would swim as *la sirena rosa* again.

She didn't know where Cluck would go. He was born among Palomas, raised among Corbeaus, and now neither wanted him. He'd spend his life coming up with lies about his real name and what happened to his hand.

Lace would remember this one night she saw him in his black wings.

She shifted her weight, easing onto a lower branch.

Movement on the ground caught her eye. A woman's shape wove between the trees. She reached the watchers, and her small, running steps stopped.

Tía Lora halted at the outside of the ring, lifting her chin and searching the tree. Her eyes found Cluck and Lace. A wince broke the line of her mouth, her lips waiting to say again the things she'd told her son. *Eres perfecto y eres hermoso.* Words she'd had to tell him now that he was a man, because the hate that lived in these woods had kept her from telling him when he was still a boy.

Those years had collected, heavy and unseen, on Lora Paloma's shoulders. Lace took them in her hands, sharing their weight.

If Lace and Cluck came down from the cottonwood, they would lose more than afternoons in the river and nights in the trees. They would become a second Lora, another Alain. The stories would go on. Their families would strap the *cuentos* to their backs. The weight of them would crush their wings. Lace and Cluck would carry them into the next twenty years.

When their parents and aunts and uncles grew old, when the story of the Paloma widow and the *gitano* widower shrank to a few embers, Lace and Cluck would be the kindling and the kerosene. They would be the story passed down to Lace's younger cousins, and the inheritance of the little girl with dishwater eyes and hair like Cluck's.

The Corbeaus would say Lace Paloma seduced Cluck and then turned on him. *He was lonely, and she flirted with him so she could do to him what Lora Paloma did to Alain.* The Palomas would say Lucien Corbeau kidnapped Lace and forced her up into a tree. *You know that scar she has on her arm? He burned it into her up there, right in front of us. We saw it.* The stories would grow too big to fit in their rooms and the trunks of their cars.

Lace and Cluck couldn't make these families, these like magnets, touch and settle. They couldn't erase the nylon nets, the slicked branches, the broken arms. They couldn't bury the things this town had said about Alain Corbeau along with him. They couldn't prove that neither the Corbeaus nor the Palomas had made those trees vanish into the lake.

But she and Cluck could make sure everyone on the ground left with something closer to the truth.

Lace slid her hands onto either side of Cluck's neck, and made him lean down to her. She kissed him so hard his breath caught in his chest.

He pulled away like she'd slapped him. "What are you doing?" he whispered.

"Making sure they know." She set her open mouth on his.

This was all they had, these few minutes to prove that everything they did to each other, they both wanted. She felt Cluck registering it, understanding. They'd show everyone on the ground that they were willing to die at each other's hands, risk the curses in each other's fingers and lips.

He gave his mouth to hers, kissing her back. He grasped her hard enough that the fabric of her dress bunched in his hands. She moved her hands over him so quickly that when a feather brushed her fingers, she did not know if it had fallen from his hair or his wings. Her mouth found the things he'd always been but had not been allowed to be, everything in him that was dangerous and passionate.

They sparked against each other like flint. Inside that sparking, Lace heard a familiar breath in, the air spiced with a soft laugh. Neither were her own, but she knew them.

Tía Lora sighed and laughed. It rang through the air like an owl's call. This was her returning the favor, her *go on*, her standing at the door and urging Lace on.

So Lace kissed *Tía* Lora's son again. She kissed him harder, their mouths growing so sore they could barely move them, until they could only set their lips together, more touching than kissing.

Cluck held her, and she rested her cheek on his shoulder. He kept her so close she could look down without falling.

All those faces stared up at them, some with eyes wide. *Abuela*, Nicole Corbeau. Some smiling. Clémentine. Lace's father, almost. Others just watching. Justin and his brothers, Lace's mother.

The face she did not see was *Tía* Lora's. She searched, and her eyes fell on where her great-aunt had stood.

Tía Lora was not there. In her place, a pillar of garnet-red feathers swirled and spun, even more than had floated from Lace's suitcase. The moon shone off them like star rubies. Then the wind took them, pulling them away.

Both families watched them fly. They drifted and dispersed, like sprays of grapevine leaves in October. They rode the wind as high as the top of the cottonwood tree, bringing with them the echo of Lora Paloma's sigh and laugh.

Cluck reached out his hand, letting one land on his palm. Lace closed his fingers over it. Another settled in his hair, the red catching in the black.

Each feather became ten more. They spread like a thousand red lacewings. They rose like every one was its own bird, full and winged. They turned the trees to autumn, all red-feathered boughs.

Cinnamon sweetened the air, the warm scent that lived on Lora Paloma's shoulders.

The two families blinked up. Their eyes drifted back to Lace and Cluck.

She pressed her hands into him. He held her harder. The watchers on the ground half-closed their eyes, the shared cringe of seeing the second time a Paloma and a Corbeau touched.

Cluck and Lace stared back, made fearless by the blessing of a woman who had become a sky of red plumes. They clutched each other hard enough to bruise. *Back off,* their eyes told the watchers. *We are not small enough that you can pull us where you want us to go.*

It didn't matter who thought they were brave and who thought they were too stupid to bother with. It added up to the same thing.

Abuela turned her back on them both and started walking, trying to hide her glances up at the red feathers.

Nicole Corbeau led Dax away from the cottonwood tree. Lace could see him dragging his fury behind him, a thing he'd killed and would eat raw. Whatever his mother's words, he took them as freedom to hate Cluck, to blame him, without the sting of him being part of their family. They were rid of him now.

Nicole looked back only once, a single glance at the second son she'd never wanted.

Lace's father left her with a last wink.

The four of them, *Abuela* and Barto Paloma, Nicole and Dax Corbeau, pulled the rest away. Both families backed toward their own sides, eyes still searching the sky for feathers. Palomas to the River Fork. Corbeaus to the old house.

Lace couldn't hear what they were whispering. But now they were all witnesses to this thing she and Cluck had made them see. They would have to carry the truth, whether or not they spoke it. It would cling to them like the burrs off sticker grass. If they twisted it, it would pinch them back.

Vouloir, c'est pouvoir.

To want is to be able.

Cluck kept his arm tight around Lace's waist. Even when all those red feathers had sailed into the highest branches, he didn't let her go. He sat with his back to the trunk, Lace lying against him, the feathers of their wings interlacing like fingers. The wind hushed the owls, and they slept.

He'd slept in trees before, when he was small, hiding all night from Dax. But always alone, never with his arm around something it was up to him not to break.

He dreamed that his body was a red-winged blackbird's, his skin all dark feathers except for two crimson shoulders. He felt raw and fearless, protective of the small place that was his, undaunted by any other winged thing.

The feel of an afterfeather woke him, the downy barbs brushing his jawline. It lifted up, tickling his cheek, and he opened his eyes. A constellation of Lora Paloma's feathers whirled through the air, like coins thrown in water.

The red danced in and out of the cottonwood leaves. He hadn't dreamt it. His mother had become a thousand of these small, jewel-bright things.

He clasped Lace's shoulder, waking her. She shook off sleep, eyes opening to the wisps of red.

The feathers wafted down through the branches, stopping before the ground. They hovered near the cottonwood's trunk.

Cluck and Lace followed them, him taking her waist to help her from one bough to the one below, guiding her through the air the way she pulled him through water.

They got to the ground, and the feathers stilled in the air, hovering like dragonflies.

Lace looked toward the Palomas' part of the woods. Cluck mirrored her, looking toward the trees that led to the old Craftsman house. Their gazes crossed. She stared in the direction of the place she'd lived when her family did not want her. He watched the space between the trees. Somewhere on the other side of them was the family that would have been his if he had not grown feathers.

Then came the look between them, the question of *Did we mean this?* And if they did, where were they going?

They could follow those feathers. They could take his grandfather's truck and drive, not turn around until they felt free of their own names, until they knew what to do with the truths his father and his mother had left them.

He slid his hand over her palm, asking the question he couldn't say.

Her fingers answered his. She took his hand, held it, trapped its heat against hers.

"Yes," she said.

"Yeah?" he asked. He wanted her sure. He wanted to know she understood. This was different than going with his family to Madera

County. This was choosing him, just him, and herself, apart from every other Paloma.

She turned her head, looked at him. "Yes."

The wind picked up. It made the trees whisper and breathe.

The feathers took off on a gust, tumbling over themselves. Cluck and Lace ran after them, following them through the new light. When the feathers floated over the old Craftsman house, the two of them got into Alain Corbeau's Morris Cowley, and Cluck pulled it onto the road.

They drove past the Blackberry Festival, where Almendro crowned a new queen who would add sons and daughters to this town.

They drove past the grocery store and the bus stop, and the truck got up to speed on the highway. A flock of birds made a V in the corner of the windshield. They had to be calling to each other to stay together, but if *Pépère* hadn't taught him that, he'd never know it from here. They seemed quiet as the clouds.

He couldn't tell if Lace noticed them. She didn't watch the sky as much as he did. She kept her eyes low, like she was always looking for the sun glinting off a ribbon of water.

They covered miles of highway, past the roadhouse. Past Elida Park, where a leucistic peacock crossed the crabgrass. Far enough that the sound of glass chimes in trees and breath through reed pipes could not reach them.

Far enough that he couldn't hear the flight calls that told him to come back, to fit himself into that small space his family made for him. His grandfather had kept that space a little bigger, held it open like pulling aside hornbeam branches. Now that he was gone, it had collapsed in on itself. It couldn't hold Cluck anymore.

Empty land flew by, studded with cornflowers. The scent, like celery seed and desert grapevine, filled the truck.

"What happened to your hand?" Lace asked.

The question drifted between them. Her words brushed his forearm like feathers.

"My brother broke three of my fingers when I was nine." He just said it, eyes still on the highway ahead, no glance over fearing her pity or wanting it.

"What's your name?" she asked.

His nickname did not wait on his tongue. It curled and hid on the back of his neck, where his feathers touched his collar. He straightened his shoulders, and it slept.

"Luc," he said. "My name's Luc." Not Lucien. Not yet. Maybe not ever. But the name was still his. His mother had given it to him. Those first three letters let him claim it.

He felt her folding his nickname up like one of her scarves, slipping it into her dress pocket. She kept it close. She didn't let it fly out of the truck's windows and drift on the highway's current like a postcard.

Luc and Lace held between them this unspoken hope, that wherever those feathers landed, they'd find an old but not old woman who smelled like cinnamon, now unafraid to cross the woods. They'd find an old man blowing cigarette smoke into the last light, ready to think of Lace Paloma as more than made of her family's stories.

They'd find the books Cluck would study from, later editions of the same ones *Pépère* had read. They'd find a house, and even though Cluck wouldn't recognize it, he'd recognize the lemon tree pressing leaves against the kitchen window. They'd find Lace's spring with all those turtles and manatees wasn't in Florida, but just under the ground where those feathers settled.

But the feathers didn't settle, not yet. They floated over the highway, tumbling on the updrafts, flying like each was a whole bird, red as tourmaline. So Cluck and Lace kept driving, chasing these things that had gotten lost.